The Historian

Six Fantasies
of the American Experience

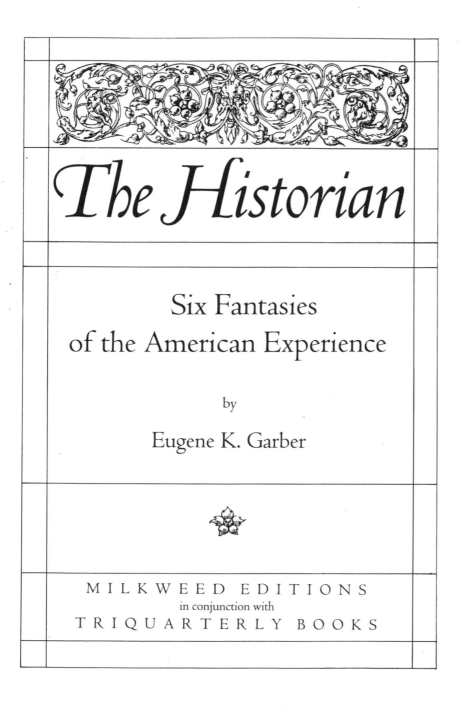

The Historian

Six Fantasies
of the American Experience

by

Eugene K. Garber

MILKWEED EDITIONS
in conjunction with
TRIQUARTERLY BOOKS

The Historian

Printed in the United States of America.
Published in 1993 by Milkweed Editions in conjunction with
TriQuarterly Books.

Milkweed Editions

528 Hennepin Avenue, Suite 505
Minneapolis, Minnesota 55403
Books may be ordered from the above address.

ISBN 0-915943-57-3

93 94 95 96 97   5 4 3 2 1

First Edition

Publication of Milkweed Editions books is made possible by grant support from the Literature
Program of the National Endowment for the Arts, the Cowles Media / Star Tribune Founda-
tion, the Dayton Hudson Foundation for Dayton's and Target Stores, Ecolab Foundation, the
First Bank System Foundation, the General Mills Foundation, the Honeywell Foundation, the
I. A. O'Shaughnessy Foundation, the Jerome Foundation, The McKnight Foundation, the
Andrew W. Mellon Foundation, the Minnesota State Arts Board through an appropriation by
the Minnesota State Legislature, the Northwest Area Foundation, the Lila Wallace-Reader's
Digest Literary Publishers Marketing Development Program, and by the support of generous
individuals.

Library of Congress Cataloging-in-Publication Data

Garber, Eugene K.
    The historian : six fantasies of the American
experience / by Eugene K. Garber. — 1st ed.
        p.   cm.
    ISBN 0-915943-57-3
        1. United States—History—Fiction.   I. Title.
PS3557.A63H57 1993
813'.54—dc20   92–41958
                                               CIP

For Norman Lavers,
a true friend and a yea-sayer

The Historian

Six Fantasies of the American Experience

The Historian

Six Fantasies
of the American Experience

The Historian

Boston, 1850

It was May, the air bearing the faint odor of the syringas, to which the boy in innocent pretense homed by smell when in fact he knew the way by a dozen other markers. Up from the bay blew salt, marsh, and mussels, as well as the news he had come to tell his grandfather.

The old statesman sat in his study, stern behind his desk, in his hand the pen with the steel nib and its own well. Mightier than the sword. The boy doubted it, for language itself meandered, full of vagary. Syringa from syrinx, panpipe. But when the wind blew through the blossoms did he hear the minor cry of the pursued nymph? Not at all. He heard the horn winded from the quarterdeck, the tantara of steel men and steel hull triumphant over old Ocean, which is what he had come to tell his grandfather. "The Cunard steamer has arrived in the harbor, sir. *Advenit.*"

The old statesman smiled, and swallowed, to moisten his throat. "Excellent," he said, barely perceptible the burr in the voice that had always, even in the Rotunda, been penetrating rather than resonant. "Now we are a meeting not only of North and South, but also East and West, which is more germane."

"You are referring, sir, to the new line from Albany?"

"From Albany and eventually points west, even to the Pacific."

The boy smiled. "Cousin Palfrey expresses from the pulpit his doubts about all this. Illusory, he says. In Him there is no East or West nor shadow of turning."

The old stateman's good eye glinted, and even the other, its blue all

milky, widened with animation. "You are witty today, my boy." He set
down his pen, rose slowly, and stepped over to the wrinkled window,
which warbled the charitable sun as it fell on his bald pate. On either
side of the drapes rose shelf upon shelf of books bound in leather,
buckram, or stiff laminated paper. Meanwhile, excited, eager for his
grandfather's reply, the boy rubbed a last year's pignut in his pocket, its
perfect smoothness soothing to his touch.

"Cousin Palfrey may very well be right, my boy." The old statesman
positioned himself so that he could see the boy or the chestnut and the
syringa, as he pleased, according to the tilt of his good eye. "In Him there
may indeed be no East or West. But here we are in a different place,
where, alas, North and South are all too real. And black and white."

"And how does your paper on the necessity of a free soil party
progress, sir?"

"Slowly but steadily according to the inexorable laws of Reason."

"And History?"

"No. In History, Reason can be found if searched for assiduously,
but most of History is an indolence in which Reason nods."

The boy knew that many years ago his grandfather had sat before
the ruins of imperial Rome and communed with the spirit of Gibbon
and cried aloud from the caverns of ignorance, "Why? Why? Why?"
And ever since had abjured the trammels of time, seeking the nature of
things in reason. But he, the boy, groveled in them. The ship and the
locomotive made his flesh tingle. Nothing did not transport him in time.
When he crushed pennyroyal and sniffed the pungency on his fingers, he
was cast back among the witches of the ancient cults and watched them
grind and brew their fabulous pharmacopoeia. On the new rails his
mind clattered out among Diggers, Pueblos, and the perilous Sioux.
"Why, sir, will they extend the railroad even to the Pacific? Is it reason-
able to do so?"

The old statesman smiled thinly and worked the spittle in his
mouth. "Well, we have made some grand purchases and know little of
what is in them. We wish to see. And there will be metals, if the western
mountains are piled as high as they say, for you cannot make such a mass
without compressing metals." The old statesman lifted his eye and took

in the blue May welkin. "But what would you have said, my boy, in answer to your own question?"

"That we must cross the vast plains and mountains merely because they are there, as the oceans were there."

"And the sky. Forget not the sky, Doctor Faustus." The old statesman's eye turned on the boy, half-stern, half-aglitter with wit. "What motive founds granaries and farms and mills and fisheries with other things useful to man, this cherish. What merely traverses and peers, this abhor."

∽

Fifteen years later, for a long ill-considered year, the historian came on weekdays, save holidays and summer, to his desk in front of the class. There on the rough-grained oak he placed his grandfather's watch and a polished pignut, the one as a promise of punctuality, the other a mystery that titillated the boys but might not stir them to inquisition, for he had forbidden it. During this year he turned them loose in the library to discover Rome of the Caesars. And his colleague Wells said, "They have sacked us, sir, dragged off all the treasures of the centuries of empire." But to him they seemed less like Visigoths than pack rats, their jaws crammed with triumvirates, conspiracies, assassinations, license beyond the dreams of the Sybarites, madness, concubinage, slavery, wine, incest, blood. And when after weeks of incredible and exhausting volubility they had heaped up the huge mole of particulars until it darkened the sky and threatened to cut them off from water and air, they fell suddenly silent, and Cramer cocked an eyebrow, half-supercilious, he whom the other boys called Reverend Mind, and said, "Why, sir?"

And the historian added, "Why? Why?" smiling. "Always repeat the ultimates thrice, Mister Cramer, as Saint Peter did."

Cramer wore thick spectacles. He took them off and in so doing removed all the light from his eyes, which fell back like shrewd nocturnal beasts into caves of bruise as dark as the sockets of a memento mori. "Alas, sir, is it all a meaningless higgledy-piggledy then?"

Winston of Virginia glowered. Wherever there was gallantry and evil he was satisfied, in whatever proportions or order of ascendancy. But Hermann lifted his voice from the penumbra of Jewry. "Sir, all this year we have studied History, but you have not told us what History is. We are lost."

And in that plaint the historian heard the whole vast cry of the diaspora, as plangent against New England stone as it was on the deserts and strands of Africa and Asia and in the walled ghettos of Europe. He nodded slowly, smiling at Hermann as gently as he could. "Perhaps, Mister Hermann, in your heart of hearts you know better than I. Do you know why Rome fell?"

Hermann shook his head like a little bird, frightened, honored, febrile. "No, sir."

"There was a time, we are told, when there was no history. The year was an eternal round, each with its mother and its king, who sprang up like crocuses at the very marge of snow and were cut down by next December's scythe. Les Primitifs. And then came your noble ancestors, cast aside the pagan gods, made a pact, and projected themselves across the desert, into Time and History, and we all have followed them. So, Mister Hermann, the wisdom in this case perhaps lies with you. But it would be a dereliction if I asked you to lecture on the meaning of History."

"Yes, sir." Hermann glowed.

Winston of Virginia glowered. The historian smiled, divining his thought. *His* ancestors had followed no Jew anywhere. Let the professor speak for his own puritanical forebears, who had adopted such foolish Old Testament names as Jeremiah, Obediah, Ezra, and the like. He, on the other hand, descended from British aristocracy, Angles untainted by the Normans.

The teacher said, "Gallant Winston does not agree, I respectfully suggest. History is not a sequence of meanings. There is only the moment—the banner's ripple, gunshot and saber, the wild neighing of a fallen steed, the evening breeze mixing the odors of powder and carrion, all more vivid than I can describe." He could not have known that within a tiny handful of years Winston would fall at the last moment of glorious ascendancy at Chancellorsville. Even so, an inexplicable poignancy echoed back to him from his own words, though perhaps to no other, certainly not to Winston, who allowed only the hint of an agreeable smile to mollify his disapproval.

The historian picked up the watch and the pignut and displayed them to his scholars. "Which might fairly be deemed an emblem of History?"

"The watch," said Cramer tonelessly, the question too obvious to reflect much glory on the respondent.

"Good." The historian nodded. "And the pignut?" The historian smiled and waited. Cramer put back on his glinting spectacles. "Would it be the timeless, sir?"

"If you keep a pignut two years, it will go punky." Rouse, the literalist, spoke.

"I am not," said Cramer, "speaking of the defunct pignut you kept in your boyhood, Mister Rouse. I am thinking of the pignut Agricola's servant roasted for him at the estuary of the Thames, which is the same as that which Charlemagne's servant roasted for him at Carcassonne."

"A bloody pignut Platonist he is, your honor," said Rouse. The class roared, Cramer joining good-naturedly and then speaking again when order had returned. "May we say, sir, that History is whatever is not pignut?"

The teacher turned the burnished object before his eyes, which were narrowed in mock intensity. "Alas, poor pignut, imperishable but historyless. Shine on through every age, but expect no chronicler."

"I shall write an ode to the pignut, sir," said Rouse. "Pindaric. It shall be foremost in my glorious canon. And thus shall the pignut enter History."

The historian shook his head sadly. "Has Philomela entered history through Keats? No. Therefore, Mr. Rouse, you and your poem may enter history, but not the pignut itself. What then, is History?"

"History is the record of the acts of great men." Winston.

"History is a repository of lessons in prudence and morality." Hermann.

"Which none heed." Rouse.

"History is the record of man's struggle for ascendance over nature and himself." Cramer.

"Which he never attains." Rouse.

The historian nodded pensively. "Do you think that History has a direction, a telos? Is it a spiral arriving at an inner sanctum? Is it a line? Is is an arabesque? An arch? The trajectory of David's stone?" The historian paused. "Or is History like the pignut after all? A grand masked ball of seemingly endless variety but in fact the elemental passions of human nature played out in disguise over and over and over again. The watch an illusion, the pignut the truth." He snapped shut the gold cover of the timepiece, pocketed it along with the pignut, and turned to leave the classroom.

"What is the answer, sir?" Hermann. And then a general chorus. "Yes, what is the answer, sir?"

"The answer!" he thundered, turning in anger that was only half-mock. "History does not give the answer. History propounds the questions." He paused to let his face and his voice soften. "Go now and begin to ferret out the questions. Write them down. And we shall meet here anon."

∽

Later he went west with his cousin Simms, self-proclaimed frontiersman, without a book in his baggage, and lay on his crude bunk smelling spruce in hopes that he would forget the blood of Indians and the fraternal blood of civil war. For the land had come to seem in his mind more drenched than Rome and no more hallowed or consecrated, even by his blood who said it was. But only a random troupe of images flitted across the dark-beamed ceiling. Memory of childhood confusions. His grandmother's Queen Anne mahogany and the field of Queen Anne's lace. In the silver breeze of June the wide white flower heads glided from stalk to stalk, laughing, as in a game of musical chairs. And in one of the chairs was a mother-of-pearl inlay that winked at him whenever he moved his head. Who was the lovely queen who strewed such delicacies in house and meadow? He imagined a white gown, a wand, and a sparkling coronet. His grandmother laughed: no, that was Queen Mab. And there was the Queen of the Bees, also hiding in the honeysuckle or behind the showers of apple blossoms. So many queens, secret and beauteous. No wonder when he saw a photograph of

England's queen, buttery little mountain of a woman, he laughed himself heartsick.

Meanwhile Simms went out with his carbine and dragged back a black bear on a skid constructed from birch and vine at the very site of the kill. And dove down to his armpits in blood and entrails, which he buried away from the coyotes. "Or their howling, dear coz, will interrupt the purification of our dreams." And scraped and salted the hide and stuffed the eyeless cranium and cured the meat in brine and smoke and vowed to subsist on jerky until the republic righted itself. But could not resist the trout and kept his gut supple in pure stream water the whole month the historian was there. "Do I understand that you're a dyed-in-the-wool Darwinian, coz?"

The historian smiled. "Until a better hypothesis comes along."

Simms scratched his head and sniffed suspiciously at the historian's words. It occurred to the historian that his cousin in his zeal for mortification should have gone south and rolled in dust and acquired lice and other parasites resulting in parched skin and bleared eyes. For the pure mountain air here immediately carried away all guilt and even the stink of bear. The historian said, "You'd think it would be easy for a pair of puritanical Bostonians like us in the depths of disgust to defile ourselves thoroughly, wouldn't you?"

"Filth has no survival value, coz. Your hunter's ritual of self-cleansing, whatever he thought it was, kept him out of the wind."

"Ah," said the historian, working his fingers as if touching the airy stops of ideation. "The principles of fortuitous change transferred from the physiological to the cultural sphere."

But Simms only scratched his head the harder and said, "If I understand aright, the criteria by which an hypothesis is to be tested are simplicity and applicability."

"Yes."

"Then I submit the case of our present great warrior president. How would Mister Darwin explain him? Are there certain caves and grots where specimens of the Silurian and Jurassic are kept hermetically intact while the rest of creation goes on its blithesome way mutating itself toward perfect adaptability?"

It was night. An oil lamp burned on the cabin table, but the two cousins sat before the fire, bathing their faces in the flames. The historian shook his head. "I'm afraid he's of the same species we are."

Simms clawed his jowls comically. "O hateful flesh. Why then, if he is man and dour Jeff Davis is man and I am man, then I say man is an absurd cul-de-sac."

"So? What species is not?"

Simms nodded. "Then what in the devil is the purpose of chronicling the descent of a dying species?"

The historian smiled warily and shook his head. "You couldn't if you wanted to. It all happens by imperceptible degrees, inside." The historian pointed to his heart. "History and evolution are incommensurate."

"Then what is History?"

The historian laughed, then pulled himself up professorially. "We shall instruct you by example, Mr. Simms. Do you remember the famous snow fight on the Commons?"

"By God I do!" Simms' eyes brightened. He got up and fetched a jar of colorless liquid from the windowsill, where the historian had remembered only a series of inverted tumblers with caterpillars under them. Or was that in his grandfather's house? The flame's beauty was corroding his sense of time. "What is it?" he said, when Simms had returned with his precious burden, holding the liquid up in the red light. "Firewater," he said, grinning demoniacally. "Purely ceremonial, bequeathed to me by a Cheyenne shaman who had inadvertently taken the form of a grizzly and whom I spared." He held the jar out to the historian. "Drink. We are brothers."

The historian took the jar and looked dubiously into its depths. On the bottom stirred an unquiet dregs that seemed to want to assume a significant shape.

"Drink, my brother."

The historian sipped the liquid, refused to cough or pant, and passed the jar back to his cousin, who sipped, recapped the jar, and set it on the hearth. "Good. We are brothers." His eyes shone. "By God, I do remember the great battle. But recount it again for us, oh sublime singer, and the Great Spirit will give you voice."

The historian saw it all very clearly, what there was to see. "How dark it was," he said. "Heaven had hidden her eyes. And the dank air reflected the glow of the gaslights back on them, as though they wore blue hoods. And we were driven back to the old church steps."

"Murk," said Simms, "quintessential Boston murk. And we in the very shadow of prelatical benightedness. Name the great warriors that closed upon us, oh sublime singer."

"By Clio, I can barely see their faces, all fogged by the great huffing of their bombardment. There was Halloran, Mahan, Puce, Carey, Fane, Bryde, and a half dozen others, including their leader Yates—neither dispossessed nor possessing, but scions of a powerful rising race, strong, coherent, brutal, and determined. And we the very emblems obstacular!"

"And sing the treasonous desertion by the comrades of our two Leonidases."

"Nay, not treason, good cousin, but a deep training in prudence that cools the blood and depresses the appetite for battle. In light of which it's a miracle that later they weren't overrun by the hot-blooded Southerners."

"All that saved them from it were the factories. But what was it that made our veins trill so strangely, cousin?"

The historian let pass across his face a bemused smile. "Nay, I know not, noble brother in arms. Unless it was simply that we were alive. The bitter snow against our faces, our frozen hands, our exhaustion, our utter hopelessness and utter faithfulness to each other told us that we were alive at that moment, whether we ever would be again or not."

"My God," Simms said in awe, almost whispering, "is that what History is, the memory of moments when someone was intensely alive?" He nodded his head slowly, rapt.

The historian mused. "I wouldn't be surprised. Consider. At a gathering there are thousands and thousands of inconsequential life moments bubbling to the surface, bursting on it, disappearing forever, historyless. Only in some corner a Musurus whispers to a Borthwick about the dismemberment of a sick empire or a Madame de Castiglione makes an assignation that will shake Napoleon III in his illegitimate throne. History. Is that what it is, great hunter?"

"You say, my sometime professor."

The historian did not smile. "I had a student who thought so, a

Virginian who had his brief moment of history at Chancellorville and is no more."

Simms nodded. "No wonder so much History is war." He uncapped the jar without ceremony and passed it to the historian. The warmth of the fire had agitated the liquid, which sent a bracing assault against the inner lining of the historian's nose. He drank. Simms drank, set the jar back on the hearth, and spoke, his voice now strangely measured. "Then there are two kinds of History, coz—written and unwritten. Madame de Castiglione's adultery and the episode of the two Boston Leonidases. Unless you plan to include us in one of your histories." Simms looked at his cousin almost hopefully.

"No, I will not write it." He then asked in a consolatory way, "Do you think the writing down matters much? Whatever History is, don't you think it all ends up in the same place?"

"Where? In the bright book that unfolds in the bosom of God like the multifoliate rose? Or in the dustbin of eternity?"

The historian smiled. "Your shaman friend must have spiked his firewater with the elixir of metaphysics."

Simms twitched his nose. "Recount, then, oh sublime singer, the last-minute reprieve of the two Leonidases."

"Aye, strange and unexpected it was. For the two were so closely pressed to the holy stone that they must flail away with loose-packed missiles, while in the rear ranks of the foe the younger warriors molded balls granite-hard, sharp-edged as flint, and passed them to the vanguard. And already the younger Leonidas had fallen once beside his cousin Simms, stunned on his ear, his head ringing. They were doomed. When suddenly out of that moonless murk, in the faint hooded light of the gas lamps, stood Yates alone. 'Stop!' he bellowed. Simms had already heaved another ball, his arm by then in methodical repeated motion, never desperate. The ball shied off Yates' shoulder. 'Stop!'

" 'We do not surrender,' said Simms, but held his fire."

The historian laughed, the firewater having descended from a stinging rawness to a cordial warmth in his bosom.

"You laugh at the bravery of your cousin?"

"No indeed. I laugh trying to remember Yates' essay at eloquence. What was it he said? 'For you two we grant remiss without surrender. To the others we swear contempt.' He spat. Remember? 'Be gone with you!' Did I get it right?"

"Close enough. But why were we spared, cousin?"

"Because you were brave. Because Yates was not an animal but had read in his schoolboy's history how the noble treated the brave."

"Bravo for History, which begets chivalry. But how does History explain that when the real war came, the once-heroic Simms issued his *non serviam* and would not fight to save the Union?"

"History is silent on this matter, as it is on the reasons that caused the other Leonidas to decline a commission."

"And the noble Irish, did they fight?"

"For the most part no, as I recall. Why should they? Had the Union taken them to her bosom?"

"Pah! No need to talk of that." Simms passed the jar. "Take another swig, coz, and we will walk under the stars of Estes Park and experience blessed amnesia."

The air was brisk. Simms said, "As we pass under the trees on our way to the meadow we will dispose of the world. I will tell you that west of here they are still scrabbling for gold, but it grows much scarcer. What are they doing in the East, coz?"

"Digging coal, laying tracks this way, accumulating huge quantities of force, engaging in enormous political venality which, if the principals were nobler, would actually be crime."

Simms nodded with satisfaction. "And what are they doing in Europe?"

"Preparing for a war which my prophetic soul tells me will forever move the center of Europe east of La Belle France."

"Really. Our Gettysburgs taught them nothing, I take it."

"No, we are brutes. In Europe wars are still a branch of the decorative arts, backdrops for opera."

"Excellent report."

They walked out into the meadow. The stars burst upon them like a shower of graces. They looked up. Tears filled the historian's eyes. He did not know what they were the effect of—beauty? The mere operation of cold air on membranes dilated by liquor? He didn't care. He welcomed the tears and let them roll copiously down his cheeks. He had

no idea whether Simms saw them or not. He didn't care. Nevertheless he
felt deeply for his cousin, nursing, as he himself also did, the bruises of
war and defection. No matter that the former was dishonorable and the
latter honorable. And his boyhood heroism, his finest hour, was not
constellated in the sky. The stars in fact had not even witnessed it that
dense dank night.

"What are you going to do, coz?"

It was the very question the historian might have asked of himself
but would not have, so uncertain and agonized the answer.

"I'm going in search of a woman."

"Is that so? Any woman, a particular woman, or Woman?"

The historian was grateful for the lightness in his cousin's tone.
Nevertheless, he did not try to match it. "I don't know," he said, frankly
mystified. "God forbid it be the last."

"In America," Simms said with some asperity, "it's impossible for
it to be only the last. Here we have no Diana of Ephesus, no Venus, no
Virgin, not even a Madame du Barry, nothing but drudges and travelling
companions. What we deserve."

The historian was stung, horrified by the cogency of his cousin's
observation, which had started up in his mind a dark figure half
occluded by shadows of willful suppression—the unrealized American
woman. The figure eclipsed the stars, brutalized by horrid alternations
of menial work and dark imprisonment.

"So, why are you going in pursuit of woman, dear coz?" Simms'
voice was slightly more distant. He had moved off across the meadow,
from a sense of delicacy perhaps—or was it possible that he intuited his
proximateness to a figure of revulsion in his cousin's psyche?

"Partly in reaction, I fear. I am sick of the works of men."

"I'm with you there, cousin. And why else?" Simms was gentle in
joining sentiment and gentler in pressing inquiry. Even so, the historian
did not know how to answer. For in his mind's eye was the sweet face of
his grandmother, she who, despite all the rigors of being a stateman's
wife in a young republic, kept something of Queen Mab about her—
fairy music welling from secret grots and dells, the whisper of the sea
in shells, stardust, ah yes and black hair that when released from her
morning snood flew down her neck like birds freed from springes, aware,

on the instant, of their liberation. So the historian could only say, "I feel a deep longing." And then he added something, virtually involuntarily, that surprised him. "But nothing of passion."

"Passion can only be excited by the particular." And for once the historian was angry with his cousin—not because of his sententiousness, for he had gone on quickly to wish the historian well in his quest, but because of a sudden recognition that came to him with all the clarity of a bitter dream. It was this, that Simms would come out of the wilderness and find a woman and marry, and that he himself never would. Never. Maimed in his sex by he knew not what.

"Cold. I want firewater, sleep," said Simms.

The historian laughed. "Me too."

But he did not sleep. The cabin, closed tight against the cold, released after all a taint of bear and sounded clearly with Simms' mild snoring. And his nose twitched. And all his fastidiousness fell upon him. He lay there irritated, sleepless, wishing that he were entirely animal, or something utterly apart, some winged thing Queen Mab had touched to life with her star-tipped wand.

Out West

New Mexico, 1875

The trouble with Simms was he never knew exactly where he was. Lily knew where she was. Well, Simms knew where he was on a map. I don't mean that. In fact he could tell exactly how he got here, on the Butter-field Overland Mail. He could tell you every damned stop after he left San Antonio—Fort Mason, Menardville, Fort Conchu, Centralia Station, Barella Springs, San Elizario, El Paso del Norte and so on. Most of em nothing but dustbins with flies eating the sidelined mules the Apaches was too drunk to steal anyway. But to hear Simms tell it they was ports of call on a royal voyage.

Simms used to like to talk to me, see? "You're a learned man, Goven," he would say, "a natural philosopher." And, by God, by comparison, he was right. Most of the jackasses around here couldn't write or cipher. Half still can't. You watch one of these pokes here try to do a sum. They'll be all right until they get to a six and then they'll stick their tongues out of the sides of their mouths and start a tight little circle down on the line and then try to swoop the tail up. Goddamnedest thing you ever saw. And all because old man Klein was here in the old days and taught everybody the German way. When Lily come she couldn't change it. Why? Because it's unnatural and perverse, the way everything else is around here. You scrabble on the ground most of your life until one day you get some good likker or a few bucks or a pretty woman and then you swoop up to the top, where the hell ever that is. Nobody knows. But that's the way they like it around here.

Say, I'm a learned man. If I don't speak well it ain't because I don't know grammar. It's because I don't give a damn. Here it ain't worth the trouble. I'm a damned sight more learned than old man Chisum, who writes a hand like a crab tree. "Goven," Simms said to me shortly after he got here . . . Wait a minute. I didn't tell you that he come all the way from Boston, by way of the Rockies, where he learned the secrets of the wilds, he thought, but not how to talk natural. It appeared he would be shot for his accent before the first sundown, but he kept it concealed as best he could. Anyway, "Goven," he says, "I bet this place has a fascinating history."

"History!" says I. "There ain't any history here, Simms. If you want history, you'll have to make it up. Or, you could ride up north with a white flag and if the Mescaleros ain't drunk, they might take you to see Old Cadette or La Paz and they would tell you the history of the whole land, from the beginning. It would run something like this. First we was here and then the white man and the Mexicans come and ruined everything. Of course our history is a little different. It says: us and the Mexicans come and run the Indians out. Mighty interesting, ain't it?" Interesting or not, it seemed to please Simms greatly.

God was another subject he was interested in. He would get up and watch the sunrise. Then he would tell me how he could feel the sun beating away off over the desert, like a smithy getting ready to create everything all over again. And the smithy would. First he would raise the hills again out of the black of night. Then he would pick out a ranch house here and a barn there and a corral or two and a worm fence crawling across the range and then the herds and horses grazing on grama grass. And then he would spring the river loose again and fill it with fish—catfish, sunfish, bullheads, suckers, eel, buffalo, red horns, all flashing silver under the brass top of the river. And finally he would get some people out of bed and lure them outdoors to stand and look at their shadows, twenty feet tall springing out of the ground. And I would say, "Mighty pretty, Simms, but there ain't even a church in this valley. It's been tried, twice, but God can't be dragged out here, even kicking and screaming. He's too smart."

"You're talking about the wrong God," Simms said, and later I reflected there might be something to that.

Well, I suppose some would say that Simms made a little bit of history here. But I wouldn't. History is something that happens once. Simms' story happens over and over. Slicker from the east comes west and falls in with the schoolteacher, to the disgust of the local boys. You know the rest.

Curiously, Simms was a dead shot with his carbine even though he hadn't been to war. Of course by the time he got here the stray Indians and Jayhawkers was pretty well cleared out or domesticated. I was in the Home Guard, which wasn't no fun. "We could of used you here a few years back," I told him.

"No, you couldn't," he says, "because I won't shoot a man."

"No matter. I'm talking about Jayhawkers and Indians."

Simms said, "You can't fool me with that show of callousness and cynicism, Goven. How many did you gun down?"

"None. But it wasn't on principle. It was failing eyesight."

Simms laughed.

After a while some of the boys began to warm up to Simms. He hadn't gotten to be the schoolmarm's man yet, and he was a good drinker and a good listener. Whenever there was a shooting spree, which we have here periodically as an emetic against biliousness, Simms dove for cover like a scared prairie dog, and only once got nicked on the heel. Twice in brawls he couldn't get out of the way fast enough and got clipped on the chin and went down like a felled ponderosa. So Simms was generally accepted as an Easterner who couldn't quite handle our ways but who took his licks without complaining. And when it was discovered that properly likkered up he could talk like a cross between a snake doctor and a book, why then Colonel Voit and Major Buster became his champions.

Colonel Voit and Major Buster. In all probability these two men never rose above private, if they wasn't actually court-martialed and drummed out, but it was the practice then to raise your rank six notches or so on retirement. Who cared? And besides, Voit and Buster was something of local heroes. They had come through the valley toward the end of the war with a picket of several other soldiers, just when the Jayhawkers was about to take us over, looting and getting after the women. And they drove em out and even produced one corpse for display, though I never was able to see where it was shot and speculated from the gray of the face that it died of overexertion. Anyway, after the war Voit and

Buster come back self-promoted and decorated with medals they had thieved or won at poker over at Fort Cooper. It was their view that the town owed em a living if they drank, talked, played cards, and fired their pistols at least once a week and on national holidays.

Anyway, it was Simms' talk that won em over. One of his early topics was edibleness. You see, Simms had a project, which was to eat one of everything that moved. "It's one of the commandments," he told the colonel and the major and the boys. "The Lord told Adam, 'Of everything that swims in the water or crawls on the earth or flies in the air, I make you master. You name it and then eat it.' " This pleased em no end. And Simms was serious. He would take his rifle out and shoot one of everything he could get in his sights and then bring it back and eat it. Before he come here he had already et several kinds of bear, antelope, deer, elk, moose, trout, char, every kind of goose and duck, squirrel, rabbit, chipmunk, and some others.

"What's the point of it?" I asked him.

"It's the sacramental view of life," he said. "I'm part Hindoo. I deny nothing. I take it in."

I didn't tell him that maybe the animals would feel more sacramental if they was left alone. Anyway he would tell about his adventures in eating. Your chicken hawk was good only if eaten young, he allowed. Otherwise the legs got so tight strung you couldn't separate the drumstick from the second joint without a cleaver. Rattlesnake we all knew about, but he claimed you could extract a broth from the skeleton that would make a Frenchman's upper lip tremble. Skunk he compared favorable to rabbit, but it had to be taken unawares. Prairie dog tasted so vetchy, he said, that he didn't wonder they were furnished by God to eat up the bitter grass so the domestic stock wouldn't get it. A buzzard could not be eaten at all. Its digestive track was defective and did not change carrion into new flesh. And so on through many other species.

Now as you can imagine, all during Simms' account there was groans and burps and forced gut rumblings and exclamations of praise for beef and pork and the like. But after a while Zack, which was his only known name and who was half locoed before he ever touched the first drop, he couldn't take it. "By God, a man who would eat suckers and mud cat ain't fit to live."

"Just a minute, Zack," says Simms. "I can understand why you might promulgate such a declaration." This was the highfalutin stuff Colonel Voit and Major Buster loved. The colonel in particular would hang on every word, moving his lips along with Simms' so he could get it into his mouth for when it come time for him to show off to another crowd. "But," Simms went on, "you have to experience the savor of one of these lowly fishes when you finish it off with cornmeal."

Now Zack didn't have gumption enough to know if he was the honored sharer of prize information or the butt of a joke. He stood there glowering down at Simms, waiting to see how the others would take it, but showing already a near-homicidal unhappiness. Simms says, "I feed em up in an old washtub Widow Graham was kind enough to furnish me." Here comes a volley of guffaws from the gang. Zack couldn't figure it out and couldn't stand it a minute longer. He launched out and torpedoed Simms once in the belly and once in the mouth before the boys could pull him off, which was the appropriate hits all right, for these was certainly the offending organs in the case. But it was Zack, not Simms, that let off the bellow of pain. Why? Because he was betrayed. "Let go of me," he cried, almost in tears. "Why're you siding with a carrion-eating varmint like that?" Which was damned good for the likes of Zack and showed that he himself had picked up a little style from Simms, who was finally getting his breath back. "They're not siding with me, Zack. They're trying to create a little society here in which men don't beat each other to death."

"Each other!" howled Zack, having detected immediately in his fumed and addled brain the blatant sophistry of Simms' statement. "You are the only one that needs beating to death." He pulled mightily against his restrainers, but they finally throwed him down and pinioned his limbs and Major Buster sat on his ribs until he promised to leave without further ado.

"So much for Hindooism and pacifism in this spot," I told Simms later.

"Not at all," says he, sunny and tranquil as a June peach. "One of these days Zack and I will come to terms." I let it go at that.

Pretty soon Simms began to get interested in Lily, and for a while nobody concerned themselves. Certainly Lily was an independent thing requiring no protection, didn't want none. That was one reason the trouble took so long to brew. And Lily wasn't no flaming beauty either. Her whole face, including the chin, was too rounded out. And her ears was pulled forward, not due to defect from birth but because her mama used em to tuck up her hair, which otherwise blowed all around her face until she got mad at it and snapped it up in her teeth like a choke-bit stallion. The transformation of Lily from the wildest tomboy on the range to a schoolmarm is another story. Let's just say she left the settlement and when she come back four years later, she was the schoolmarm, Miss Proper. She was a corrector. She corrected speech, manners, writing, dress, table setting, just about anything you could name that had rules to it. If she had been an outsider, the men would of rode over the objections of the women and scatted her out of the settlement. But she was our own Lily, who used to skin up the *higueras*, ride bareback, swim the river, and so on. And still when she got crossed, the old mischievousness would come out again. One day Abner Cubb put his boy Jeptha up to asking her what was the proper way to hold the fingers and what was the proper order of teats when milking. "Like this," she said, making Jeptha dangle his fingers down while she pulled on em one by one clockwise all the while holding her little finger out like she was lifting a cup at the queen's garden party, which caused all the other boys in the school to commence to laugh and make contented mooings. And for weeks after that whenever Jeptha trudged up to the schoolhouse he got heifered with moos and laughs, which caused him to have hot words with his daddy and which discouraged others from trying to pull one over on her. It was no wonder that none of the farmers or pokes had ever come a-courting. But when Simms started to hang around her, why then it dawned on em that she was a woman after all and one of the few unattached. Still, they was afraid of her tongue and her cleverness, so there never was no chance the field would get crowded. Finally one come forward. And who else would it be but Zack, who had no doubt put himself up for no other reason than to cross Simms.

"Simms," I said, "he probably don't give a damn if Lily never gives him a look, as long as it gives him a chance to shoot you."

"Fie," says Simms. "Lily's gentility will sooth the savage beast and protect me from all harm."

Well, we have a saying here. Those who do not heed must feel.

Meanwhile, Simms fell in love with Lily's tomboy past. After the children were gone and she was straightening up in the schoolhouse, inspecting the desks and papers, he would come by and get her to talking about her childhood. She told him how on the trip from Texas, when her family first come to the valley, she couldn't abide the confinement of the wagon and the company of her little brothers and finally growed so vexed that she quaked like an aspen. So her daddy let her ride the oxen, first a wheeler, where he could keep an eye on her, and then up on one of the leaders, where she said she kept watch for Apaches, which led to another story. The first year they was in the settlement she traded an ignorant squaw a calico doll for a baby girl. And when the Indian woman come back at the end of the day for the papoose, and Lily's mother made her give it back, she set up a terrible howl, that she had been cheated—not out of the doll, she didn't care nothing about that, but the baby, which was to grow up and run and ride wild horses like the wind. Ever after that she called a squelcher an Indian giver. But still she went on companying with those not of her own kind, like the Mexicans, because she wanted to learn how to balance an olla of water on her head like the Mexican women, which, of course, she did, and cajoled one of the old potters to throw and fire one for her, and in the process learned Spanish. Nor would she ever after that carry a bucket up from the well, though her daddy gave her a licking. Every day you could see the one *gringa* in the whole settlement carrying water on her head. Lily was bell metal. Nobody could crack her, not even her daddy. That's what fascinated Simms. She told about being a roamer. She would ride out on her pony in the morning and show up again at sundown, and the lickings did no good, nor would she tell where she'd been. This drove her daddy wild until one day he bellowed up a fire and branded her on the foot, barred K. By God, he swore to her, every day she rode out without permission and report he would brand her again, and did on the other foot, but couldn't bring himself to disfigure her any further. Lily showed the marks to Simms.

Well, this kind of rough and tumble butt-headedness was why the locals didn't rush up to the schoolhouse and declare themselves for courting. Was Simms courting? It wasn't clear. It seemed more like he was having a romance with the primitive frontier. Down by the river he had built himself a little adobe, but he wouldn't gyp it, so it stayed ugly brown. He run a little ditch from the river right around by the door and baited it with cornmeal and scraps until he had the dang fishes eating out of his hand. And all around the casita he planted two each of apple, peach, plum, pear, and cherry. He laughed when I asked him if he thought they were male and female. "Goven," says he, "I'm the Noah of the fruit world. This is a new creation."

Maybe. But Simms smelled decidedly old. He had shot himself a bear and salted the skin out and commenced to wear it wrapped around him like a winter brave. "Simms," says I, "why don't you wear merino like everybody else? When it gets a little wet with sweat and rainwater it stinks good enough, don't it?" But he only laughed. Also he stitched himself up a pair of moccasins which caught the sweat of his feet pretty good. And he burned mesquite and buffalo chips in his fire, which was all right if he had made the flue big enough, but he soon picked up the fragrance of jerked bear, which was what he was eating along with his other vittles unheard of around here. The Mexicans said he had become a *natrix*, a witch doctor. It was Lily who showed Simms how to make soap out of *amole*, or Spanish dagger root. But he didn't take it as having nothing to do with cleanliness. It was just the next phase of his romance of the frontier, which was to have Lily show him all the old ways of the settlement. So she took him to watch the farrier, and you would of thought to see his eyes bulge and glisten with fire that Simms had found the great smithy of the desert that re-creates everything at dawn. She also showed him how the women dipped sperm candles because we still didn't have any coal oil at that time. She took him to the mill to watch it grind and to watch Old Man Jessie sharpen the burrs, which he said were of French flint, the finest made. She showed him the rolling sweep old Chisum had invented to gather acorns for the hogs. She told Simms the same thing she told the school children. "Mr. Chisum is the long-headedest man in the settlement. That's why he's the richest. He can always see a possibility that nobody else can." She was right. For instance, at the height of his holdings, when he had maybe

60,000 head, he never tried to stop the rustlers cold, which would of meant an army of cowboys and a river of blood. He just kept his best cattle close and fed off some sickly animals to the outside to be taken. In that way his herd was purified.

Lily took Simms out to old Chisum's and showed him how they gingered up the goats and then turned em loose to trample the wheat. She took him across the river and showed him how the Mexicans made their corn sieves of rawhide, serendas they called em, and how they beat the ears with saplings until the kernels fell through. "It's like the old scapegoat rituals of purification," said Simms. And when they throwed the kernels up with their shovels, he stood downwind and caught the pieces of husk and silk against his face, like a blessing.

So it was time for Zack. He come to Lily and declared himself for courting. And by God he got himself up real decent. His shirt and britches was washed, and his boots and hair was shined. He chewed rosemary to sweeten his breath and he carved the dung out of his fingernails with his knife. Lily let him walk her home from school some days. And on Saturdays she let him take her to store. Some was surprised that she didn't turn him away. Others figured she let him tag along just for the sake of decency and good grace. Others said she done it for Simms, or otherwise Zack would come down on him. That, of course, was what didn't work. It was bound to happen that Zack and Colonel Voit and Major Buster and Simms and a bunch of us would end up in the saloon one night and Zack would get likkered up. He had carried Lily's basket and bags that day and he was preening like a cock. "Why don't you let her be, Simms? What the hell woman wants a Boston Indian around her with the stink of bear and a skunk-tail beard." That both pleased and angered Zack. He had the knack of riling himself up, discovering in his own words worse corruption than he had originally imagined. "And God knows what your breath and your belly rips must smell of, eating suckers and bear, for God's sake!" Zack fumed. "Ain't there a gentleman among you that will free Lily from this dung heap?"

Colonel Voit laughed and stroked his face. "You can't hardly get on him, Zack, for the bearskin, because he has learned bear talk and called his brothers off. Remember how they used to break down the corn and eat it and trample down the banks of the irrigation ditches? No more, thanks to Simms. Why the major and me was thinking of taking up a community collection, in gratitude to Brer Bear Simms."

"Goddamn it," says Zack, "all the more reason to shake him loose from Lily. You want her to marry a bear?"

Then Major Buster come in. "Sometimes, Zack, a woman will take on two beaus just to scare into action the one she really wants."

"But which-a-one?" says the colonel in a witchy voice. "That is the question, Zack."

Zack threw down another shot of whiskey. "Naw, it ain't the question, goddamit. If I thought there was the puniest chance in the world this carrion-eating varmint could slick Lily into marrying him, I'd tie him to a skid and drag him off downriver for the coyotes."

The colonel laughed the way you do when a braggart has finally crossed the divide. That tipped Zack over. "Goddamit, I'll show you." He lit into Simms, swinging as heavy as he could. But Simms just hunkered up and wrapped his skin around his head and twisted and humped and grunted. Zack couldn't get a clean hit. He commenced to kick, which was more telling. Simms groaned. The colonel and the major and a couple of boys figured that was enough and dragged Zack off, him flailing away the whole time. "Goddam filthy bear!"

They got him sat down in a chair panting. Simms come out from under his skin and blinked about him, for all the world like a spring bear. The colonel gave Zack a lecture. "Lookyhere, Zack," he said, "this settlement is a little oasis of civilization out here in the wilderness. We ain't going to have you tear it up like a savage. If you want to challenge Simms to combat, you throw down your gauntlet. But remember, the challenged one names the weapons and the distance."

Now, of course, Zack had his gauntlets with him all right. He took great pride in em because they was supposed to been Bill Boney's, Billy the Kid, but nobody ever proved it. He threw one, but not down, instead right into Simms' face, where it smacked a little and dusted his hair.

"All right," hollered the major with great vehemence and happiness, "the gauntlet is throwed. If you accept the challenge, Simms, you pick it up. If you don't you can slink out of the settlement and be titled a yellow-livered coward ever after." Everybody gave a rallying whoop, including Zack. But Simms didn't need no urging. He stooped right over, picked up the gauntlet, and throwed it gently into Zack's hand.

"All right, then," says the colonel, rubbing his hands with pure joy, "you choose the weapons, Mr. Simms." Somehow I knew Simms wouldn't name rifles, though he could of cut Zack down easy. For a time he didn't say nothing. "What'll it be, Mr. Simms?" says the colonel, pretending impatience but loving the high drama of it.

"Snowballs at twenty paces," says Simms, squinting down and showing his teeth like a mad dog. For a minute then everybody wore a face of puzzlement—brows tucked, mouths screwed—until one of the pokes says, "Snowballs! What the hell?"

"Yeah! What the hell! Snowballs!" was the general outcry.

But Simms rose up in the din. "Shut up, you ignorant pokes! Snowballs it is, and without face masks or chest protectors, without greaves or shields!" Simms made himself stern as an old bear.

The colonel hemmed. "Mr. Simms, although the choice of weapons do fall to the one challenged, the idea is that one of the regular weapons will be chosen, like fists or pistols or sabers, suchlike."

By this time Zack had got his voice. "Snowballs! There ain't any snow short of a two-day ride up the Thompson Trail. And besides, we ain't talking about kid stuff. I throwed down a pistol gauntlet, goddamit!"

Simms spoke again. "On the steppe of Kharsakov young Prince Alexei of the house of Romanov met his fate at the hands of Ivan the Terrible, who squeezed his snow down to the consistency of diamonds. The first missive tore off the young prince's right ear. The second extirpated his left eye. And the third sliced away the cap of his cranium and strew his brains over the glacial hoarfrost, gray on gray. Everything is in the packing." Simms made his fingers claw and crimp, like a hawk's talons. "Colonel, I name you my second. Will you have the major as yours, Zack? If so, let us provision ourselves and ride to the mountain."

Now it was hard to tell whether the boys was going to swallow this or roll Simms out into the night. He went on. "And I promise you, sir, that your corpse will be brought back on your steed and buried with all due rites as benefiting a warrior. And you shall do the same for me if fate fall your way."

That decided it for the colonel, and he decided it for the rest. "The challenge has been made and accepted. The seconds have been named. All that is left is the deed itself."

I was the official witness. It was a strange ride up the old Thompson Trail. Late November it was and unusual gray. I had been up many times, for antelope, bear, and even mountain goat, which we never got, and once after a party of Mescalero raiders, which also escaped us. But I never saw it so gray and foggy. Our riding order was the colonel, Zack, the major, Simms, and me, in a single file, so there wasn't no talk, just the ruckle of hoofs and the snort of the horses, and even that was muffled by the fog. When we got to the tree line the pines and firs would rise up in front of us and pass by like it was them was moving and not us. Then past the tree line was the needle rocks filing down on both sides like giants that could strike down on us if they took a mind to. The sun was mostly behind us both morning and afternoon except every once in a while from a switchback we faced out on it, all gauzed in fog like something once bright but dying. I wished I was back in the valley. At first I had thought of the snow duel on the mountain as a fine joke that only Simms could put on, with, of course, the conspiring of the colonel and the major. But even before we set out I saw it wasn't no joke with him. In his little adobe he went down on his haunches praying, purifying himself before battle. And also the colonel and the major had throwed off the barroom dramatics and was all grim business. And Zack was dark as a skulking scout. Something had gone wrong with the joke. Nature itself was against it.

Even at night when we set camp nobody had nothing to say except the necessary. Zack tried glowering at Simms, to spook him, I suppose, but Simms was entirely inside himself. His eyes never looked out. That was two nights. The third day we hit the snow line about midday. "Here it is," declared the major, but Simms shook his head. "Too thin."

"The challenged party," said the colonel, "judges the weapons insufficient." We rode on. Zack didn't say nothing, him who was likely to be agitated by a whisper. It worried me. I figured he had something up his sleeve. I watched. I was the witness.

A few hours later we come up on a little flat. We was high enough that the sun might of shined through, but it was late. Even so, I thought I heard it humming and zinging with the effort. Something, by God, was vibrating, something maybe over by the bank of snow that mostly covered the wall of rock at the far side of the flat. Simms got off his horse, tramped around and dug down in the snow with his hand. "This will do," he said. We hoppled our horses, which was snorting fog like dragons.

"Goven," says the colonel, "will you step off the twenty paces?" I went on into the flat a ways before I stepped it off and marked the spots. This got the horses out of the line of fire. It put one man up near the wall of rock and the other near the edge of the flat.

"Combatants remove all outer garments," said the colonel. Simms throwed his bearskin off with a swirl and Zack done the same with his merino. The major stood by Zack. "Gloves and hats to remain, colonel?" says he. The colonel nodded, then said, "Which position does the challenged choose?"

"I relinquish choice of position to the challenger."

Zack didn't say nothing but stomped off to the spot I marked near the rock wall. The major went with him. The colonel stood by Simms. I walked halfway in between, off to one side.

"Are the combatants prepared?" hollered the colonel. Zack and Simms nodded. The colonel and the major backed off, in a line with me. "At the ready!" hollered the colonel. The two men commenced to pack a snowball. When I was back in the valley this was the place I had warned myself I couldn't laugh, for Simms' sake, unless of course he got to laughing himself. But this wasn't no more funny than if they was drawing pistols. "Fire when ready!"

Zack fast as he could, heaved a ball that busted up on Simms' shoulder. And throwed two more that was too fluffy to do any damage. When Simms finally throwed his, it was tight packed and thumped into Zack's belly with a whump and staggered him back, but it give Zack a piece of good ammo and he got it off into Simms' chest and knocked him back some. Simms went on packing, and Zack packed, but you could see he was just waiting for Simms to throw a good one so he could get it. And Simms did. It was way off, down at Zack's feet, but it was only a decoy. While Zack dug it out of the snow, Simms pitched another ball right into Zack's head and knocked him down, out if it hadn't been for the hat, which flopped off in the snow. Now Zack had two balls

Simms made, while Simms had to make another one, but Zack was
woozy. His aim was off. Both balls missed. Simms lambasted him, one
ball on the gloved hand that Zack throwed up, but another one in the
throat. Zack went down gasping. Before he could get his breath, while he
was still down on his knees, another ball come slashing across his cheek
and ear. The blood come, and Zack sunk down on the snow.

"Major," called Simms, "you should advise your man to ask for
quarter or you yourself declare him incapable of carrying on."

"What do you say, Zack?" said the major. Simms was packing
another ball but holding his fire.

Zack shook his head. I couldn't tell if he meant no or if he was just
clearing it. The light was bad. The blood on the snow was dark purple.
Then suddenly Zack staggered up on his feet, ripped back the chap on
his right thigh, and pulled a pistol. "Goddamn carrion-eating varmint!"
He fired. The shot boomed out like thunder, but Simms didn't go down.
The bullet went ringing over the ledge and down the mountainside.
Maybe Zack shot wide on purpose because now he was grinning and
hollering, "What about it, bear? You ask for quarter? Colonel, better
take care of your man!"

"Zack!" The colonel put all the sternness in his voice he could, but
Zack was locoed with hatred and snowball hits. And anyhow, this was
what he'd planned from the first. The colonel and the major had pistols,
but they couldn't draw for fear that Zack would cut em down. I had a
rifle in my saddle, I turned to go get it, but another shot thundered out,
and snow spat up at my feet. "Stay where you're at, Goven!" He looked
at the three of us, seconds and witness. "Everybody just keep real still."

The mountain groaned. I couldn't tell where it come from, but I
heard it. Then, with a leap quick as a cougar Simms flung a ball that
zinged into Zack's thigh so hard it took him down, but he come up
fanning the pistol. He must of thought Simms was coming in behind the
ball, but Simms had flung himself down in the snow. Three shots thundered out, and then down come the wall, snow, rocks, and all. The major
barely got away, debris tumbling at his heels. I had to cut and run, the
colonel slogging out in front of me. And even Simms had to jump up
and scramble back. The horses neighed and reared, but we had em
hoppled good.

As soon as the avalanche had settled, Simms led us back to the heap. "Hurry," he hollered. We dug into the snow as hard as we could, having nothing but our hands to work with. It went slow. Some of the boulders took all four of us to roll away. The only hope was that Zack was covered with snow and the rocks had missed him, but it wasn't to be. When we finally reached him, just at nightfall, he was still half under a flat slab that had stove in his chest and sent blood gushing out of his mouth into the snow. He was already cold.

Simms never would of finished Zack off, we kept telling everybody. It was Zack that killed himself trying to kill Simms unfair. They had to believe us. They didn't have no choice. But in the end it didn't stick. We should of had one of the boys with us, but who could of believed it would end up that way? Maybe it didn't matter finally that me and the colonel and the major might be seen as partial to Simms, because I believe the thing that got to the boys was the sight of us riding back into the settlement, me and the colonel and the major all bearded and hag-eyed from riding down into that whirling sun, and Simms all hooded like an Indian natrix turned bear, and worst of all the corpse of Zack, which was all bled out to a blue white. And when we untied it from the horse, it stayed curled over, like a wind-tortured juniper. And the eyelids, rolled halfway up, didn't show nothing but the whites. And the body couldn't be straightened out for burial, but had to be wound up crooked and buried in a wide hole.

There was no way the boys could stand it, no matter what the truth was. I felt it. "Get out of the settlement, Simms," I told him, "at least until this thing blows over." And he did lie low—kept away from Lily, and even stayed out of sight around his own place. But he wouldn't leave. So one night a big posse rode down on the casita with torches and drove him out. I got on my horse and followed as close as I could. They drove him down to the river hee-yawing at him like he was an animal. And he did look just like a big bear. The moon was not half, so it was hard to see. Yet I couldn't make myself believe a man would shamble that way and go down on all fours. They ran him into the river, and when he come up on the other side, they forded and herded him toward the ravine. Nobody fired a gun. They just drove at him with fire and kept him circled until they had him to the edge of the ravine, where he scrambled around in the rocks, dodging the torches this way and that. I saw him slash at the horses with his claws and saw him bare his fangs in the firelight. But the riders hollered and ran at him and whooshed the fire in his face until at last he lost his balance and tumbled down the ravine.

Then the posse dismounted and held their torches out over the edge of the ravine. "There he is!" hollered one. I could see a dark thing down there in the rocks. The posse began to roll stones down, faster and faster, bigger and bigger, until there was nothing but a general thunder and a cloud of dust rising up under the light of the torches. They waited until that settled and then they surveyed their handiwork, which was a huge heap of stones down in the bottom of the ravine. "Let's see the carrion-eating varmint get out from underneath that!" They rode off with a whoop, and I rode home slow, thinking two things. One, it was the strangest posse I ever saw. Not a shot was fired, not even in the air. Either they had agreed against guns, or something about Zack's fate had scared em. The other thing I thought was that I didn't know for sure what the critter in the ravine was. I wanted to know, but how could I? It would of taken a six-team of mules two days to move all those rocks and a day-long drive down from the south end of the ravine before that.

Christmas passed. Spring come on. One evening I went to see Lily. She was all alone now. The boys wasn't interested in her. Nobody was. Nobody so much as lifted a hat to her when she come to the store on Saturday. Still, she held her head up, so nobody insulted her directly. But she felt the sting. When she come to the door she looked at me cold. "What do you want, Goven?"

"I want to know if you talked to Simms after we come down from the mountain." There was no need to beat around the bush with Lily.

"Yes. Now let me ask you a question. How did two intelligent men like you get involved in that assininity? Zack, Voit, and Buster I can understand. But how did you two?"

"How else was Simms going to deal with Zack? After all, you taken both as beaus."

"Took. Did not. I only abided Zack for fear he would be even more violent toward Simms, hotheaded as he was. So if I could play a game of patience with Zack, why couldn't you and Simms?"

I had wondered if she would show sorrow. All she showed was anger. "Well, what did Simms say about his plans?"

"Plans for what?" All this while she kept her eyes hard and never offered me a step across the threshold.

"Plans for the future in general. Did he plan to go away?"

Her eyes got even harder. "What difference does it make? He's dead now."

"That's what I ain't sure of."

"Am not. What do you mean?"

"I mean I ain't . . . am not convinced he's dead."

"Thrown off the edge of a cliff and buried under stone and not dead! Goven, you must've left your senses up on the mountain."

"Maybe," says I, "but I was thinking of hiring a bunch of boys and going down to give him a proper burial, if it is him."

"Maybe you would find a carved stone saying, 'Stranger, ride on. Forbear to disturb these bones.'"

I squinted at her. "Now who's cracked?"

She give me a smile but dropped it quick. "Goven, let it be."

And I did. But I noticed that Lily rode out alone sometimes of a Saturday or a Sunday. Well, she had always been a loner, but I kept my eyes out. And the more I saw her ride out, the more convinced I got that she was meeting somebody on her rides—Simms, I figured, who was not what was buried under the rocks in the ravine. So one Sunday I trailed her on foot. If I followed on horse, she would see me. And I figured I could keep up on foot because she rode an old mare that was stove up in the shoulder. Lily rode west out past old Chisum's long house. I remember the day when Voit and Buster and the soldiers rode in that way just before the war ended and the Jayhawkers had us down. They had a banner, the Second United States Dragoons. Even they was a pretty sight that day, but not as pretty as Lily. She had let her hair down and the afternoon sun caught in it and flickered like a young fire as she jaunced up and down on the mare. I stayed low and scurried from cover to cover, once among old Chisum's *carrizo*, where I saw that the bears were coming back to sup now that Simms wasn't there to discipline them. Then I ran among Chisum's sheep. I remembered people thought it was crazy, a cattle man bringing sheep onto his land, but it turned out to prove again just how long-headed old Chisum was. These sheep concentrated on the pip grass and so kept the cows from getting alkali poisoning.

When Lily got to the foothills it was easier for me to stay hid. The trail rove around curlicue through the rises and the stands of mesquite and juniper. I hadn't been this way since Simms and me come out to hunt black rabbits to enlarge his sacramental diet. So the country was not bright in my memory, but I didn't worry when sometimes I lost sight of Lily because I trusted she would stay on the trail, and the nag couldn't get too far ahead of me. To tell the truth, I had half forgotten what I come for, watching Lily disappear behind a clump of juniper or a hillock and come back again with the sun in her hair. I couldn't see the round tomboy face or the poked-out ears. So I just went on that way, dreamy, for quite a while. And then she rode behind a hillock and I followed to the other side and come out on a kind of mesa butted up against a sharp hill. The trail petered out. And Lily was gone. I couldn't believe my eyes. There wasn't no place for her to go. I run out to the edge of the mesa to see if the trail picked up on the down side. There wasn't no trail, and the side of the mesa was too steep for Lily's mare even if she led it down. Besides, I would of seen her because below the mesa was another flat running five mile or more to the next ridge of hills. I run along the edge of the mesa just to make sure there wasn't no defile where she was hiding out with Simms.

I was breathless, more from the mystery of the thing than from running. I went over to the face of the hill and commenced to search for a secret trail through, but the hill was a blank wall except for one outcropping of ragged rocks. Behind it I found a little cave. I stopped and listened. I felt foolish. You can't lead a horse into a cave, not even Lily's old mare. I listened. I didn't hear nothing. I took a few steps in. It was black. I didn't hear nothing but the tiny sizzle you get in a cave, more in your ear than in the air. I come back and looked around. The sky was blue except down by the rim, where it was going pink. I had time to get back to the settlement before dark, but I couldn't leave. I sat down in the middle of the mesa and kept watch while the sun set toward the next ridge.

It was a quiet place. The jays and sparrows and magpies we had

back in the settlement didn't come out there. A hawk had been hunting
on the way out, but he was gone now. No rabbits came. There was some
nice hot lava rock out at the far end of the mesa, but no snake sunned
there. As the light dropped, some insects took up, but very pale.

Where was Lily? I was hungry and a little light-headed. I tried to
picture in my mind what had happened. Was there a passage through the
cave? Had Simms come with a torch and let her through? I thought I
should of run around to the other side of the hill where she would of
come out, and the next day I did, but all I could find was hill rolling up
on hill toward the mountains. Anyway, I didn't leave that night. I stayed
on the mesa. I had hope that they would come out of the cave, Lily and
Simms, and say something to me before they went on. Or that a piece of
the hill would open up and show a hall inside, all lit up, and Simms and
Lily would let me in. That got pretty thick so I shook my head clear and
walked around the mesa. It was quiet. A couple of crickets and away off
some coyotes, nothing else. I had nothing to be scared of, but still I felt
childish sad, like I had been deserted by my mama. It was silly, but I
couldn't help it. Tears come to my eyes and splayed the stars.

After a while I scratched up a little dirt and weed, folded my hat,
and laid my head down. Nobody came. I thought maybe Lily would, but
she didn't. Then I went to sleep.

The sun slapped me right in the face the next morning. I cocked an
eye and saw a prairie dog freeze against the sunrise like a stick and then
scamper off when I moved. I took another turn around the mesa. I threw
a rock in the cave. It made a flat hollow sound. I hollered, "Anybody in
there?" Then I went around the hill.

Back at the settlement I went by Lily's place. She was not there, was
never there again. I went home and et bread, beans, and bacon and drank
coffee and tried to figure out what it all meant.

There was two things I could of done. One was to take my mules
down into the ravine and move the stones. The other was to take a load
of pitch pine out and explore the cave. I didn't do neither. They had left
me without a word. So I would not humble myself to look for em.
Nevertheless, the next year, '76, I went in search of wisdom, by stage and
by train, to the Centennial, where I saw many things, among which was
President Grant himself, bearded, high-collared, and sober as a judge.

But most interesting was the famous Corliss steam engine, which it was said produced the pull of two thousand and five hundred head of horse. It had a flywheel about the size of the planetary system. And the pistons and their hoods was taller than old Chisum's barn and stomped up and down like a mad giant. The engineer sat in a little box reading a newspaper, except every once in a while he would dash up one of the long ladders and drop a little oil on a spot he could hear the giant complaining about, whereas the rest of us couldn't hear nothing but a terrible rattle and thunder. What would happen, I wondered, if the giant's little friend wasn't there to tend his sore spots? I bet the giant would go crazy and run wild. I got back on the train, and on the way south I was thinking that with the giant I could move the stones in a hour or bore a hole through from the cave to the Cordillera del Norte. But I saw that was foolish. It was foolish thinking about the giant and Simms at the same time at all. And I said to myself, "Simms, you and Lily stay in the country. The world of the giant ain't your world." And I was sure it wasn't mine neither.

Clio
New York, 1877

The historian was giving instructions to his agent, Rothman. "How will you know her? You must use your intuition. The fame of your intuition is the reason I retain your services. Keep in mind that as the embodiment of Clio she suffers all the ills of the age."

"Who's Clio?" Rothman wore a striped cloak that was like a prayer shawl, and his jutting forehead was like a phylactery of bone.

"Clio's the daughter of Mnemosyne, goddess of memory. She's the muse of history."

"What do you want with her?" Rothman's black eyes bore insistently into the historian.

"I want her to liberate me. I'm an historian. My head is crammed with the things we are, but it's stoppered. The woman will restore my memory. When you bring her here and she tells me her tale, I'll remember everything. I'll write again."

"Women are suspicious in this age, sir. I can't tell them I'm looking for the embodiment of Clio."

"No, of course not. Tell them that an eccentric millionaire will pay handsomely for stories of American lives." The historian continued to meet Rothman's dark gaze, but allowed himself the hint of a smile. "And if she's not amenable to the mercenary aspects, then tell her that she's to assist in the making of a gorgeous and unique pearl. Have you seen the pearls in the museum at the Vatican, Rothman?"

"Never, sir."

"They're marvelous—some humped like Indian elephants, others

elongated like fish, others folded and carapaced like scarabs or like trilobites, or self-paired like Siamese teardrops. What do you think determines the shape of the pearl, Rothman, the irritant or the oyster?"

"I don't know, sir."

"Then tell her that."

"This is a hard job, sir, all in figures—not a definite woman with a real name."

"If I'd wanted merely a certain Mrs. Smith, I would have hired any agent at all. I would not have troubled to find the one whose intuition is reputed to be a net so fine that nothing can escape it."

Rothman leaned back but didn't shift his gaze. "Why not go out and look for her yourself, sir? You'd recognize her more easily, and save my fee."

The question gave the historian pause. He turned and looked behind him. Not a ray from streetlamp or moon lanced the velvet drapes closed tight in front of the French doors, beyond which lay the fallow winter garden where even the junipers had gone gray and withdrawn from the air their mildly acrid pungence. The historian looked the other way. Behind Rothman was the massive door that gave out upon the impressive portico commanding the street. Over their heads a single green-shaded globe hung from the high ceiling and illuminated the desk and a small circle beyond. Out in the penumbra, on the long shelves, stood Schleiermacher and Scott, Pausanias and Polybius, and hundreds of others, including his own dust-sealed oeuvre. He felt securely immured. To Rothman he said, "It's not safe for me to go out. An historian without his muse is like a somnabulist on a battlement. The fog curls up around his feet. He dare not move. One false step and down he goes into the chicken-shat courtyard or down into the outer darkness of the unknown."

"Another figure, sir."

"Yes, I'm afraid so, Rothman. When I have nothing to write, words are a mere passage from any one thing to another. Rothman's cloak might become the memento mori on the back and wings of a magpie in flight." The historian made his eyes lachrymose and a little desperate. He took from his desk drawer a ledger, wrote out a draft, and handed it to his agent. "The advance I promised you."

Rothman took the draft. "It's more than you said."

"I'm asking more of you than I realized."

Rothman held the draft absently. "All the ills of the age," he repeated slowly. "Her spirit would need great strength to bear up under that."

"Yes, and great sensibility to receive its full weight in the first place."

Rothman nodded slowly. Then he took a deep breath and relaxed somewhat the rigor of his gaze. "We'll see, sir."

"Go now," the historian said, "you'll find her."

When Rothman had departed, the historian lay down on his couch and called the familiar sequence to mind. It began always at the city gate, where the Lord Mayor's men met the ancient Voltaire with an ermine-lined litter. Their livery was all of gold and white. The horse guard formed a cordon of sword and clatter. In the litter, open to the admiring throngs, only the face was visible, the famous nose severing the thick city air, as mind and pen had cut away the illusions of the ancient régime. But that night when the ladies of the court came to pay homage they plucked hairs and threads and even bits of embroidery and buttons from his coat. And later Madame de Fleury—she who had posed as a serving lady during the fete at the palace—recounted the report of his valet that the aging body had already begun to turn to amber like the miraculously preserved saints of the Vatican, that it gave off a faint incense, that the shanks were translucent and the bones luminous.

Great Enlightener, Pontiff of Encyclopedism. The historian smiled. How cleverly the old Philosophe had cozened the Roy du Soleil, crept into his soul and manner like a hermit crab. The historian considered himself a direct heir of the great Philosophe, for he proposed to creep into a soul, too—not of a king but of a woman, and discover there not only the lineaments of an age but of Clio herself, the muse of history. The historian closed his fist. Yes, by God, he would have her. The noble Rothman would find her. That was the way of the new history. You didn't seek in the sacred dust where ancient papers gave up to the air their mortal fibers mote by mote. You sent an agent out into the street to bring back the thing itself, in the flesh, vibrant, warm, and brimming with all the ills of the historical condition.

∽

When Rothman walked rapidly, especially if the wind was in his face, his cloak rippled and revealed a continuous unfolding where black stripes and white stripes arose out of each other in the unsettled moiré of an eyeblink, ever changing. His forehead thrust forward and pierced the emanations of any street whatsoever—the elegant passage of carriages in the park, the curses of congested carters in the Garment District, or in this case the furtive stridence of the tenderloin, where he came upon the scene of an eviction, a below-ground off Fulton. The law was breaking it up, a sergeant and six, brass-buttoned to the throat and wearing gloves against the miasma and filth. But it was no use. The straw ticks were rotten and the bedding fell apart even as they lugged it out. The bedsteads were verminous and so were the bunks that had been triced up in the cubicles. Rothman's nose wrinkled involuntarily. And now the officers piled in the gutter an incongruent conglomeration of chattels—stoves, straw hats, soup signs, looking glasses, perfumes, holy pictures, and the like. Beyond the stir Rothman saw a magazine sketcher drawing on his pad at a furious rate. A woman stood beside him in a state of controlled agitation. "Where are the stays on the corsets? Where are the eyelets and drawstrings?" She spoke with bitter mockery in a distinct southern accent. "How will your readers know how it feels to be cinched up in a bee waist? And the stink—how will they know that? How will they hear the cries?"

"From the faces of the officers and the prostitutes," replied the sketcher, still drawing away furiously.

The woman turned and accosted the sergeant. "Well, you've come at just the right time to avoid catching the gentlemen callers."

"I would have avoided being here altogether if it was left to me," said the sergeant in a surly tone. The woman snapped her eyes at him and started to speak again, but was distracted by the appearance of the madam, who came up out of the stews screaming, "The devil take you! What cause have you to disturb my boardinghouse for young ladies?"

"A routine eviction," said the sergeant. "Don't tempt us to look for evidence of misdoing."

"The devil take you!" said the madam through clenched teeth and plunged back down the stairs, perhaps to rescue some memento of the establishment. No doubt she had already stuffed her cache of earnings safely into the bosom of her dress.

Rothman turned his attention again to the woman, who gave an angry shake of her head and said loudly, though to no one in particular, "I *will* do something, so help me." She turned and walked away. Rothman followed her. Two blocks away, the progress of both impeded by the passage of several carriages, he addressed her. "Excuse me, madam. May I have a word with you?"

The woman, lost in thought and utterly unaware of her pursuer, now turned and looked Rothman full in the face. Annoyance and interest contended in her gaze. "Who are you?"

Rothman tilted his head away from the corner and the two of them stepped aside to a storefront. "I'm in the employment of a millionaire who pays handsomely for American stories."

The woman's brows plunged down. "What do you think I am?"

Rothman allowed a shadow to pass over his usually implacable gaze. "And what do you think I am, a procurer?"

"I don't know. You don't look like the ones that work around here. You look like some kind of mystic."

"Then believe what I tell you."

"About the eccentric millionaire? All right, what does he want? A spicy story about the stews of Fulton Street? Tell him to read it in *Harper's*, and look at the lurid pictures."

"No, he doesn't want that story. He wants your story."

"My story! What on earth does he know about my story?"

"He knows that it's significant for the history of our time."

The woman allowed a hint of smile to play over her face. "Well, I declare. How does he know that?"

"He's an historian. It's his business to know."

"And what's your business?"

"I'm his agent."

"You mean the one who locates—what do you call them?—the subjects?"

Rothman said nothing.

"And did you say I'd be handsomely paid just to tell stories?"

"Your story."

The woman reflected for a moment. "And if I say yes?"

"Then tell me where I may pick you up and what night. I'll come with a carriage. I'm warrant for your safety. You can trust me."

The woman looked in Rothman's face. "All right then, let's say I trust you." She took from her purse a small pad, wrote on it with a stub of pencil, and handed the sheet to Rothman. "Come by around eight. I won't be armed." She gave a rich, almost tuneful laugh, turned away, and left Rothman to look after her.

∽

Therefore, at an hour made indeterminate by his self-immural there came the agreed upon tap-tap-tap at the historian's study door, which immediately he opened to two: a lady in a dark cape and Rothman, his cloak still disentangling itself from the mist.

"Please enter."

Rothman ushered in the lady. "Signora Victoria Azeglio." The signora swept forward and flung back her hood, revealing a head of bright auburn curls that even the darkness of the study couldn't dim.

"Welcome, signora," said the historian, offering to take the lady's cape, a wonderfully handsome thing lined with orange silk like the famous tunas of Seville, but she occupied herself for some moments slipping off her fawn gloves finger by finger, looking about, and finally singing out almost gaily, "Well, Victoria, what kind of inkiness have you gotten yourself into this time?"

"There can be no inkiness, now that you're here, signora," said the historian, bowing slightly and holding himself ready, like a footman, to receive her wraps, which presently she deposited on his arm and he took to the coatrack. Returning, he said, "Please come and sit down, signora. And Mr. Rothman may join us."

"No, sir," said Rothman stolidly. "The night has invaded my gullet. I'm not fit for talk."

"But perhaps our guest wouldn't like to lose her escort."

"Let him go. His courtesy speaks well of his master."

"Your graciousness, signora, will sweeten his dreams. Good night, then, Mr. Rothman. The cab is without, I trust."

"Yes, sir." Rothman departed.

The historian seated his guest in an armchair just within the circle of pale yellow light and himself took a seat behind his desk. From a crystal decanter he poured them each a tulip of sherry. "To your health, signora."

"And to yours, sir."

After a suitable pause the historian said, "And what story have you come to tell me, signora?"

"I could tell you years of stories, sir. I'm a book with more than a thousand and one nights."

"You're fortunate. I'm a yellowing parchment from which everything seems to be fading. But if you tell me the right story you'll quicken my memory. You'll restore me."

"Phoo," said Victoria Azeglio, "you make me sound like some kind of hair or potency medicine."

The historian smiled. "That wasn't my intent at all, signora. I meant to say that I would take your story and make history of it."

Signora Azeglio nodded thoughtfully. "Yes, your man told me you were an historian. But if you want to make anything of yourself, you'll have to do much better than the other historians."

"In what way?"

"You'll have to tell the story of women, children, and the poor. You historians only tell about parliaments, great men, wars, and syphilis, which don't have much to do with real life, though syphilis is more germane. Don't smile, sir. I know poverty firsthand. It was the first thing I came to understand, it and the ridiculous names of my parents, Zenobia and Orlando Pitkin."

"Of the Old South?"

"Of old nothing. Of low birth—probably descended from the criminals Oglethorpe brought over to Georgia. You know all about that, sir. Anyway, to get away from them I bestowed my buds at the tender age of fifteen on Hector Pradl, who doesn't appear in your books, I don't imagine." She made a wide arc with her eye, taking in a considerable expanse of shelves.

"Not to my knowledge. What was he?"

"A cracker snake doctor."

"And what did he inscribe in your book?"

"Lots of things—the world's gullibility, the evils of drink, the pleasures of the body, the art of talking yourself into and out of anything you can think of."

"If he taught you all that, then he was an apt teacher, whatever else."

"He was a brute and I left him."

"Well, I knew, signora, you weren't the wife of a country healer. So your story won't be about him, I take it."

"It could be about him or any of them, sir. All of my steps from the shack of Orlando and Zenobia Pitkin to this dusty dark have been men. I gave them pleasure, all of it they could stand. And what they gave me back was some very interesting knowledge." The signora leaned forward into the center of the light. "Did you know, sir, that in those sleepy minutes after lovemaking a man's body comes unstitched? It's true. You can put your thumbs on each side of the cranium and open the seam and look into the brain."

"And what do you see there?"

"All the snaky gray of male stupidity. For instance, men don't understand that the body is more than a husk to house the kernels of ambition, bravery, and other such nonsense, so they burn it up in money-making and war. That's why men can't be allowed to govern."

"So women must govern?"

"Yes."

The historian nodded eagerly. "Your experiences and your views are fascinating, signora. I long to hear your story, for which, if I may be so mercenary, I'll pay good money."

"Your man made that clear, sir. But I have to tell you the truth. I'll spend the money on a new order that'll make history lick its feet."

"You can do with the money entirely as you please, signora."

"All right. Then I'll tell you a story so full of darkness and light that it may even set you free from this dust you have buried yourself in." The signora swept her eye with distaste over the files of books that seemed to stretch indefinitely out into the darkness.

The historian removed the ledger from his desk, made out a draft, and gave it to her.

"This is very generous, sir."

"No sum is generous enough for the kind of story you promise."

Victoria Azeglio sipped her sherry and then concentrated her ener-
gies so brilliantly in her face that even the auburn curls seemed to fade
and recede. And then she began. "A while ago I fell in with a man named
Zubin Attleboro. He said he was the son of a great pasha who'd married
an Indian mystic. His mother taught him psychic powers and how to
mix up every potion known to white and black magic. He didn't pretend
to be a medium. Such tripe was beneath him, he said. Instead he claimed
he could put his clients in a state of receptivity so they could be visited
by their deceased loved ones. The long passage from the foyers of eternity to the porticos of the mind can be opened, he told them. His
words. I told you he had the gift of gab. And how did he open the long
passage? By drugs, or by ecstasy, especially if the client was female and
comely." The signora paused and looked frankly into the historian's eyes.
"I hope you're asking yourself how I fell into such a vulgar cliché."

"Yes, but I know that you must have had good reason."

"No I didn't. It was pride. I had learned so much about male illusion, spying into my lovers' heads, that I thought this one last conquest,
of the pasha's son, would make me omniscient. I'd be able to twist the
male world around my finger and create a new future. Pride goeth before
the fall." Again the signora paused and looked searchingly into the historian's face. "Do you really know why I'm telling you this dark tale? Do
you think it's money?"

"Perhaps, signora, you feel compelled to tell it."

"Perhaps. But suppose I've found out exactly who you are, your
fame, and all the rest."

The historian smiled gently and nodded. "So you're using me to
get your story told to a wider public, to forward your cause, and you
don't wish to conceal your motive from me. Is that it?"

"That's it."

"You're honest, indeed, signora, but you're mistaken. If your
story's what I think it is, then it's using you to get itself told and I'm
merely the recorder."

Victoria Azeglio revolved the historian's words in her mind for
some moments and then said, "I never thought of it that way. But never

mind, just as long as you and I aren't playing false with each other."

"I assure you we're not, signora. Please proceed."

"Well then, let me tell you about Zubin Attleboro. He was a gorgeous creature with black eyes and skin like an old penny and ringlets of black hair, like a prince of Persia. God knows what he really was. And I imagined I'd experienced everything in the arts of love, as you gentlemen call them. I was mistaken. But what do you think he wanted from me, sir? I told him right off that I was wise to his charlatanism, and he knew I had no money to pay for illusions like his other dupes. What do you think he wanted from me, sir?"

"Perhaps he longed at last for a taste of true love."

Victoria Azeglio threw her head back and produced a sharp volley of laughter. "No, sir. What he wanted was for me to play an interesting part in a charade he was putting on for a rich young man who had tragically lost his bride of less than a year. I was the reincarnate spirit of the preternatural boudoir. That was the game, sir. And to make sure I played my part with passion he guaranteed me a third of the fees paid by our grief-stricken little widower. Have you ever heard of prostitution dressed up any fancier? And I agreed. Why do you think I agreed, sir?"

"I think it wasn't the money, though I know that the extortions of these spiritualists are enormous and your dedication to your cause is deep."

"Thank you, sir. Indeed, what I wanted was to get my hands on their heads, Zubin's and the little widower's. I wanted to look into their brains, hawk and gull. I wanted to inspect this exact picture of the two sides of male madness. With such knowledge, I thought, I'd be invulnerable in my work for a new order."

"A noble enterprise, signora."

"No it wasn't, because I planned to use them the same way they were using me. Anyway, you're no doubt wondering why I didn't just get my look into their heads and leave."

"Yes, I was wondering that."

"Because I couldn't pry Zubin open. His will was like steel. And besides, every night he put on my tongue what he said was an Indian aphrodisiac, a tiny seed, a thing you could stick under your thumbnail. How could I know that every one of those little seeds was like a link in an iron chain, and that one day I'd crawl and beg at his feet for the next one?" The signora suffered a visible shudder, but held up her hand to show that she didn't want the historian's sympathy. "And in the meantime I couldn't look into the little widower's head either because we were leading him on step by step, payment by payment. Zubin said, 'These are the tantric exercises that lead into the arcanum of desire.' I'll never forget it. We kept him excited for days on end in the cruelest ways. I can't bring myself to describe them—veils, lights, music, distant sighing. Imagine it for yourself, sir."

"I have the picture."

"Then when Zubin finally decided he'd played him to the limit he gave me to him and I was the receptacle for his torrents. And then I did look down into him. And what do you think I saw, sir?"

"I don't know."

"Nothing but me, as in a mirror, except that I was all shining with the oils of desire. Nothing else was in his head, no picture of his real wife or anything else—just this horrible anointed me. I tell you, sir, Narcissus himself would grow vomitous on such a fixed image."

Victoria Azeglio took up her tulip of sherry as if to drink, but quickly set it back down. "And then the little widower was gone— disgusted with himself and with me no doubt, but at least free of illusion. Well, Zubin moved us immediately to another house on a back street and closed it up tight with drapes, like this place. And that very night I tried to climb up out of my depravity. When Zubin gave me the little seed, I slipped it out of my mouth. I wonder he didn't notice that my flesh was cold and clammy. After he'd had his fill of me, I lit a candle and stooped over him laughing as if I was playing a little nymph's game, though it was all I could do to keep my hands from shaking. And he said, 'What're you doing, dear Lady Victoria?' That was his game, that after unspeakable practices we'd call each other lord and lady. I said, 'I am the great phrenologist Madame Zenobia. I will read the shape of your skull.' He laughed and I looked in."

A cloud passed over the signora's frank blue eyes, and it was some moments before she resumed. "I saw chaos, sir—crowds of black nothings. I was supposed to plumb male illusion in the name of my cause, remember? But all I saw was deadly chaos. Zubin laughed his hellish laugh. 'Haven't I warned you against prying, Lady Victoria?' he said. 'But you would go down. And having gone down, you're doomed to dwell there for certain seasons evermore.' "

"And are you so doomed?"

"Let me finish, sir. The next time I ate the seed and let him alone. But I wanted to get away. With all my heart I wanted to get away. I got into his casket of drugs, which he didn't even try to hide from me. I thought maybe I could fight fire with fire, get free from the seeds with another drug. All I did was create for myself horrible dreams. In one I tried to escape by climbing down a ladder made of my own hair, but it turned into a rope of fire and burned me until there was only a bone with a wristlet of steel around it. So I was still his slave. And in other visions, when it tickled his fancy, Zubin would come to me wearing a black crown and would spit me on his long teeth and his sex. And more along that line.

"One day—why, I can't imagine, after my experience with the little widower—I looked in a mirror. What I expected to see was a haggard face with the cheekbones pressing up like a death's-head and the eyes all tunneled out. And if that's all I'd seen I would've just slipped on down into death. But what I saw was worse—a horrible thing made up of nothing but wisps like the fox fires in the swamps of Georgia, a stinking thing that any breeze could blow away." And now the signora did take up the tulip and finish the sherry.

"May I, signora?" said the historian, lifting the decanter. The signora covered the lip of her tulip with her fingers—but said nothing and continued silent, so that after a while the historian mused softly, "I wonder what marvelously resourceful thing you did to free yourself from those iron bounds."

"I tried to think. But you know what came of that, sir. I could only think what men had given women to think for centuries. If you are a damsel in distress do you think up some clever strategy of escape? Of course not. You wait breathlessly for your Prince Charming to come and set you free with his lance and his kiss, pricking bravely across the plain on his mighty stallion Amogard or some such. Well, do you think it amusing, sir, that a woman on the very edge of annihilation would be the victim of a moldy cliché?"

"Please go on, signora."

"I did the only thing I could think of. Whenever I could slip away from Zubin, I went to a window and stood there, naked. I was desperate. But my eyes were so dilated and dazzled I couldn't see anything—street, passersby, nothing. Maybe all I was facing was a blind alley, a blank wall. So I took my bony nakedness from window to window. I tried to mouth the word *help*, but it's not a word you can mouth, so I just opened my mouth as horribly wide as I could, like a Greek tragic mask." Victoria Azeglio paused and her expression softened. "But someone did see me after all."

"Your prince came and is now your husband."

"Yes, he knocked on the door. Zubin wouldn't answer, so he left a card saying that he'd lost his wife and wanted spiritual instruction. But Zubin was afraid he was an agent from the rich young man's family. So my husband-to-be left another card saying that he'd seen in the window an apparition of his dear departed and was deeply desirous of Zubin Attleboro's instruction. Zubin looked at me and said, 'Are you ready, Lady Victoria, for another randy gentleman who imagines that he pines for the dead?' Yes, I was ready, I said. He took me by the wrist and inspected me. 'You're too thin even for a revenant,' he said. 'We'll have to feed you.' I told him I'd eat. I didn't tell him that the seeds had made food repulsive to me, or that I knew he'd have let me die if it hadn't been for this chance to get more money."

Victoria Azeglio looked into the historian's eyes. "You see, sir, somehow I knew that this time it wasn't another gull but someone to help me. They say that hope creates what it hopes for, and what did I have but hope?"

"You're a courageous woman, signora." The historian saw that despite her imminent rescue by her husband there was still a shadow on her face.

"This great good being took me to his house, where I began to shudder like a cold bitch. My bowels knotted up and my lips curled back from my teeth. I began to whimper for my beloved Zubin and his amorous seeds. The good being sat in front of the door. I begged to get out. I groveled. I licked the palms of his hands and his feet. When he didn't move, I raked at him with my nails. I bared my teeth. Then I

sweated and vomited. I lost consciousness. When I woke up I was
wrapped in cloth soaked in sweet oils of sandalwood. After a while the
good being unwrapped me. Like what, sir? A chrysalis? Anyway, I wasn't
a fox fire anymore, a stinking swamp gas. I was a creature that might
grow into something decent."

"Something very beautiful, I would say, signora."

"Thank you, sir." The signora reflected for a moment. "I'm never
going to tell that story again. It's too dark."

The historian nodded. "I can understand that, but will you
continue with it long enough, signora, to tell me how your husband
wrested you from Attleboro's iron grip?"

"If you could see my husband, sir, you'd understand immediately."

"Then you must provide me with an image of him, signora."

"I can't do it with words, sir."

"Have you a picture then?"

"A picture wouldn't do either. You have to have his presence in
your mind, the great being himself."

The historian reflected. "You always call him the good being or the
great being, and never a man. Is he not a man?"

The signora didn't answer directly but said, "I have him in my
mind wherever I go—ghettos, stews, deathhouses, the dark and dusty
rooms of mysterious men." The signora allowed herself no flicker of
smile. "I'm always protected."

"Can you convey to me the presence of your husband, signora?
Otherwise I can't understand the story."

Victoria Azeglio inclined her head toward the historian. "Do you
trust me, sir?"

No, the historian did not trust her. It came to him as simple as
that. The blue eyes were too bright, the flesh of the face too youthful
and luminous for the ordeals it was alleged to have endured. But the
historian trusted his resilience. And certainly the prospect of having
Azeglio present in his mind was worth a small risk. "Yes, I trust you,
signora. What do you propose?"

"I told you how I used to look down into the snaky gray brains of
my lovers."

"Yes."

"Well I know now how to do the opposite."

"What is that, signora?"

"I mean not inspect but project."

"Do you mean you can actually project an immense presence like your husband?"

"Yes, when the cranium of the recipient is unstitched."

"And how is that to be done?" said the historian, detecting a hint of playfulness in the signora's voice.

Victoria Azeglio looked up into the yellow light and sighed. "How horribly closed up we are, sir, all bound in sinew and bone. All of us, women as well as men, will have to learn how to open ourselves, especially you who must write down our story."

The historian nodded meditatively. "I seem to be able to open, signora, but only in the dark, like a night flower."

"Then at least the dark doesn't alarm you. Shut your eyes."

After scarcely a moment's hesitation the historian did as he was told. The images of smooth face and auburn hair faded, leaving in his mind a pregnant darkness. He heard the signora arise and come to him. He smelled the odor of fabric, followed by the more appealing and precise aroma of flesh and soap, and then her breath, washing over his face, sweet but also powerfully digestive. "We are in a bare room," said a warm voice. The historian had the impression that his head was now a diminutive thing hanging in the vestibule of a large but benign mouth.

"Signor Azeglio is sitting on a mat. The light's coming in from the window. Is the light coming into your head?" The historian nodded.

"Good. Your eyes are growing accustomed now. In a minute you'll see him." The signora's thumbs pressed against the historian's temple and her fingers against the top of his head, a kind of gentle mastication. He felt himself soften.

"Yes, you can see him now." The voice within the wash of warm breath droned on. "Yes, you can see him."

"Yes, I can see him," said the historian. And there indeed was Azeglio, sitting as the signora said, on a mat just beyond the swath of sunlight streaming in at the window, a huge personage of immemorial jadelike flesh, translucent except in the deep crevices of his flesh where a rich verdigris had settled. His head was bald and he smiled fixedly. His

arms grew down like banyan roots. The trunk of his torso rose up from
the great bulb of his belly. His feet, tucked beneath, clung to his
buttocks. His benign genitalia lay in the soft cup of contiguous thighs.
Above, his full breasts were neither clearly male nor female but were
perhaps moist, lacteous. Nowhere visible was there a hair on Azeglio.

For long minutes the historian concentrated all his attention on
the figure. Was it the miraculous similacrum of a real being or was it a
purely imaginary projection, the whole story in fact made up? Azeglio
didn't move. The historian couldn't detect the minutest expansion or
contraction of breathing. After a while he opened his eyes, aware that the
signora had withdrawn her breath and her fingers. She was sitting again
in the chair on the other side of the desk looking somewhat quizzically
at the historian, who nodded slowly before he spoke. "A remarkable
figure, signora. Remarkable. And you say it's your husband. But he's like
a bodhisattva. Surely you've never lain with this man."

"It would be unthinkable, sir."

"Then you can never part his cranium and learn the infinite
wisdom within."

"I never could have anyway, whether I lay with him or not, because
that was only a way of spying on the meanness of the male." The signora
paused and called into her face a gentle smile. "But what if I were to
look down into your psyche, sir? It would be different, I'm sure."

"I'm afraid you'd only see a misty darkness."

"Then we'd have to blow it away."

The historian smiled. "My darkness, signora, isn't principally the
darkness of confusion or denial but of gestation."

The signora lifted her brows. "What's to be born?"

"I am. And my work."

"Then your man has found the right woman. Nobody knows
about rebirth the way I do."

"How would you midwife me, signora?"

"I'll tell you stories."

"What story could you relate, signora, more profound than the
one you've just told me?"

"Many, sir—from the dark past and the still dark present, like this
room, and then about the bright new order that's coming." The signora's

hair blazed in the light and her blue eyes fell passionately on the historian's. "We'll be exactly right together. I'll be your memory and you'll write in my book."

The historian smiled sadly. "I'm afraid that after such notable company you'd find my prickings disappointing."

"Oh no, sir, because the best writer is the one who can write on a crowded page. Isn't that true?"

"I'll think about it." The historian rose slowly and made his way with deliberate step to the coatrack. Returning, he said, "Already I'm thinking about it, signora."

Victoria Azeglio rose and slipped over her shoulders the orange-lined cape the historian offered. Before she put on her gloves she touched his chin. "What a pity it'll be if we don't come together."

✍

Rothman sat where Victoria Azeglio had sat, on the verge of the small circle of light from the hanging lamp. "In what way was she defective, sir?"

"Defective?" The historian's tone conveyed unpleasant surprise.

"Then why didn't you keep on with her? I have to understand before I search again." Rothman stroked the bridge of his nose, an ancestral gesture perhaps, by one not accustomed to having his judgment questioned. Behind him on the coatrack hung the furled cloak like the wings of a huge bird of night.

"There'll be many, Rothman, who aren't defective but who also are not her."

"She knows the city in its depths, sir—the destitute, the diseased, the women with the rickety belly-bloated babies."

The historian nodded. "Death by marasmus." He looked up at the dark ceiling. "The touching case, for instance, of the infant harpist of Fifth Avenue, a prodigy, a Savoyard. Dead by marasmus in the middle of a melodious lay. A platonic disease, we speculate. The child, longing to return to a remembered realm of sweetness and light, declines to tarry with us."

"They die of filth, malnutrition, and dysentery."

"Yes, Rothman—the feet billowing with edema, the nates and anus raw. You think I'm hoodwinked by this nefarious romance? What do you take me for?"

"An historian, you say."

"That's correct. But poverty and disease aren't the essence of history. Oh, some of my brethren think so. They create a history made of numbers—charts of crops and slaughters, studies of nutrition and changing dietary habits. They perform the autoptic weighing of organs. They disinter the dead and inspect them for abnormal ossifications and God knows what else. But I tell you, history is not pathology."

Rothman looked seriously at his employer, obviously deeply engaged, "What is history, sir?"

The historian furrowed his brow. "I'll tell you something else it's not, Rothman. It's not a parable about God and Mammon, Dives and the poor man, and so forth."

"What is it, sir?"

"It's a woman." The historian was utterly serious and intent. "The most extraordinary and complex woman ever scribed, and she's here, in this very city at precisely this pen prick of the infinite panorama. And only I know that she's here. And only you can find her." He looked into Rothman's black eyes. "Anybody else would think I'm mad. But you know I'm not."

"I'm not sure that I'll recognize her, sir. I thought Victoria Azeglio was her."

"No wonder, Rothman. At first I thought so too. She's certainly a close cousin, beautiful, brimming with sensibility and consciousness, a true child of the Zeitgeist. If you can find Victoria, you can find Clio herself."

"In what way did Victoria fail, sir?"

"She was too self-consciously revolutionary and mythic, too intentional. You understand what I'm saying, Rothman? The one we're looking for will be revolutionary. But her essence won't be purpose. It'll be pure sentience."

The historian withdrew the ledger from his desk and made out a draft.

"Again, more than agreed upon," said the agent.

"Take it, Rothman. Your services are priceless. Go now and find her."

∽

Rothman got word of a fabulous woman who had unveiled Isis and was now, with the assistance of a retired army officer, a reknowned linguist, writing a universal history of the Spirit. At the Caravansary on West 48th Street Rothman announced to the woman and her consort that he hadn't come to gain mastery, through denial and meditation, over his desires, and that he did not yet wish to enter into the realm of pure ether. What did he want, then? He wanted madam to visit his master, an eccentric millionaire who would pay handsomely for stories of America. About Rothman's feet were bear skins, tiger skins, a lion's head, a stuffed crocodile on wheels with a leash around its neck, hassocks, and prayer mats. Against the wall was a suit of armor, a cuckoo clock, and a huge laughing Buddha. The prayer mats were thickly padded, he was told, for the neophytes who levitated and didn't yet know how to return safely.

What did the millionaire want with stories of America? The millionaire, Rothman revealed, was the most famous historian of the age. From the stories, he would put together a new history. The woman expanded noticeably and declared that she herself was writing a book, of all the manifestations of the Spirit. The Colonel, who knew many languages and scripts, was helping her with it. Yes, Rothman knew this and thus opined, as optimistically as his deep voice and jagged face would permit, that she would be eager to assist a fellow writer. The woman smiled, and at length declared that she would come.

∽

Twice the historian dreamed of the fabulous Azeglio. In the first dream he was olive and androgynous, just as the beautiful Victoria had projected him. In the second dream the historian, seeing all too clearly the ahistorical temptations that Azeglio represented, made him as black-thicketed as Silenus, mounted upon him a Priapian projection of larger than human dimension, and thrust him upon his wife. Thus, having

disposed of Victoria and Azeglio and having also resisted parting the
drapes and looking out into the garden, where he knew the gray-berried
junipers were creeping forward under cover of soot-flecked snow like the
soothsayer's inexorable army, and having held hand from pen by iron
resolve while the sap of memory accumulated, the historian was
rewarded by the agreed upon tap-tap-tap at his study door on a night
and at an hour made indeterminate by his self-immural.

Through the opened door entered a woman under a fantastical
scarf, a huge paisley-like star-shower of zodiacal signs. Behind her came
Rothman. On the shoulder of his striped cloak, fallen from eaves or
limb, sat a tiny fist of snow, which scuttered away like a white mouse the
moment he entered the study. "Madame Lotta," he announced, so
fretted and furrowed that the woman might have just sprung full-blown
from his prodigious brow. She plunged forward and seized the historian's
hand, which he in this sudden, not to say furious, entry was not aware of
having offered. Her flesh, ungloved and fresh from the snowy night, was
still oven hot. Hatless and crinkled to the roots like the fleece of a ram,
her black hair was brightly beaded with recent snowflakes. Beneath the
wide scarf was the quilting of a long, gray dress, gold-striped.

Rothman rushed forward like a tardy courtier in the train of a
precipitous queen, but then stood aside like a dumb supernumerary. The
historian said, "Madam, please have a seat." He wished to free his fingers
from that hot hand and to disengage his eyes from those black pools.

"Thank jhu." The hand relaxed the grip that the historian understood he never could of his own power have broken. Rothman slid a
chair under Madame Lotta's ample body. "He say jhu look for stories of
America." The woman had a voice full of timpani and tuckets. "I yam
America." Ahmayricka.

"Indeed," said the historian. "May I offer you a cordial, madam?"

"I doan take. But permiss to smoke?"

"Of course."

From a wallet belted to her waist Madame Lotta took paper and
tobacco and with an expert rolling of plump fingers and an adderlike
flicker of the tongue produced a fat cigarette with crimped ends. Then
ensued a search for matches, Rothman slapping his pockets, the historian
rummaging in the drawers of his desk. "I got," said Madame Lotta,

holding up a stout kitchen match and firing it with a quick scratch of her thumbnail. She lit the cigarette, breathed deeply of the smoke, released it through sharp teeth, and said, "Jhu can send jhu man away."

The historian gave a slight nod and Rothman receded.

"Thank jhu and good night," said Madame Lotta. "Jhu know where jhu can find me."

"Yes." Rothman nodded and departed.

The historian sat down behind his desk. Madame Lotta said, tilting her head toward the cold black hearth, "Why jhu doan have fire?"

"It's in a furnace in the cellar."

"Jhu need to see fire." She rolled her black eyes up to the ceiling lamp. "And jhu got this new light with no fire."

"Yes, electric. I finally relented a year or so ago."

"I tell jhu this man in a minute."

"What man?"

"Electric Man."

"Is it his story you've come to tell me?"

"One."

The historian looked at Madame Lotta through laminations of gray smoke, latakia-laced, pleasant to the nostril. He relaxed a little. Her massive face (Calmuck, Georgian, Turk?) seemed benign. She smoked and squinted at him. He noticed that her fingernails were a dark amber under the edges. It was not dirt, he was sure, but a mixture of spices, masala or harissa. If he could put the fingers to his nose he might guess the proportions of cumin, turmeric, coriander, cardamom, etc. "You say you're America. What do you mean by that, madam?"

"I yam writing a book," said Madame Lotta.

"Which explains how you're America?"

"Yes, but also why my fingers stain." Madame Lotta smiled omnisciently. "I read jhu thoughts from air. I write the book with mix of ink and iodine."

"Why?"

"To show how words slide and wink in the sun. You can't depend."

"I see. What language are you writing the book in?"

"Various, for each gods."

The historian felt slightly dizzy. Perhaps he was unconsciously keeping his head empty to protect his thoughts from Madame Lotta's interception. As a consequence he seemed to be bobbing loosely along waves of perfumed smoke. "Still, you haven't told me how you're America."

"I yam here fifteen month, in the city, which is America. In this time I enter all people, same jhu great white poet."

"I see. And one of the people you have entered has something to do with electricity?" The historian felt the distinct need to establish a sequence.

"Yes. The one I said, Electric Man. He worship god of technic. Shut jhu eyes. I take you to him." Madame Lotta bore into the historian with her black eyes. He felt a palpable weight on his retinas, but shutting his eyes seemed at least as dangerous as sustaining her gaze. Shocked by his disobedience, she arched her brows and repeated imperiously, "Shut jhu eyes!"

The historian obeyed. It was unpleasant—like walking into a dark chamber all abuzz with a portentous emptiness, where one struggled to remain thoughtless for fear of interception.

"Doan think about me. Look at the place. Jhu got forest of wire here. Jhu got a man in his lavatory all full with electric . . ." Madame Lotta's slow voice boomed on, but the words at the very moment of their vocalization changed, through the medium of the historian's mind, into images: the gaslit laboratory, the huge magnets bending the space around their poles like fine spume from a fountain, a great bulwark of bluish retorts and beakers filled with vitriol, all catching a ghoulish glow from the gaslight. And there stood the familiar figure, the archetypal American inventor, thin, slightly stooped, gray. But alas, the face was horribly strained. The flesh was pulled back as though moving forward at a tremendous speed against an onrushing wind. No wonder. The scalp and the skin under the ears had been severed, gathered, and sutured so that the integument was horribly taut. "What happened to him?" cried the historian.

"This I come to tell jhu."

The historian tried to open his eyes, but the lids were weighted.

"The story of America and its god."

The historian shook his head violently and tried to open his eyes.

"What's the matter with jhu?"

"I'm in the dark."

"Open jhu eyes." Obediently the historian's eyes popped open. Madame Lotta had rolled and lit another cigarette. The layers of smoke, even more complex than before, made in the air of the study a curious script. "If jhu want to understand the story, jhu have to put your own thoughts out and come in the dark. I told jhu, I yam America. I know dark. Now I tell jhu story of Electric Man of America."

Madame Lotta paused to take in and exhale a great gust of smoke. "He come from farm, like all Americans. What he love there? Cow, chick, piggie? No, he love lightning in clouds. He learn electric. He take cat and wire it and rub its fur to make electric. The cat doan do, so he make wheel and brush and snap electric between balls.

"Now jhu go with him to city. He see prostitutes in all steps of the ladder. He see the fifty-cent-for-my-body down on Bleecker and Greene—what jhu call sisters of the pave." Madame Lotta laughed with an unpleasant gusto that shook the smoke under the lamp. Meanwhile the cigarette had gone dead in the ambered crux of index and middle finger. She threw it onto the hearth.

"I've never used any such phrase," the historian declared.

"No? Shut jhu eyes." The historian obeyed.

"Remember. Jhu see what he see. We going to climb the ladder." The historian entered the dark uncertain but expectant.

"Jhu Electric Man now. Jhu coming from Houston and Worster on Amity Street. Jhu got better class here and lesser drunk." A wavering image of half-familiar gray streets passed behind the historian's eyes. Vague female figures slid by smoothly as though on well-oiled trundles. "What jhu feel, Electric Man? Pity? No, jhu see system. Jhu got two, three thousand walkers. Each group got its own bound it circle round and round. Systemic."

"I never thought that."

"Yes, jhu did. Jhu technic man. Now jhu in parlor houses with false business front—tobacco, papers, pawns. Jhu got to move jhu eyebrow so the man know what jhu want." In the historian's mind the merchandiser was a big fellow with a black band on his upper right sleeve and a black patch on his right eye. The good eye, furious with its partner's blindness, bulged and blinked an angry red.

"Behind jhu got rug and rocker chair and sofa like home, but not baby picture and flowers and little things. But we not stopping here. It doan interest. We going to highest neighborhood, grand saloon. Jhu got gold ceiling and all little gods of love with bow arrows and wings . . . how jhu call them?"

"Cupids." The little winged creatures were as pink and luminous as Tiepolos. Below them ran a golden frieze of prancing satyrs. And just below that, over the high windows, hung purple drapes. And between the drapes there shone a red wallpaper flocked with velvety fleurs-de-lis. At regular intervals sconces burned with blue gaslight.

"The madam come and take jhu money first, even in a fine place like this." The historian proceeded down a dimly lit corridor to a tiny boudoir of soft decor—pink floral carpet, lacy dressing table, and a bed with a gauzy canopy, almost a child's bed. On it sat a beautiful blond-haired young woman wearing a black negligee, which still failed to give her any air of the illicit. What was desirable about her was an innate, scarcely nubile charm. The historian stood gazing at her, not with desire but with the studied look of one trying to unravel the meaning of a complex symbol. And then suddenly the face broke into an expression of shock so intense that it shattered all its own beauty. Horrified at being the cause of this terrible transformation, the historian withdrew into the dim corridor with the intention of returning to the main salon. But he lost his way and found himself in another boudoir, this one more sumptuous. And there, on a chaise longue, completely naked, lay Madame Lotta. The huge face was gemmed with onyx eyes and pearl teeth. The thick throat was a pillar of unctuous flesh, the teats below peaked and surrounded by an indelicately rich welting of chocolate. The historian, transfixed, lowered his gaze, but suddenly omphalos, mons veneris, and the colossal pillows of thigh tumbled onto the oriental carpet and splattered like spilt mousse. Madame Lotta laughed her percussive laugh. "I yam not there, Mister Historian. Open jhu eyes."

The historian obeyed promptly. And there, as before, sat Madame Lotta, encased in her high-necked quilted dress, her black eyes still as sharp as augers and her marvelous lips inaugurating with their super-abundant motility the following, "Who jhu saw?"

"I don't know. You tell me. You put her in my mind."

Madame Lotta waved a finger vigorously and shook her head. "I doan put in jhu mind. I call what is already in it. But we going to talk about that later. Now I tell jhu the young woman was Missus Wayne Winslow, wife to the assistance of the big shipper man. She from jhu same farm town. She know jhu from child day. Jhu watch lightning together. She terrified to see old child friend." Madame Lotta paused. "Why jhu think she want be whore sometime? Jhu think she conquered by lust?"

"I don't know."

"I tell jhu. At ball she in Egypt quadrille. She want a little gold snake for her white arm, with ruby eye and emerald in its tooth. All these room doan have whore but wife and fiancée need silk, jewel, ostrich boa. Jhu understand?"

The historian nodded. "I understand." A phalanx of vermilion-lipped wives advanced upon the wings of his inner eye, receding, however, when Madame Lotta spoke again.

"And what happen to technic man when he see old friend in black? He understand systemic greater than human, so he run find fastest train. Speed change his molecules on track to world fair of West where he see dynamo with stomping legs higher than jhu house, which is *efreet*, which say, 'What jhu wish, Electric Man?' Electric man say, 'I wish to find all technic of modern world. I doan have time to be man.' So *efreet* of machine sew up all parts except for the holes he need for technic work."

The historian nodded. "So that's why he looked man-made, like a Frankenstein."

"He his own monster. Yes. In English jhu got Doctor Frankenstein to warn and in German Doctor Faust. But in America jhu doan got. Everybody Faust. Jhu got Benyamin Frankel and Electric Man play with lightning. Jhu got Missus Vanderbilt in her ball wired like big tree of electric shine. Jhu got poor Missus Wayne Winslow acting whore. Everybody in America worship power and Mammon. America the Frankenstein for the whole world."

"And you are America?"

"Almost. I got some little more thing to put in my head. Then I write and free myself from this hell."

"I wish you all success, madam."

"Doan wish me nothing. We each going to help the other with the things in our head. I told jhu I doan put, I call. And what I see in jhu mind I write in my book. And what jhu see jhu write in jhu book."

"Then my mind is merely a stage for your players."

"My players!" Madame Lotta widened her black eyes. "I told jhu I call. Jhu the historian. Jhu got the memory of everything. Now I tell jhu the story of Red Dancer, Big Bible Man, and all these Americans. Jhu remember everything. It doan matter where jhu stop and I begin. We parts of one. I write book of Universe Spirit in all its form, America one, and jhu write the America history book." Not taking her eyes from the historian's face, Madame Lotta reached into her tobacco wallet. "Now, Red Dancer."

But the historian held his hand up. "Not tonight, Madame Lotta."

"What's the matter with jhu? Open jhu mind. I yam going to call Red Dancer. Jhu will remember her taking up all the airs of Tiflis with her cloths of dance."

"I can't do it now, Madame Lotta. There's a substance, they say, that washes colors from the eye so that it will be ready for fresh images. But you've painted so indelibly that I need time to get ready for new ones."

Madame Lotta bore into the historian with her black eyes, apparently saw evidence of genuine fatigue, and at last relented. "All right then. Jhu man knows where I am."

∽

Rothman sat where Madame Lotta had sat, his nose and brow making deep shadow where the light had lain in undulant swaths on her broad face. The historian was nodding meditatively. "Oh, she has great powers all right, Rothman. No doubt of it. She projected me into the inner sanctums of electricity and prostitution, which in her mind are intimately connected." He looked closely at the agent. "Tell me, did she favor you with one of her transports?"

The agent's face darkened. "In the carriage, sir. I was tired."

"Where did she send you?"

"Into the old city in the desert. I held the shofar in my hand. I lifted it to my mouth and sounded the summons for the Day of Atonement."

"And it seemed very real?"

"Yes, sir. I felt the heat of the sand and heard the horn echo from the hills."

"Until she burst the illusion with that brassy laugh of hers—was that how it was?"

"Yes."

"What did she say?"

"She said I was a poor little Ashkenazi gone to work for the goyim, and my brothers would help them make science, which they would turn on us, and then there would be a real Day of Atonement, not just one of memory."

The historian nodded. "She told me that America is the world's Faust, that we worship the *efreet* of the machine."

"Yes, sir. She knows these things through objects and words."

"What do you mean?"

"I mean the strange collection at the Caravansary. The Colonel says she has an uncanny eye for things invested."

"Invested, eh? Numinous objects, precipitates of the Zeitgeist."

"You're ironical, sir."

"No indeed. And what about the words?"

"Between her and the Colonel they know many languages. Behind the differences, which are like veils, stands eternal being."

"The word as spirit. I'm not being ironical, Rothman."

Rothman nodded. "She's writing a book about the ultimate nature of things, like yours."

"I'm not writing a book," said the historian sharply.

"That's the point, isn't it, sir?"

The historian sighed. "Yes, Rothman, that's exactly the point."

After a brief silence Rothman said, "How did she fail, sir?"

The historian rubbed his chin carefully. "She has great insights, greater than Victoria Azeglio's. When she said she was America she wasn't far off the mark. But both of their insights are undermined by a false premise. One thinks history is the record of the battle between male aggression and female wisdom. The other thinks it's the record of the battle between science and spirit. It's neither."

"It's a woman," said Rothman flatly.

"Yes."

"A child of the Zeitgeist, suffering all the faults of the age, brimming with sentience."

The historian smiled. "Precisely. But now you're being ironical, Rothman."

"No, sir, I'm not. And I'll try once more."

The historian took the ledger from his desk, made out two drafts, and handed them to Rothman. "One for you and one for Madame Lotta."

Rothman took the drafts, but before pocketing them he said, "Once more, sir."

"Go now. You'll find her."

♋

Rothman had no difficulty finding the place. He walked in through the large double door without knocking, as instructed. The theatre was dark except where a muted shaft of silver fell down from a snow-dimmed skylight. It was a queer place, old in its appointments and yet with a feeling of newness. He sat, as instructed, in the front row in the dim light. The apron of the stage was also partially lit, but the rear, wings, and flies were dark. The silence was uncanny, as if the noise from the city street had fallen away into a different time.

After a while a woman came out from the left wing. She was dressed in a motley of colored cloths that flowed down variously from shoulder and waist to thigh and knee. On her feet were buskins that rose to the calf. Rothman peered intently into her face, which, though shadowed by a bush of bronze hair, was rosy. From his vantage across the narrow pit he could also see that her eyes were intensely blue. She returned his gaze.

"Will you speak to me, madam?"

"Who sent you?"

"Voltaire," said Rothman, as agreed upon.

The woman laughed a remarkable laugh, melodious and yet so piercing that it caused Rothman to blink involuntarily, as when a bat veers at the last moment. "What do you want?"

"My master wants you to tell him your story. He's an historian."

"An historian!" repeated the woman, in a tone not entirely comic.

"Yes, an historian, and also a millionaire who pays good money for stories of American lives."

The woman said nothing to that. Rothman stood and gave his shawl a definitive swirl. "Come. You can tell him your story and make money."

"Tell him that stories are fatal. Tell him to come here and I'll dance for him."

"He can't leave his study without his muse, Clio."

The piercing laugh again caused Rothman to blink and thus almost miss the amazing leap that took the woman from stage to aisle.

∽

Above all else the historian had loved to watch the script writhe at the end of his pen like a spitted snake, he the master of the sinuous track, and to glance up now and again to see beyond the autumn garden the neighbor's lean elm lower the failing sun from arm to arm down the evening sky. But that was a long time ago. Now, self-immured, he allowed himself no ink. A third time came the tap-tap-tap at his study door, which he opened upon a woman whose face appeared above a fantastical assemblage of cloths. Behind, Rothman kept station in the dark winter air.

"Please come in, madam." The woman entered. Rothman receded. "I'll be outside in the cab, sir."

The woman looked around the room and smiled. "Perfect."

"Perfect for what, madam?"

The woman didn't say, but went to the hanging lamp and pushed it so that it threw a yawing light over desk and books and made on the floor a shifting platter of pale gold. Immediately she began to dance along the rim of light, making beautiful complex arabesques. Presently the lamp quieted and the light resumed its steady illumination.

"Quite beautiful."

"I have come to teach you the inner stillness of each thing."

"I'll try to be a good student," said the historian, at the same time indicating with a chivalrous sweep of his hand the chair in front of his desk. "Won't you sit down?"

The woman came forward and took the chair, the swatches of cloth rising and then settling into a fragile leaflike repose. How contradictory she was, the historian thought, kinetic and still, her very walk not continuous but a series of beautifully discrete instants. He sat down behind the desk, smiled hospitably, and looked into the woman's intensely blue eyes. If they were pricked, he imagined, peacock would runnel the rosy cheeks. "What story have you come to tell me, madam?"

The woman smiled mischievously. "I haven't come to tell you a story. I've come to dance." She cocked her head and the lovely cowl of bronze flared. "Story was for the other two."

"The other two?"

"Yes, the two who wanted to tell you fables of reform. Neither was Clio, was she?"

"No. Are you?"

"I am the one you've been waiting for these three years."

Three years? Yes, three years to the season, his pen suddenly mute in his hand that winter, his mind wandering aimlessly and then fearful of moving at all as the immemorious fog thickened. And now came this strange blue woman speaking of inner stillness as though it were a talisman granting passage across a historyless bourn. He said, "All right, what are we to do then?"

"I dance and you speak." The woman made a musical laugh that blinded the historian momentarily. When he regained his sight, she was careering along his bookshelves, making unimaginably rapid glyphs at the border of light and dark. "Come with me."

"I'm afraid of the dark." The woman said nothing to that, but continued to dance. The historian took out a sheet of bond and laid it on the desk. "You dance and I write." He took his pen out of its case, unstoppered the well, and smelled the sharp caustic of the ink. He dipped the pen, put it to paper and scratched, saying, "The Story of the Mysterious Blue Lady." But nothing appeared on the page except infinitesimal instants of black that were immediately whisked away into the trail of the woman's dance. "Why are you not letting me write?"

The woman stood still. "I can't stop you from writing, or make you write. Anyway, it's not writing that's at issue. It's stories."

"What's the matter with stories?"

"They always come to an end. Everybody dies."

"What does not come to an end?"

"Dance. Shut your eyes. Go into the inner stillness."

The historian shut his eyes, but warily, having twice before submitted in this way to false muses. He felt the air stir again.

"Speak."

To his amazement, the historian began to speak, word and image simultaneous. "I see a beautiful dancer sheathed in blue light, like a phrase from an urn of chased silver."

"Very elegant, but put a little tooth into it." The woman laughed her musical laugh.

"New York. Oysters, champagne. Tangoing with the infamous Russo. Stealing daisies from the park, strewing petals on the floor and whirling and whirling until the petals rise up in whirligigs about your thighs. And then lying among the petals and being deflowered." The historian paused, eyes still shut.

"Flowering and deflowering are only two sides of the same membrane."

The historian chuckled. "Europe. At Bayreuth with Cosima, but your dance of the Rhine maidens too undulant for the Teutonic spirit. Eleonora Duse, Rome, but in Verdi's Italy all passion is in the throat." The historian opened his eyes just in time to see the woman finish an incredible wheeling that carried her into the dark by the coat tree. "When is this? Who are you?"

"I am a body dancing and you are a voice speaking. Who and when do not matter."

"I am an historian."

"Don't be, because then you have to tell stories. Shut your eyes. Speak."

The lids of the historian's eyes fell shut. He went flying under a blue sky to the isle of Salamis, to a temple of dance erected on an outcropping of rock, columns washed with fading cerise, friezes olive. "Eager nymphs rush from every corner of the continent to study with you. Spume of Anima Mundi, the wild old Celtic poet calls you. Old men on the seawall chirp that your body is carved of Parian marble and never will decay." The historian opened his eyes. The woman was by the bookcase again, bluer than ever. "Speak."

The historian shut his eyes and spoke in a strangely plangent voice. "Stupefied as I am by the fumes rising from the tripod, and uncertain of the will of the fathers, still I prophesy—that you cannot go back. You must go always east, into the dawning of the new destiny of mankind."

"Do not prophesy. Prophecy is story. Story is the fatal trap you historians have fallen into and taken us women down with you." The woman's voice sank. "Down . . . down . . ." The historian fell into a thick darkness. By the time he managed to struggle back up, the woman was gone. He rushed to the door and looked down the street. A cab clattered away into the fog.

∽

The next morning the historian stood at the French doors and peered through a narrow parting in the drapes. A contention of sun and lingering snow scratched his eye. And the junipers were signaling by a new vesting of gray-green the change in season. The earth shuddered on its axis. So he knew that when the woman returned, another war would have come and gone. The temple would be no more.

Tap-tap-tap. Rothman entered, slipped from his tent of black and white, and joined the historian by the drapes. "Are you all right, sir?"

"Yes, I think so."

"Is she the one?"

"Yes. I knew you would not fail."

Rothman inspected the historian closely. "You look more youthful, sir. The skin of your face is smoother."

The historian touched his cheek. "That's good, isn't it?"

"Yes, if it's a natural rejuvenation, not a bargain with Satan, as in the old stories."

"I assure you I have no intention of selling her my soul, but you speak of stories. She is utterly against story."

Rothman frowned. "What does that mean, sir—against story?"

The historian mused. "Very strange, isn't it, Rothman—the idea of speaking without story."

"An historian without story? It would unman you, sir."

The historian smiled. "Unman me, eh? Is manhood so fragile that it depends on narratives?" The agent said nothing to that. "Well, Rothman, some say that it was your people who invented history—destroyed the old cyclical gods and made a pact with the God of time and destiny. What do you say to that?"

"I can't tell whether it's an honor or another calumny."

"Neither can I. But according to her, stories and histories are crimes against woman and dance. We must rediscover the inner stillness."

Rothman nodded reflectively. "So, what is she doing if she's not telling you her story?"

"She's dancing and I'm shutting my eyes and speaking. Things come into my head, strangely."

"What sort of things?"

"Colorful scraps, prospective notables in New York, France, Germany, Italy, Greece."

"Prospective notables? What are these, sir?"

"Persons who will be famous," the historian said almost absently, but then continued with animation. "We are going east, through the flames of a great war, into the dawning of a new era. I have prophesied it."

Rothman looked dubious. "You are an historian, not a prophet."

"I was transported to ancient Delphi. I spoke in an oracular voice."

Rothman's brow creased. "I'm afraid she's a dark spirit come to lead you astray."

"She will help me write again."

"She may betray you, sir."

The historian narrowed his eyes. "On the contrary, I will find out her story. She has cleverly snipped it up into patches with her scissoring steps, but I will put it back together. Any woman as beautiful as she must have an extraordinary story. I will find it out and write it."

The agent looked into the historian's eyes. "Tonight I'll stay, sir. I'll hide behind the drapes."

"It won't pass. She would detect the slightest change in the contour of the room. She has danced the whole space around the axis of her being." The historian was touched by the look of consternation on his agent's face, but he said, "Go now. Bring her tonight."

⌒

Tap-tap-tap. The door of the historian's study opened again on the varicolored swatches of cloth that cascaded down to the tops of the buskins. "Come in. It's cold." In fact, however, the woman seemed not to have entered from the snowy street, but rather to have materialized there just inside the open door, which now shut behind her with a clap that sent a shudder along the drapes and a puff of dust up from the shelves where Niebuhr stood against Novalis. The historian stood dumb, smitten by the woman's beauty.

The woman crossed the study and sat down in the chair in front of the desk. The historian sat across from her and looked into her blue eyes. The woman tilted her head. "Tonight you have one last chance to get free of story. Shut your eyes."

"I'm afraid to shut my eyes. I'll see you in somebody else's arms, then not at all."

The woman shook her head, but smiled gently. "If you come to me out along the edge of light and speak the dance, no other lover will come. I will not go away. There will be only the dance."

"And if I cannot?"

"That will be sad. You will go back to your stories and your false Clios, and I will keep looking for my muse."

"Then I will come."

"Good. Close your eyes."

The historian's lids slid suavely shut. The air changed, cool and prickly on his face, as if it were blowing across a wide plain, plucking up scraps of hay, darts of flax, fresh and stinging. The wind of revolution. "Where are we?" Silence. The historian knew from the winnowed sound beyond his desk that the woman had gone whirling out along the margins of light. He saw a huge concert hall full of people, the woman all in red turning upon the axis of revolution. "*Tovarishch! Tovarishch!*" he shouted. "*Comrade! Comrade!* We are in Russia."

"We are on the axle of perpetual revolution."

"Yes. A grand school of dance. No sculptural Greek this time but revolutionary whirling. Moscow. You and your students dance the heaving earth of the new Russia, from Crimea Square down Ostozhenka or Prechistenka until the two avenues converge upon Christ the Redeemer. You dance the brown waters of the Moskva. Neskuchny Park, the Novo-Devicky monastery, where light settles in lemony curds. You dance the old Kaluga Road, by the river Pakra, the white birches in the breeze turning up their silver undersides like laughing girls showing their slips. You dance the dark way to the canted old house where wise Kutuzov waited patiently while Napoleon's army lashed and writhed like a wounded snake in the invincible heartland of Russia."

"Not lashed and writhed but lashes and writhes. Always. Revolution is always. Do you understand?"

"Of course," the historian said, watching the dancer's body gather up all the images into a rose so fiery that the worm of history could not gnaw it.

"Go on."

"You and an army of revolutionary children dance Scriabin, flaming and transcendent. Tchaikovsky, sweet Ilyitch, soul of Russia. The 'Pathétique.' For long minutes rising and yearning upward in a single motion while the children sway like windswept grain." The historian looked out through half-closed lids at the woman's body weaving all the swatches of her motion. He longed to uncase his pen and dip it into the caustic of story. But he leaned back in his chair. "*Tovarishch! Tovarishch!* Lenin himself shouting *Tovarishch! Tovarishch!*"

"Are you with me?" The woman's voice came so vibrantly to the historian that it was as though she had leaped into the very portal of his ear and danced there, her feet beating on his timpani.

"Yes, I am with you! We are in the East. Everything is turning about the axis." But then the inevitable lover appeared. He and the dancer wore tarpaulins, like black versions of Rothman's cape. They went into a strange flying machine. On the front of it something turned and turned on its axis. Then it rose into the air and flew west.

"Speak!"

"A baroque salon of the Bundschu. Bach himself might have composed it—golden medallions, gilded scrolls, Gobelins of the hunt, silken gentlemen on silver horses, a hooded falcon, and whippets lean as the wind." The historian felt the passing of the sharp tippets of the dancer's varicolored cloths. "You in a beautiful red gown. The beaded portiere swaying as though on a Litz-wagon rushing through the German night. I see a little man in a white jacket, black britches, and spats, a poet aflame with revolution and vodka."

"Pietyr. Pure lyric! Speak!"

"This was your most strenuous dance, because Gorky and Tolstoy's son were there in exile, unmoved by the revolutionary toils of Mother Russia. Did not listen to the poems the poet recited for them. Cared nothing for the revolutionary Stall of Pegasus, where they would be vastly celebrated if only they would come home. Cared nothing for the dancing school on Prechistenka or the thunderous applause at the Bolshoi. The old count behind his bush of beard like an aging virgin. Gorky saturnine, casting on poet and dancer baleful eyes brimming with jaundiced moralism. Dialectic. History."

"No, not history! Speak purely. Enter the dance."

"You leap up in a fury and snatch the damask from the serving table, the chafing dish spinning across the room with a final whoosh. The oracle at Delphi extinguished! The West dead! Revolution forever! You whirling and whirling, twisting the damask. *'Tovarishch!'* " The historian was astounded. She had done it. Raveled time up in a red whirligig, raveled up the unrevolutionary two, their pitiful little heads dangling over the tight coils of the damask like strangled fowl. The historian felt himself begin to wheel slowly out from his desk toward the axis of the woman's dance, the inner stillness.

Now the dancer made a soft loop of the damask, drew the poet to her and kissed him on the mouth. The historian felt the kiss on his own mouth, burning with all the heat of her dancing. He became aroused and tumbled back into time.

∽

The lamp was out. But the woman was there, by the parted drapes, against a pale light from the garden, the colors of her motley indistinguishable in the diffuse light. The historian rose from his chair and went toward her.

"Is this what you want?"

"Yes."

"It will make a story, you know. It will come to an end."

"I know." The historian went on toward her until at last he found her lips and kissed them.

Her body swelled against him and then receded. "I will do my last dance for you." Turning slowly, she detached a swatch of fabric from the motley, laid it on the air and let it sink softly, then repeated the action with another swatch, which was diaphanous and almost weightless. And another.

"Are these the scarves of Tiflis?"

"Yes."

Over the historian's face flowed the warm air of the Black Sea and into his nostrils poured the fragrances of the Maydan. Swaying, the woman removed one by one the sheer panels and laid them upon the air until there were dozens of them floating down the dim midnight. The last two were long scarves that curved in opposite directions on the same axis, meeting once between the breasts, again at the navel, and finally at the mons veneris. And then these slipped down among the others at her feet.

The historian stepped back and disrobed. When he returned to her, his bare feet made little pucking sounds, like kisses. He thought of the marble dancing floors in the great halls of her schools, in whose veins their complex fate was long ago foretold. The fragrances of the Maydan gave way to the natural perfume created by her dancing and stored on her body, into which he now sank.

∾

Tap-tap-tap. Rothman looked sharply at the historian. "Are you all right, sir?"

"Yes, I'm all right, Rothman."

"Your voice sounds broken, sir."

"Does it? I suppose because I'll never see her again."

"I can find her for you, sir. Once I know a woman, she can't escape me."

"But you don't know her, Rothman. Neither do I really."

"Then she wasn't what she seemed. I knew it!" Rothman's eyes flashed. "What was she?"

The historian shook his head meditatively. "Pure dance, timeless, historyless—unimaginable to us mere mortals."

"Well, at least you're safe, sir."

"No, not safe, Rothman. The only safety is in her unstoried place. As it is, I must die. You must die." Rothman's brow loured. "You think such a place is an illusion?"

"Yes. Everything is history, just as you've always known." The historian could think of nothing to say to that.

"Tell me, sir, did you . . ."

"Lie with her?" The historian looked out into the middle distance. "Yes, probably so, but it was more like a violation, Rothman, a forcible entry into time."

"How strange, sir."

"Yes, everything about her is strange, passing strange." The historian looked into Rothman's craggy face. "But if she'd been a she-devil, you would've burst through the door and saved me, wouldn't you?"

"I would've tried, sir."

"You would've succeeded, Rothman." The historian took his ledger from the drawer, wrote out a draft and gave it to Rothman. "Now I can write the book. I have betrayed her for a book, but I have been true to myself."

"The book is your destiny, sir."

"Yes, I'm afraid so."

"What is the book, sir?"

"Her story—though she is against story. It will contain all that she danced for me, and more, more, because once the sap of memory begins to rise, everything comes."

"Will it make us better, sir?"

"I don't know." The historian paused and then said, "I understand that you give all your fees to the wretched among your people."

"Not all."

"Nevertheless, you're a good man, Rothman. And she is dance. But I'm only an historian . . . something dangling between goodness and dance." The historian stood up. "I'll miss you, Rothman."

"I'll miss you, sir."

They went to the door together. "Good-bye, Rothman."

"Good-bye, sir." The agent drew up his cloak and winnowed the thick fog that haunted the city street. And then he disappeared.

∽

On the historian's desk lay a blank sheet of paper, the inkwell unstoppered, the pen uncased. Under the drapes crept an inexorable seepage of light from the garden in its everlasting throes of season. The historian sat nodding in reverie. Across the confused stage of his mind came again the old Pontiff of Encyclopedism. "She is fair, as fair almost as *ma belle France.* She will give birth to an age if you can write her, my son."

The historian nodded.

Another time he heard a great clamor in the garden, thinned by the glass of the French doors and muffled by the drapes but still demanding. The historian knew what he would see if he were to open the drapes. There would be the garden, the mise-en-scène: in the north corner the last polyp of snow gnawed to a nub by the advancing sun of March, and the junipers creeping forward in fresh gray-green. And the reformers of course, flown in over the roofs of the city like huge heraldic birds, and now chorusing, "Write the story of the betterment of mankind!"

On the right were Madame Lotta and a gentleman with a lovely russet mustache, the Colonel, master of many tongues. On the left were Victoria and Azeglio himself, the bodhisattva, his eyes mystic but bright with interest in the world. The four made again their vigorous demand. "Write the betterment of mankind! Raise the poor and the afflicted!"

The latakia-thick smoke from Madame Lotta's cigarette made an ambiguous scroll above their heads, emblem of the disturbed city, or of their angelic mission. "What is this wild woman I see in jhu mind? Not even of our time! Put her out and write the book of the Spirit!"

The historian imagined himself opening the doors and appearing as on a papal balcony. "Be still, my children. My history will include all of you, just as I promised."

"History!" They flung the word away as so much merde among the rotted leaves. "Free the women!" shouted Victoria Azeglio. "Free the children!" And all together: "Write the betterment of mankind!" They began to lift their wings. In another moment they would fly at him, headed by the beautiful spindrift of auburn curls, flanked by the black ewe's head, the russet mustache, and the verdigris of the bodhisattva. Nothing to do, after one last fascinated glance, but close the door and drapes and consign them to the darkness outside of his imagination.

After a while the historian took up his pen. He listened with satisfaction to the slowness of his heartbeat—like a horned toad's in hibernation. To finish his monumental task he would need time and peace. He lifted his pen to write, but there was an alien presence in his mind. He set his pen down and surveyed the stage of his imagination uneasily. But when he recognized the presence he smiled. There, propped up against the wall, where she had left him, was the sad little revolutionary poet, his fine blond hair mussed, his natty white jacket soaked with vodka, his ringed fingers limp in his lap, his trousers wrinkled, his spats soiled. Poor little miscreant.

"You weren't watching lovingly, were you, when she danced the revolution. You were supposed to write pure red lyric. But you were dreaming of Sophia Andreyevna Tolstoy, the great man's granddaughter. What a glorious union in the history of Russian letters, you thought. And I was dreaming of my book." The historian shook his head. "Alas, alas for us." He picked up the poet, limp as a rag doll, light as an effigy, eviscerated by self-deception. Nevertheless, in honor of the significant role the little man had played in the dancer's story, the historian grunted theatrically as he made his way to the coatrack. There he proceeded with the terrible ritual. A length of crimson cloth was ready to hand. He knotted it expertly, cinched it around the poet's neck, and secured the other end to a horn of the rack. Then he dropped the body and sent the poet skipping off to eternity. But there was no jerking, no bulging of eyes, no fatal erection. Because the act had already been done by the poet's own hand and the historian was merely recording it.

The historian returned to his desk and took up his pen. He knew that eventually he must write the terrible return to America, the dancer all in red, the vituperative audiences. And then he must write the final

trip, to Nice, the axle of the motorcar turning and turning in the hub of its evil fate, the long crimson scarf with its beautiful Chinese asters looped sweetly about her neck, one end lolloping innocently in the breeze. Up, up into the hills, never to return. Her story—which he had forced on her there in the dark of his study.

The historian clenched his teeth. No, by God, he would not write that, not now anyway. He would start where his love of her had bubbled up like spring sap, seizing him in every sense, there at the Maydan in Tiflis.

I am writing, my love, that Georgia surprised us with her gaudy sun and with her women no less gaudy and with her succulent jewel, Tiflis. We took the funicular to Ptatsminda, remember, and saw the town lying like a bedizened girl by an imaginary sea. But our first experience of her was the Maydan with its thousand voices and stalls. Remember the cucumbers in disorderly layers like the shakes of old roofs, and the tumbling pyramids of tomatoes, and the corn and the mirror-bright eggplants and the grapes and plums, pears and quinces, and the cracked figs doomed by their own sweetness. And remember the flowers bursting into the sun like geysers of color the earth could not contain. And out on the street they were frying thin cheesecakes over braziers, and the zithers were humming and hissing like an infinity of bees, and the dicers rolled, for what stakes we could not see.

But the best was down at the little bazaar where the wind circulated more freely. For there were the unforgettable scarves of Tiflis billowing against the sun, all the colors of the rainbow. What did you think they were? The sails of Greek dance that plied your imagination those sunny afternoons of Salamis? The fiery panels of revolution? What did you think they were? You bought them by the dozens, remember? And draping them over your breast, one and then the other, and fronting the wind and the sun, you ran and leaped into the air of Tiflis. And the women of Tiflis laughed and the men of the Maydan came out from their stalls and slapped their knees. You disrupted the whole market, but at last you had too many, they raveled you up like a fish in a net, the scarves of Tiflis. So I had to carry many myself, and the wind wrapped them about my neck and mouth. And you laughed and shouted, "Come out of purdah, you benighted woman." Away we went to the hotel, the wind whipping up the scarves about us like children of Iris caught meddling in our mother's colors.

The historian stood up from his desk, his eyes brimming, his mouth overflowing with sweetness. "O my beloved, I will write it all. It will be greater than history. I promise."

Something, perhaps the very violence of his rising and speaking, caused the yellow globe to sway, the circle of light to turn rhythmically among desk and chairs. But the volumes in their faithful rows kept an echoless silence. The garden beyond the drapes went quietly about the business of spring. And the city, whatever disturbances yeasted in its bowels, was noiseless at the moment. "I promise," said the historian, and sat down to work.

The Courting of Martha Tewkes

Connecticut River Valley, 1807

Noah Parker was a boy of twelve when Simms came to the valley of the Connecticut River. Simms was not the first queer person Noah had encountered, however. Two years earlier, a woman had come all the way from the city to escape the horrors of the tenements, but the silences and the stirrings of the nocturnal animals had driven her back. And there was always the chapman who brought in salt from the Jersey coast and yarn and indigo and axes and nail rods and all manner of doodads. His head was not set steady on his neck, and the saliva pooled in his lower lip. Still, he made honest weights. And there was Martha Tewkes, who had been queer all her life, but she had also lived in the valley all her life, so she was familiar to Noah.

Simms' queerness, however, was altogether different. First of all, there was the question of his origin. One day he just appeared walking down the trail by Crowfoot Creek. Noah saw him and ran to tell his father. They thought he might be an Indian. He wore hide leggings and moccasins and a bearskin. But he carried a knapsack and a rifle and he whistled and hummed, and presently they saw he had a beard.

"Where are you going, stranger?" said Lemuel Parker.

Simms smiled and looked around with his bright blue eyes. "Well, I think I shall stop hereabouts for a while."

"All the good land has been homesteaded. What's left is bog and rocky acres."

Noah was a little ashamed of his father for being so unwelcoming. Besides, he found the stranger fascinating and did not want to lose sight of him right away, so he was pleased when the stranger said, "I wouldn't plan to stake a claim, sir. Just settle in for a while and live off the land." He stuck out his hand. "Simms."

"Lem Parker," said Noah's father, taking the stranger's hand. "And this is my son, Noah."

Simms took the boy's hand. Noah had never felt such a hand. It was not so much like fingers and a palm as it was the paw and pad of a big friendly dog, or a bear.

"We'll get to know each other, Noah," said Simms.

"Yes, sir."

"Well," said Lem Parker a bit gloomily, "it's good today, but it can get bad yet this month, and on into April sometimes." He took his hat off and looked up. There were rolls of dark cloud under a high cobwebby sky.

"It doesn't matter, if you're half grizzly. You just make a tent of your own skin and puff up a fire in your innards."

Noah did not know whether to smile or not and was grateful when his father spoke again. "Where are you coming from, Mr. Simms?"

"I was in Boston and then I went west and now I'm back east. It's a long walk. Seems like half a century."

∽

"Well, he does sound like a queer one," said Noah's mother. "Why didn't you bring him home for supper so I could see somebody new for a change?"

"I didn't know what you had."

"If there's enough for three, there's enough for four. And I just baked."

"Well, I'm not sure you'd want him in your kitchen, Tess."

"Poo. We've had Indians."

"But this fellow smells even worse."

"Your son doesn't agree with you." She looked at Noah mischievously. "He thinks this Simms man is a wonderful mystery. Don't you, Noah?"

"I don't know him yet," said Noah with such obvious diplomacy that it made his mother laugh outright. How he wished she would not put him athwart his father, for these days there was already a mysterious little tension between them. Still, he loved his mother passionately. He was proud of her. She was a beautiful black-haired woman with eyes like chestnuts. The other women were afraid of her beauty and of her ways. At meeting he had overheard one say, "She's too quick for her own good," and another, "She's saucy and forward." She made them nervous.

She made his father nervous, too, for ever so often the blood would beat up in her and drive her to a kind of wildness. For instance, every week or so she bathed at night in the wooden tub behind a screen of muslin. The scent that rose up from her discarded clothes and the sound of sluicing water warmed Noah all over and made his scalp tingle. And then sometimes she would commence to sing and the singing would rise to a fine la-la and the fine la-la would ascend into a crooning that was still melodious, until Noah was almost breathless. Sometimes Lem Parker would step to the screen and hiss, "Tess, for God's sake! The boy." And the woman behind the screen would stop crooning, but presently she would begin a lyrical laugh that turned into a singing that turned into a fine la-la and so on. And then she would stop suddenly and come out from behind the screen all trussed up in a long gown and housecoat and wearing her clogs on her feet and a white night bonnet on her head. She looked at them severely. "Why don't the two of you find some useful occupation while I bathe?"

In fact, Lemuel was trying to make entries in his ledger with a crow quill pen. And Noah had begun reaming out a soapstone with his hand bit to make an inkwell for himself, but long ago the bit had gone still in his fingers and the half-routed stone had blurred in his eyes. Tess continued to look sternly at them for some moments and then with deliberate awkwardness she clomped several steps in her clogs and laughed. "If you would only make me a wooden floor, I could curl my toes at you."

"I shall make you a wooden floor, my dear, I promise, but not until we have completed the bridge and the mill."

Noah did not catch his mother's reply any more than to note that it was surprisingly muted, for suddenly his attention was focused on the fantastical designs she had scratched with a stick into the packed dirt of the floor—wild arabesques that looped out under the table before they curved back toward the walls and lost themselves among their own tails.

The other women made simple borders of leaves or squares—except Martha Tewkes, of course, who had once seen Tess Parker's floors and made hers of the same kind, only wilder.

After a while Noah climbed the ladder up to his bed in the loft and tried to stopper his ears with his blanket, but what he might not actually have heard he imagined he heard, and so he could not resist touching himself. Afterwards, when all was quiet, he looked out into the night through his bottle window. And there was the moon five times, splayed wickedly on the curved glass. Someday soon, his father promised, he would have the chapman bring a pane shipped over from London. But Noah did not think a mere pane would straighten out his crooked desires. They were a great burden to him these days.

Before they could get started the next day digging out the last of the east bank where the abutment for the new bridge would go, Simms appeared, vaulting over the stone wall up the hill and bearing down on them with a jolly rolling step like the very harbinger of spring. He wore his hide leggings and moccasins and a jerkin. His arms were bare to the late March breeze, which was pleasant but crisp. He was ripping the skin from a bruised crab with his incisors and wallowing it in his mouth as lusciously as if he were eating an October Maiden Blush.

"Where did you get a crab this season of the year?" asked Lemuel Parker.

Simms crushed the core in the back of his mouth, skeeted two pips into the creek, and said, "Woman lives over the hill there. She gave me some sassafras tea, too, and a cup of milk, and all for the one hour's work of making her a well sweep."

"Martha Tewkes."

"Is that it?" said Simms gratefully. "She never said."

"Her family was massacred by the Indians when she was a child."

"I'm sorry to hear it," said Simms. "Many in the West are badly damaged." Then he brightened suddenly. "But Martha Tewkes isn't damaged too deep, I don't think, just quared a bit." He did not wait for Lemuel to comment on that. "So you're going to build a new bridge, are you?"

"Yes."

Simms stepped out onto the log and slat bridge and bounced up and down. "What's the matter with this old girl? She feels firm to me."

"Oh, she's all right," conceded Lemuel. "I built her with my own hands, but she won't carry the big wagons, so we lose all the traffic to the Conniston Road. When our new bridge is up, we'll get easier to market. And there shall be tolls."

"Ha!" said Simms, pointing his finger suddenly at Noah. "The world will come and get you, Noah. Nothing there is the world hates worse than not being able to get to a place."

"We must go to work," said Lemuel.

"I shall help," said Simms. And he did, dug and hauled dirt. By noon both sides of the creek bank were scabbed out and ready for the placement of the abutment stones.

"Well," said Lemuel, "we must go back to the house now and do the rest of our tasks." It was obvious to Noah that his father suffered some embarrassment. "If you come on the day the neighbors help us raise the king post and beams, we'll give you food and switchel, though my wife will put no rum in it. But we're grateful for your help this day."

"The pleasure was mine," said Simms, "and the instruction was invaluable." He smiled and gave his naked hairy arms a friendly pump. "Don't worry about my belly. I'm adequate with my rifle, not to sound boastful. Soon I shall have a buck to feast on and jerk. My springes are out, too, and I shall have rabbit as often as I like."

That night, because Noah had forgotten again to drop the shutter outside, the devil moon made its five wrinkled grins in the bottle window. And he thought about Martha Tewkes. He had always stayed away from her, on the road or when she came to the house to visit his mother. She was wild and pungent, her skirts brambly and her hair all tangled and her eyes bright with frank interest. He thought she must be closer to his mother's age than his own age, but she had no restraint. On the road she might break into a skipping gait or twirl about suddenly as if something had grabbed her by the hair. And once at his mother's table he had seen her teeth and lips stop upon a peach as if her mind had been seized by an awful power and not let go for a whole minute while the sweet fluid welled up in the corners of her mouth. And then she chewed on and laughed and took his mother's hand and slid her own around it, slick with peach juice. Noah could not understand her. "What ails her?" he asked his mother.

"Nothing. Nothing at all," said his mother, mischievously pretending surprise. "It's just that the Indians sheared all the fleece of society off her when she was a child, so now she's only what you and I would be without our wool."

"But even the Indians don't act so wild," said Noah quickly, not wishing to think of himself shorn of his concealment. His judgment of Indians was based on the two stolid old traders who came down the road ever so often with ash bows, herbs, and beads.

"No, of course not. Indians are very thickly coated with society. Only it's not ours."

∽

Noah and his father were late to the creek the next morning because Noah's mother had made them take down the banking from the sides of the house. "There may still be chill winds, Tess," said Lemuel.

But she was furious. "Take them down, I say. They're dead and they stink."

She was right, Noah conceded, for as he pulled away the old corn stalks and pumpkin vines and hauled them to the compost bin they smeared on his fingers an oozy brown swill that had the smell of pure corruption. The very sight of the stuff infuriated his mother. "Get every last scrap of it! Too late already. Which is the trouble with this ignorant valley, forever dabbling with the old year, with the past. The devil take it." She kicked the rotten old vegetation viciously. "Snails, slugs, and grubs!"

Noah and his father went swiftly about their appointed task, grim and sullen but not daring to voice complaint. As soon as they were done they struck off to the creek, where they found Simms and Ben the ox by the stone pile. Simms had apparently fed Ben the leaves of a sapling and now, tickling his nose with the remaining switch, had hypnotized him. A slaverous rope hung from the great beast's jowls, and his eyes were fixated on the ground. But as soon as father and son appeared Simms released the beast from his trance and leaped up to greet them. "What I want to know," he said, "is where you found these fine stones and how you got them here."

Lemuel smiled, purged at last of the aftertaste of his wife's fury and pleased by Simms' wonder. "From the field just under Placket Mountain, where the stones rear up every year new. And old Ben hauled them for us along last month's ice."

"We were lucky," Noah chimed in. "You must have a thaw and then a freeze, or else you must haul a great quantity of water from the creek to make your own ice road."

Simms stroked his beard smiling. "How long ago do you suppose it was the savage old Titans planted these stones?"

Noah looked at his father, saw there only a mirror of his own wonderment, and understood that it was his place as a boy to question. "Did the Titans plant the stones to build bridges with later?"

Simms smiled grimly. "No indeed, Noah. They harvested them for war. They assaulted the gods of Olympus. And lost of course. Assaulting the gods is a foolish business at best. Avoid it."

"Yes, sir."

Simms turned his attention to Lemuel. "But tell me, how will you get the stones in place and mortar them?"

Lemuel brightened. "I will not mortar them. I will dry mason them. How will I get them in place? Old Ben will move them for us, eh Ben?"

The great beast slued his eye slowly to his master and switched his tail lazily, not entirely pleased, it would seem, to have returned from Simms' trance to the workaday world.

"Watch us," said Lemuel. But of course Simms did not merely watch. He helped roll the stones onto the sled and followed with excited step as Ben hauled them to the edge of the excavation. There Lemuel had driven a stout fulcrum post. With a sling of hemp and a long lever, Noah and Simms lowered the stones into place, Lemuel standing below to direct the exact placement of each. Once they lost one into the creek, but Ben hauled it back up for them. By noon they had a third part of the east abutment done.

"By the Lord, that's a fair morning's work," said Lemuel swatting his pants leg with his hat. "And we're much beholden to you, Mr. Simms."

"The debt is mine," said Simms. "Think what I've learned, and in such good fellowship too."

What an odor Simms put off, Noah was thinking, too rich to untangle man, ox, hide, earth. Then suddenly he was alerted by what his father was saying. "I'm thinking you must come to supper with us this day."

"You're kind, Mr. Parker, but your valley is so rich in society that I'm already spoken for. Miss Martha Tewkes has invited me to eat cornbread and maple sugar with her and perhaps a root from the cellar, and drink mead." Simms laughed. "I'm sure it'll be a rare meal. And I am to pay for it like the troubadours of old with a tale of the Wild West. Later, of course, I'll bring her a rabbit and some venison though it'll be a little high this time of year. And then when I've plucked a proper sinew and the water warms we shall have a trout." Simms bowed his head momentarily, as if in obeisance to the richness of the countryside. "But my thanks to your wife, sir, and a blessing on your table."

∽

"Well, we asked him to supper," Lemuel said to his wife. "He's a mighty help."

"But he wouldn't come?"

"No."

"Alas. I so want to see Noah's big bear. Why wouldn't he come?"

"He was spoken for—by Miss Martha Tewkes." It was the moment Lemuel had been waiting for, and he followed it with a raucous laugh. Noah thought his mother would tweak his father's ear or swat his buttocks with the broom, as he had seen her do before, but this time she only fell into smiling thought.

"Well?" said Lemuel after a bit, "aren't you going to feed your men? Miss Tewkes is to give Mr. Simms cornbread and maple and mead and who knows what else." And then he did get a rap on the head.

∽

That night Noah had a sweet winter dream. He was walking beside Ben, who was pulling the big sand-filled snow roller down the road and making from his nostrils huge plumes of steam that floated up into the trees. Noah carried a whip, but it was only a symbol of authority, for the great beast labored willingly. Behind them came a stream of grateful journeyers: a townsman driving a sled laden with milk and syrup, an old woman in a grandma's chair behind a pony, a handsome couple in a cutter, and many others. Oddly he had the impression of having just been to meeting house, where the preacher stood on a box of coals and all the congregation had their lap robes spread out to catch the heat of their foot warmers, so all the air was snuffy with smoke. And then he was home in bed. His mother had put a hot stone at the foot, and the last of the heat of the kitchen fire lifted up into the loft. And then he remembered in his dream that it was Christmas Eve and out in the barn Ben and Gertha the cow would be conversing and he ought to run out and stand in the warm straw and listen, but he did not. The next morning his mother would fly all about the house with a fire pan of hot embers like a spirit of flame and light the candles that stood within the hoops of laurel. And there would be presents: a table and a stool of his own to take to the loft and a fine tin lantern his father had made, all punched out in concentric circles with his initials in the middle, shining bright: N.P. For he was now to become a scholar and read and write. This was well before the time of his trouble with himself.

∽

Simms was waiting for them at the creek the next morning. He had bathed. His hair was still plastered down with water and his beard was all runneled and rutted. His leggings and jerkin were damp. "You will catch the ague, man," said Lemuel.

"Not if you give me some good warm work to do."

So they laid stones for three hours and then they stopped and rested. "Yesterday," said Simms, "I gave Martha Tewkes the jaw of a deer I found buried in your creek bank these many years. I washed it and polished it up very nice. There were six teeth left, three of them almost perfect."

"What a fine gift for a woman!" said Lemuel. Noah was surprised by his father's jolly irony.

"Yes indeed, and I presented it most formally, and she accepted with a curtsy."

"Curtsy indeed!" said Lemuel with amusement. "Martha Tewkes never curtsied in her life."

"Perhaps not until yesterday," said Simms, and then went on in a facetious, ruminative way. "No doubt the deer's jaw opened up to her vistas of time, for she peered deeply into the grain of the bone. She recalled another life when she was a queen's handmaiden but got sent out into the country when the king required her favors."

"Back to work," said Lemuel.

Simms rose to his feet, but not until he had said, and this time with unqualified seriousness, "I tell you, Lemuel Parker, Martha Tewkes is not the quaint country hoyden you think."

"I think nothing," said Lemuel, rather defensively.

Then Noah, to his own surprise, spoke out boldly. "My mother says she's only us without the wool of society."

"That's a nice way to put it," said Simms. "Your mother must be a clever woman."

Noah was glad that they took up their work immediately, for he did not know what to say to that.

∽

A week later, several neighbor men helped Lemuel, Noah, and Simms raise the king posts. Already Lemuel had assembled posts, braces, and beams on the ground. He had used no iron nails, not even those beaten from rods at his own forge, for they would rust. He had used only trunnels—ash into oak so that seasoning would cinch the structure even tighter. These he had driven with his great ironwood beetle. Simms had shaken his head in admiration and amazement. "No one but your father could swing that instrument." Looking at Simms' bare arms, Noah believed that the bear-man from the West could swing anything humanly possible, but he did not say so.

When the bridge beams were hoisted into place by men and ox and the king posts raised and the crossbeams added, then Noah climbed to the top and placed a brush of green pine on the crest and recited the lines his mother had prepared and taught him:

> Over Crowfoot Creek we have raised a frame
> And Parker Bridge will be its name.

And then Tess Parker passed around mugs of mead and generous gobbets of sweetbread, and one of the neighbor men led them all in a great hurrah. They tipped mugs, drank, ate, accepted refills, ate more, and then, like the busy countrymen they were, soon departed, feeling no doubt more than amply rewarded for their morning's work.

Then Tess Parker came close to Simms and smiled in his face. "I'm much obliged to you for the help you've given my husband and my son."

"It's an honor to be apprenticed to such bridge-builders," said Simms with his sunny, uncalculating smile.

"But I would be offended," Tess continued, almost as though Simms had not spoken, "by your failure to eat with us if I didn't know you were courting Martha Tewkes."

"Ah," said Simms as brightly as before, "we haven't come to that."

In the background Noah, come down from the king post, stood besides his father, who was staring in amazement at Tess's brazen approach to Simms.

"Not come to that?" said she, her face clouding a little. "I hope we're not speaking of a springtime dalliance, Mr. Simms, for as you know, Martha is unusual in her innocence."

"Indeed, madam, and loves you especially."

Tess laughed. "Do you mean that one must be unusually innocent to love me?"

"To the innocent, madam, all things are innocent."

Lemuel and Noah, knowing all too well the unpredictable excesses of mercurial wife and mother, stood still and silent, impaled on the barb of uncomfortable expectation.

"And are you innocent, Mr. Simms? Have you really come to us from out of the West in a state of nature?"

Simms said, "I will answer the question you are too gracious to ask directly. Yes, I mean to treat Martha Tewkes with honor—and more, with the affections required by her unusual innocence, as you say." During this declaration Simms still kept his face open and affable, its

candor burnished by the sun and the brisk airs of March, by the ruddy
effects of demanding labor, and perhaps by Tess Parker's mead, which
had in it more than a hint of fermentation.

Tess Parker did not reply immediately but studied Simms' face. At
last she said, "Then you are indeed decent and honorable, Mr. Simms."
She paused. "But are you wise in the ways of the heart? Will you understand Martha's unique requirements?"

"No, madam, I am not wise, but where the will and the heart
intend good, they do not often go widely awry."

Tess Parker gave Simms a definite and yet somewhat pursed smile.
"That's as far as we can go, Mr. Simms." And then abruptly she added
with something approaching vehemence. "Do not come to me for
counsel."

"I'll not trouble you, madam. But I suspect that Martha will come
to you."

"She will not—not about you. She'll keep you swaddled and
hidden in a secret corner of her heart. So there'll be just the two of you.
That's the danger." With that Tess Parker turned away from Simms and
went to her son and husband, deftly slipping her arms under theirs and
drawing them to her. Then she smiled back at Simms. "In any case I
have no time to counsel lovers, because I'm taken up with these two.
You understand that they are making history here with hammer, forge,
and saw."

"I do indeed, madam. That's why I've apprenticed myself to them,
but I fear I'll never attain such deep communings with stone and wood."

"And iron," said Tess Parker, "when the mill is done." And then
she added, "I sometimes think my husband has made a secret compact
with the demon of the mechanical arts." She smiled at Lemuel, who
obviously was now required to speak, and did so without the awkwardness that Noah had feared. "If my hands were as quick as Tess's tongue
we'd have machines that would teach the creek to plow and milk and
harvest for us and we'd have to invent games to take up our time."

Simms laughed and looked at Noah. "Do you think, Noah, that I
should be required to choose between your father's genius and your
mother's wit?"

"No, sir."

〰

As the spring advanced, Noah found his quill and paper both fractious and fascinating. To begin with there was the choice of three inks, each of which sat stoppered in its well on his desk. He and his father had made them: the brown from boiled walnut and butternut hulls made fast with vinegar and salt, the black from the brown dyed with soot, and the blue from indigo, madder, and bran. So the brown and the black were pungent and went on with a sheen that never entirely faded. But the blue had the secret fragrance of fields at night and hid its shine so well that no turning of the paper would catch it out. So when he wrote a lesson of practice words, he put them down in brown and rolled out the letters as carefully as he could. When he wrote some facts of his life in the valley, he set them forth in bold black. "The bell of the meeting house rings at seven o'clock, twelve noon, and nine, after which the day of the month is tolled. Births are tolled in the morning. Six bells is for the death of a woman, nine is for a man, after which the deceased's age is tolled." But if he were ever to write a secret diary, he would write it in blue. How it would frighten and thrill him to see his secrets flow out of the quill— recording that night, when, in the crooked light of the bottle window, he touched himself and suddenly there was a spasm and a slick sprang out of him. And after that when he touched himself again the slick could not be held back. It sprang out of its own accord and from that he understood it was the source of life. And the blue would also tell how he was disturbed by his mother's bathing and by her fragrance. It would tell how at night sometimes the body of Martha Tewkes would come to him wild with the smell of primroses and honeysuckle and brumming like bees. It would tell how the uninhibited smell of Simms, which the creek water never could wash away, made him think of women.

Fortunately his father gave him practical tasks. He copied out the text for a handybill to be printed in Conniston and posted throughout the valley. It informed the populace of the new bridge, its convenience, and the modest toll for its use. He also drew out with pleasure—after some miscues and frustration—a sketch for the mill. At the top of the drawing was the dam that created the mill pond. From the pond a long wooden sluice ran down to the mill wheel. At the head of the sluice Noah drew a gate and showed how, when it was open, the water ran down into the baffles of the big overshot wheel and turned it. Just

behind, Noah drew the stone foundation of the mill house, through which the shaft of the wheel passed. All this he put down in black except for the water, which was blue and which showed by its splashing and rippling its great power.

Lemuel looked at the drawing with satisfaction. "It's fine, Noah." He showed it to his wife. "Very pretty," she said. "Tell me, will it replace my old quern?"

"Indeed," said Lemuel, "and save us much other labor too. You will see."

Tess smiled, looked at her hands, and gave her husband's cheek a gentle stroke. "Why then if I put away my old quern stick, my hands will become as soft and velvety as a London lady's. How will you and Gertha like that?"

Lemuel Parker did not say, but he smiled in a way that Noah found foolish and moving.

ᔕᓄ

The work on the mill went apace. Simms came every day to help, but never came to the house to eat. In scarcely two weeks the pond was dammed and walled and the trestles for the sluice were raised. "Are there enough stones left for the foundation?" Noah asked one day.

"Shh!" Simms wrinkled his brows mischievously. "You want to throw old Ben into a black funk?"

"There will be," said Lemuel, "if we lay them carefully."

"If any man can do it," said Simms, "you can."

Good Friday they did not work. It also happened on that day the bluebirds came to the valley, slipping among the bushes like errant little freshets of creek water. Noah grew very restless and went out into the woods. He wandered high up on the hill with no purpose other than to expend energy. But presently he began to see Martha Tewkes' syrup tubs mounted on maple trunks beneath little spiles of sumac. And these seemed to direct him inexorably toward her house. It was April and the air was full of a confusion of fragrances and of temperatures. He could not tell whether it was warm or cool against his face. And when suddenly he heard in the distance a woman's laughter he did not know whether it was real or not. He went on toward it. Presently he came to the edge of the woods and there around the clearing was the root fence that old man Tewkes had put up years before. What an ugly thing it was—upturned stumps of twisted roots striking out like serpents. You might think it was a dragon's corral, except that there in the distance under the single huge maple was the cottage made of rough-hewn poles. It had a bark roof and a clay-and-stick chimney. It canted dangerously to the west. How it had stood these many years Noah did not know. The barn had not. Raised without a stone foundation, it had long ago sagged down on the north side and looked now like a huge lean-to. Off to the side of the cottage Noah saw the garden, but all else was a riotous contention of field grass, weeds, and flowers. By the front door a forsythia bush pushed up bravely, blooming already with a bright yellow splash. And along the front of the house the Boston ivy and the creepers and woodbine were taking on their new spring sheen.

Noah, though he heard nothing at the moment, stood cautiously just within the shadow of the woods. And then he did hear something— a gay whoop. It was Martha Tewkes. But it was not she he saw first. It was Simms, and what a fantastical sight he was—ropes of clover and a garland of tiny white wildflowers around his neck, and on his forehead a double fillet of honeysuckle. Out from behind the cottage he shuffled like a wild beast, his feet moving crudely in the tall grass and his arms held out heavily as if to improve an uncertain balance. Behind him came Martha Tewkes, her hair as always a fanciful whorl of sunbeams, her skirt tucked and tufted up by burrs. She had a switch in her hand and whipped the air behind her beast with jolly abandon, laughing and yelping while he in turn made deep throaty brumblings and shambled on, driven by lashes that never fell, ill-tempered but obedient to his bondage.

The sight sent Noah's memory swimming back to an earlier spring. His father had taken Ben off for the day to another farm. Now he remembered. It was the farm of Owen Fetler, who had galloped up on his horse like a king's courier and said that it was time. And before his father had left with Ben, his mother had draped the beast's horns with plaited vine of wild grape and laughed. Now Noah crouched and watched the wild woman drive her beast. Around the house they went and back out again. Noah sighed. It did not seem to him a game that

was going anywhere. He slipped back into the woods. But he did not
return down the hill to home. Instead, he began to look for Simms'
place. Presently he saw a red fox, or at least the fleck of it in the brush
like a tiny fire within the dark eye of the forest. Other small beasts scat-
tered at his coming. A rabbit, in temporary confusion, bounded toward
him, then pivoted away in a great scuttling fright. Squirrels and chip-
munks scampered off. All the birds went quiet, except one that called
over and over with a strange liquid stridence, compelled, impatient. He
followed it and found Simms' hideaway.

The hideaway was a roof of hides that sheltered a round fire pit
and a raised platform of poles and bark that obviously served as a bed.
On a rope depending from the ridge pole of the roof hung a stout box
made of oak shingles—jerky and other foodstuffs, Noah assumed. The
general smell of the place was smoky, but by the bark bed Noah picked
up Simms' special odor. The familiar smells of smoke and man were
comforting, for the place otherwise had a strange atmosphere that made
Noah nervous. In fact, if he had not known what he was looking for, he
might have thought that he had stumbled upon some queer Indian
worshiping place. Even Simms' little birch-bark bucket took on a spooky
quality. Its stripes and soot-blackened bottom made it seem to Noah like
the slough of some huge snake. He felt a tingle on his neck and in his
scalp, like the prickling that warmed him when his mother sang her wild
bathing song. He squatted down on his haunches, but that must have
constricted his blood because when he got up he was a little light-
headed. He looked up toward the crown of pines, which seemed to be
turning slowly under a halo of misted sun. Everything around him faded.
He felt utterly alone. So he went down the hill home. And two days later
at meeting house he sang alleluia as loud as he could, not because he
understood anything of the miracle of the stone rolled away in that dim
time past but merely to join his voice with others, at least for a moment.

∽

The sluice box ran its route down from the pond. The stonework
to support the mill shaft and to serve as the foundation of the mill
house rose almost magically under Lemuel's hand. The wheel also was

soon completed, its vast hoops made of various woods banded in a certain order to insure binding when they were wet, each section a half-quadrant linked to its neighbors by wedged tenons. Simms shook his head and looked at Noah. "I thought I'd seen fine wheels and mortising out west, but it was to this mere journeyman's work."

Lemuel let Noah make a joint and it was fine. And then, very carefully, they rolled the wheel to the bank of the creek. "Don't let her get loose, men, or she will run away from us and stop who knows where."

"Don't worry," said Simms. He was the brake, keeping his back against the wheel, letting it roll only little by little. Lemuel and Noah steadied the wheel behind and hauled back as best they could to take some of the load off Simms. "If she starts to get away," Lemuel told Noah, "I'll jump around to your side and we'll push her down." But Simms was good to his word and presently they tipped the wheel over gently there on the grassy bank of the creek just upstream from the stonework. Lemuel let out a great puff of relief. "There! When the shaft comes, Ben will have to help us lift her again, but we've got her where we want her for now."

Lemuel had had a great debate with himself about the shaft. Noah and Simms had listened, commenting little. On the one hand Lemuel believed he could make an arrow-straight axle from the heart of oak and save the money for an iron one, though it would be a long labor. But the man at the foundry in Conniston advised him against it. Lemuel recited. " 'You'll think it's as true as God's will,' he says, 'but it'll have a warp in it that you can't see, even when it's turning, and slowly the warp will wear your master gear and all the gears to everything you attach.' "

"Why worry?" said Simms. "You have your toll money and will get more."

"Yes, and a little crop money, too, but I'd hoped to send Tess into town for a new dress." He sighed. "Well, it will have to be. We can't have a crooked shaft."

The next day he constructed a plumping mill and brought Tess down to see it—a clever little thing: water box and pestle at opposite ends of a shaft mounted on a fulcrum. An attenuated flow from the sluice fell into the water box, lifting the pestle. Then the water spilled out from the box and down came the pestle into a mortar that Lemuel presently filled with dried herbs. Up and down went the little mallet, pounding the herbs into a fragrant powder.

"Very nice," said Tess, chucking her husband's cheek with pleasure.

"And this is just a trifle to what's to come," said Noah.

"I believe it." Tess smiled at her son, and then looked at Simms. "Take some herbs to Martha."

"With pleasure."

When the pestle lifted, Tess quickly scooped up a small handful of grindings and put them into a piece of rag she pulled from her apron pocket. This she twisted up into a little ball and handed to Simms. "Martha will like that."

"I'm sure she will."

"And how does the courting go?"

"Slowly. So slowly it can hardly be called courting. We're still children. I'm various animals—a dog, a bear, an old horse, an ox." Simms smiled patiently, apologetically. "You see, we must pass through childhood to youth and then to womanhood."

"And what if she will not or cannot."

"Then so be it. But I think she will, for this childhood has been put upon her and is not from inside." Simms grew more serious. "Fear me not."

Tess Parker reached out and closed his fingers over the little sachet of herbs she had given him. "Be careful."

"I will."

To all this Lemuel listened with unusual complacency, and when Tess stepped away from Simms, he took her place. "Here is a coin," he said, pressing a large silver piece into the palm of Simms' hand. "It's a toll from the bridge you helped us raise."

"What would I do with a coin?" said Simms.

Lemuel's face darkened, whether seriously or not Noah could not tell. "Take it. Do you want to be a good fellow, or do you want your generosity to be a burden to others?"

"I want to be a good fellow." Simms laughed.

"Then take it."

Simms held the coin up between his thumb and forefinger. "It's a handsome old thing, isn't it? I think it was die cast by hand. I'll give it to Martha. She'll like the stern old face and the Latin."

And that made Noah remember the time when coins were also not to him things to be exchanged for shafts and books but were curious objects tingly to the touch. It was a time when the wraiths of Indians and bears fled before him as before a wizard with a magic wand. Those were the days before his troubles with himself. Well then, was Simms wise to lead Martha out of those days? Suddenly he realized that his mother was looking at him. "If you see such curious things down inside yourself, Noah, why not look out at this fair May."

And it was indeed fair. The sun had sunk behind the barn and the swallows were dipping and diving over the mill pond. But even the swift beauty of their flight could not lift Noah above his confusion.

∽

The shaft came from Conniston. To it Lemuel fitted the big master gear, a foot thick with twenty stout oak cogs. Then with Ben's help they raised the wheel, slid the shaft through the hub, and rolled the assembly into place. The shaft rested securely in three iron sleeves, one atop the stone foundation wall of the mill house, another atop an exterior buttress wall, and a third mounted on a pillar in the basement of the mill house.

"Let's open the sluice gate and see how she turns," said Noah.

"She'll turn all right," said Lemuel, "until the day water runs uphill. But first we must build the mill house."

And every morning Tess Parker said, "Go to the mill. Go now." She smiled and said, "I'll milk the cow and do a few chores and then I'll take my basket and a-maying I will go — for passionflowers and maypops and dandelion leaves and chicory and magic roots."

Noah wished passionately that he could follow his mother and spy on her. He believed that she would go up the hill to Martha's and that they would laugh and croon together and maybe even fling off their clothes and do some wild woman's thing. He was beginning to believe that all the earth was nothing but a giant saphead and life the bucket that caught it. At night he could not keep his hands off himself. In the wry light of the bottle window he would watch the slick leap out, now farther and more copious than before and in three and four pulses. And even then he was unrelieved because he had nothing to attach himself to and he hated the world that would not partner him. And his mind turned to Simms, who was always there, every day, waiting by the creek, always bathed, his black hair slick and his beard runneled with creek water, and yet as rank and yeasty as ever. Still, he did not believe that Simms lied to his mother about Martha. But he could not think of Martha, because she who had once seemed frowsy and silly now seemed ultimately desirable, and maybe he could have had her if it weren't for Simms, because she was nearer his own age really. Noah shook his head. All this was only a wild farrago of frustration and anger. He never could have touched Martha, for what if she told his mother?

While Lemuel dry-masoned the chimney, Noah and Simms laid the sills on the foundation walls and then the cross beam and then the floor joists, cutting their own tenons and mortises without recourse to Lemuel, who shouted ever so often, "Fine work, lads! Fine work!" Yet he seemed to shout not to them but to the skies, as though he had the assistance of a host of heavenly laborers. After the floor was laid all around the shaft pillar, Simms raised the flared corner posts and set in the plates and girts, but still Lemuel, climbing his scaffold and laying stone, called, "Hurry, boys, or I shall reach the sky before you." And just as they were raising the end rafters, he finished the last course of stone and helped them with the ridgepole. And Noah, even in his time of confusion and anger, saw that his father was in his glory and rejoiced for him.

Simms was a less certain case. Sometimes Noah thought his mind was up on the hill with Martha, though his hands were always careful with the wood and his eye always attentive. At other times Noah sensed that Simms was much further off than that, away out west. At such times Noah could spring a little story out of Simms, about a bear in a canyon or a catfish in the Pecos River or an old Indian living at the snow line, but there was never much story to it. Just the animal itself living there, being there, always. And then would return to Noah the wonder of Simms' first coming and of the huge vitality of the man, the great paw-like hand that had taken his and sent a hot tingling into his body. But then the odor of the man would rise up into Noah's nostrils and throw him back into the confusion of anger, love, and desire that tainted all his relations these days.

They worked on, the three together now, setting in the single window, pegging on the clapboard siding, and laying the roof shingles. So it was still May yet when one day Lemuel led his wife down from the house to the mill. Noah saw that his father was extended upward like a hearth fire that catches a draft. Lemuel said, "Today we're going to open the sluice gate and start the wheel. You go in the mill house with Noah and Simms." Tess, subdued for once by her husband's authority, went in without a quip. "Noah, Simms," said Lemuel, "you stand by the sleeves with your buckets and keep them wet. I will open the gate only to a slow wheeling, but even so the first turns will be ratchety until the shaft finds her sockets."

So Noah stood by the wall sleeve and Simms by the pillar sleeve. Tess looked out the window at her husband. Presently Noah heard the gate lift and the water splash down on the baffles and then slowly the great shaft began to turn. And just as his father had warned, the rote of it in the sleeve was terrible to hear. And even though Noah poured water on the shaft, he could feel in his teeth the grinding and the brittle tremor of metal against stone and metal. "The wheel is turning," said his mother. Then Lemuel came quickly through the door of the mill house and inspected the two sleeves. "Keep them wet," he said. He glared down at the shaft in Noah's sleeve. "See how she wants to rear up and out. She wants to walk with the wheel down the creek, destroying everything. But will not, if only you keep her wet, boy. Keep her wet." And then he dashed out shouting, "I must keep my own sleeve wet!"

For a long half hour, that seemed to Noah a week, they watched and listened as the shaft was slowly tamed to the sleeves. Its motion smoothed, its harsh gnawing dropped to a creaky complaint and then to a liquid glide. "There," said Lemuel in the sunny door of the mill house, cocking his ear. "I hear her singing. I will now open the gate full."

Noah was not ready for what came. He thought the shaft would only run faster in the sleeve, gliding through the water. And it did do that. But he had not known what the force of the torque would feel like. The whole mill house commenced to shudder and weave. The floor snaked under his feet, filling his bones with quaking. It took his breath away. But there stood his father in the mill house door, a dark demon smiling in the shadow of the sun and shouting, "Are your mortises sound, men? Are your pegs locked tight? This is the hour we shall find out." He beamed. "Had you known there was such power in our little creek?"

"Will it always be like this?" said Tess, her voice still strong but somewhat muddled by the shudder of the mill.

"Yes, it will always be like this."

"What will you do with all this power, Lemuel?" asked Simms.

Lemuel strode into the room. "There above the gear I will mount the millstones. From this end here I will drive a pit saw. Here under the chimney I will set my forge and work the bellows with a crook shaft. Oh, and I will think of other things—a trip-hammer, a die press. Who knows?" All of this was already vivid in his father's eye, Noah knew, but he himself cared nothing for these things. He was totally absorbed by the mere turning of the mill. His whole soul went out into it, the magnificent churning of the thing, its weaving up of the very air of the house. Even his mother was a diminished thing here, her bonnet a frail burr in the sun at the window. Even Simms' big bones were as nothing to the huge turning of the shaft. Only his father, the demon of the machine, seemed to move above the forces he had called up. But such distinctions did not really interest Noah, for he had gone out into the machine. In his very bowels he throbbed and churned no less than the shaft in the sleeve, the wheel in the water. They were brothers.

∽

It was a bad time for insects. The flies hived like bees. The grass-hoppers were so thick that in their blind leaping among the grasses they beat a tattoo against Noah's pants. The black gnats hatched by the millions and stung wherever Noah sweated through the peppery liniment his mother anointed him with. The walking sticks ate their stilted way up every branch and stalk. The aphids were so thick and vicious that neighbors fell to arguing about their nature and names—plant louse, green fly, blight, gall worms, ant cows. Then came the corn borers and the gypsy moths and bagworms. Tent caterpillars made camp in the apple orchard. The ditches stank like a swamp and were overrun with water skimmers. All the day long Noah was required to help his mother pick and swat insects in the orchard and among the young shoots of corn and the melon vines.

"They want to starve us," said Tess Parker. "They want the whole world to themselves."

In the evening dozens of swallows swooped through the swarms, but did not diminish the pests. Lemuel made a noxious gas by wetting a mixture of root and quick lime, and in the heavy dusk it hung among the trees and garden plants just as he had hoped, and the day after, the insects were fewer. But they were always plentiful. Like his mother, Noah hated the insects, but not because he feared starvation—he could live off the land like Simms and the animals. He hated the insects because they kept him away from the mill, where already the millstones were in place and had been tested with some old corn and where the pit saw was ready to lighten the labor of any neighbor building a house or a barn. But it was the brute force of the mill he longed for, the feel of the floor writhing beneath him and the shudder of the roof above. Meanwhile, Simms still helped his father.

One day the two old Indian traders came to the farm. Tess communicated with them by signs and mouthings, at which she had an uncanny knack, no doubt because she found the old men fascinating, fantastically dressed as they were in skins and white men's hats. One had moccasins on, the other boots. One wore on his forehead a fillet of snakeskin and on his little finger a signet ring. Perhaps he had inherited it from some marauding ancestor, but more likely he had traded for it.

Tess knew better than to offer them chairs. They sat on the earthen floor, careful to arrange themselves so that they did not cover any of the design she had inscribed there. Tess did not smile. "Sit down, Noah, and we'll talk." And she gathered her skirt up between her legs and squatted down with them.

One of the old men made along his knee a creeping and then struck it down with his fist. And Tess nodded. "They'll rid us of the insects."

"Ask them how," said Noah, disbelieving of course, but now also amused and interested.

Tess made motions. The old man with the snakeskin fillet took out a rattler of more than a dozen cells and shook it. He was the chief, Noah saw. His assistant brought forth a tiny gourd and rattled it. They commenced a low murmur and then stopped abruptly, all this in a matter of seconds.

"They'll call on the magic of their gods," said Tess. She fashioned flowing motions with her hands, which made Noah a little uneasy because it seemed to him that she was offering herself, her breasts. The assistant rocked his fist gently under his chin.

"In return," said Tess, "they want things to eat and drink."

Here followed a complicated series of offerings, refusals, acceptances. At last the Indians found adequate a jar of honey, a half bottle of black-berry juice fermented with brown sugar (Tess would not give them more), some currant preserves, and a sack of dried apple quarters, which with many motions she advised them to soften in water or imperil their teeth.

"What a bargain," said Noah, with more irony than he had intended. "This little bit to rid ourselves of the pests. Father will be proud of you."

Tess, now with all the vivacity she had repressed since the arrival of the Indians, slapped her son gaily atop the head. "Have you no belief in the spiritual, man of the earth?"

Noah laughed. The vibration of his mother's blow loosened the saliva in his mouth like a sweet berry. The assistant allowed himself a grin, which had exactly five teeth, three above. Presently, then, they went out to the field, where the old men performed their ritual, and then again in the orchard. They raised their rattles to the June sky. They chanted and tamped their feet carefully on the soil. At a certain point they were seized by the powers—their eyes closed and they swayed dangerously in the light breeze. But at last they successfully returned to earth again and gave a final blessing.

During the last of the ritual, Lemuel, alerted by the noise, came with Simms to the mill house door and looked up. Tess saw the two men and with stern face put her finger to her lips. But when the cere-mony was complete, she hollered, "Hallelujah! We are free of the insects!" And then Lemuel laughed and Simms shouted, "Hallelujah!"

But it seemed that the traders were not quite done. The chief made a great rolling motion with his hands, and Noah saw in the dull eyes and in the crimp of the old mouth a flicker of animation.

"They want to see the mill wheel turn," shouted Tess.

"Then bring them down," Lemuel shouted back without hesitation.

When the Indians were properly stationed on the creek bank for an advantageous view of the wheel, Lemuel directed Noah to open the sluice gate part way so that the Indians could understand the operation of the wheel. Then, at his father's bidding, Noah closed the gate and the wheel stopped. Lemuel invited the Indians to visit the mill house. This they conferred about at some length and at last cautiously approached the door but would not enter until all the whites were inside and would not proceed more than a step or two beyond the threshold.

"Tell them what we do here, Tess," said Lemuel. And Tess with pantomimes of grinding and eating and with frequent repetitions of maize managed to clarify the purpose of the millstones. The explanation of the pit saw was simpler, for already on its bed was a plank that Lemuel had been cutting. He showed the Indians how the teeth of the pit saw gear engaged the cogs of the shaft, repeating the operations several times to that they might understand. Stoically the chief nodded.

"Shall I go out and start the water?" said Noah.

"You needn't go out," said Lemuel. "Just reach out the window."

And there indeed was a lever his father had contrived so that one could regulate the mill wheel without leaving the house. Noah opened the gate wide, knowing full well the effect of the sudden torque, ready to pretend, if his father scolded him, that he had not understood the operation of the lever. In a very few seconds the house began to shudder and weave. The millstones made a low thunder. And the pit saw went fiercely up and down, up and down, with a life of its own—"Put something in my teeth, in my teeth," it seemed to say.

Now the assistant would have bolted, but the chief held him by the arm—stayed in part by pride no doubt, but not only by pride. Noah followed the wide eyes of the square old face from the awful machine to Simms, a personage in whom he saw perhaps some rudimentary kinship. And Simms was reassuring, standing composed with his arms folded in front of him, undisturbed by the din and the shuddering. But the assistant, though held fast and also supported by the hand of his superior, was not entirely reassured. He needed a prayer, which he directed, so far as Noah could determine, to a spirit beneath

the floor. At any rate, when the chief was satisfied that they had shown
that they were not daunted, he held his hand up, said something to
Lemuel, and led his assistant out. With deliberate step and with great
dignity they walked the path to the road, crossed the bridge, and soon
disappeared in the bend at the foot of the hill.

"Close the gate," said Lemuel to Noah, and when the mill house
was quiet, Noah said, "What do you think they thought?"

"Nothing," said Lemuel. "They were terrified."

There followed a small silence, and then Tess said to Simms, "You
don't agree."

"Oh, they felt terror all right. But it went beyond that. They felt
the spirit of force." Lemuel frowned, but Simms went on. "It's something Indians spend a lifetime observing, the spirit of force in the sun
and the water and the wind."

"Then why have they never put it to work for them?" Lemuel asked.

"Because to them it would be like yoking a god and making him
walk a circle, like a mill horse. They would be afraid for their souls."

"Should I be afraid for my soul?"

"Not you, Lemuel, because you will always put the spirit to
gentle uses."

"Then who should be afraid for his soul?" said Noah.

Simms looked at him steadily. "Those who would use it to gain
power over others."

Lemuel said, "We'll only charge a little fee for its use, enough to
pay us for our labor and our shaft. And you'll take some," he said to
Simms sternly. And when Simms only smiled, he said, "You say you're
courting this woman seriously and yet you have nothing. And she has
nothing but a tumbledown house."

"I told you," said Simms, "we are scarcely beyond childhood. We
aren't thinking of houses and such."

Tess smiled. "Consider the lilies of the field. They toil not, neither
do they spin. And yet Solomon in all his glory was not arrayed like one
of these."

Simms, looking from one to the other of them, began to laugh, at
first a jolly laugh, and then a bigger laugh that reached out and embraced
them all in its generosity. It had something in it of the thrum of the mill.

It shook a sympathetic laughter out of Noah and his mother. It made Lemuel smile and rub his face. But when again that night, after it had started to rain, Tess laughed until the tears streamed down her cheeks, Lemuel's face darkened. "Why're you laughing, woman?"

"Because my foolish old Indians performed the wrong ritual. They did the rain dance." She could hardly choke the words out. And Noah began to laugh. He could not help himself no matter how black his father's looks. Then, just as suddenly as she began, Tess stopped laughing and gazed at her husband. "Why do you look so black, man?"

"Because I cannot laugh with you."

"Why do you envy us our laughter? We don't envy that you can commune with the soul of wood. No one has everything." She leaped up suddenly and put her hands on his knees there where he sat in the chimney corner. Above them the rain beat plumply on the roof. She looked into his eyes. "This reminds me. Where's my floor? The bridge is up and the mill is done. Where's my floor?" Lemuel softened but did not speak. "Well, where is it?"

"You shall have it."

"And not your glutted planks all ridged to catch the dirt, but planks sawed and pumiced smooth. Yes?"

"You shall have it. Noah will pumice the planks." Lemuel chuckled.

Tess now stepped over to her son and, smiling with mischievous wistfulness, took his hands and said, "Alas, poor Noah's hands. How tired and worn they shall be." She kneaded his fingers with a gentle pressure. The tingling rose up into his scalp. And above them the rain beat plumply.

∾

So the summer wore on and was hot. All the humans smelled rank, and the animals too. Gertha steamed, and rope after rope of thick slaver slopped from Ben's mouth. The floor was dug out and the dirt hauled by Ben on sleds up to the garden for fall plowing. "What will the things taste like," said Tess, "that grow out of the very soil we have walked on all these years?"

"What cares the soil who walks on it?" said Lemuel. But that did not reassure Noah, for he was a despoiler of everything. His hands, he imagined, were still tacky with last night's slick. He was an outlaw from the family of Parker, from the meeting house, and from the society of the whole valley. He was alienated from Simms, for he could not bear to think of Martha. He was a hater of insects and earth. The only thing he loved was the mill. The hours he spent with his father at the pit saw cutting joists and planks were heaven. The hours he spent in the house laying the floor and pumicing it were hell. The very grit of the stone stank, and that was nothing to the ripeness of the wood or his own rank sweat.

Around and around the finished floor his mother walked, like a child in a fairy place. Barefoot she was and worked her toes against the wood. "Doesn't it feel fine, fine." And the table and chairs had to be moved this way and that, this way and that, and then moved all over again when the tie rug was complete and threw the room out of balance. So in the end Noah despised the wooden floor and wished they had again the hard-packed dirt with the wild lines that the Indians had been careful to avoid.

One day at dawn Noah's mother and father yoked Ben to the wagon and went to Conniston to fetch home the panes that Lemuel had ordered for Noah's loft and for the mill house window. Noah said that he wanted to stay back for the rope walk and Lemuel permitted it. But before he went to the rope walk, he went to the mill. He disengaged the millstones and the pit saw. Then he opened the sluice gate and let the wheel and the shaft run free. He lay on the floor and gave himself over to the spirit of force. He lay there for an hour or more until the weave and the shudder had penetrated his bowels and mollified his bones. When he got up he was such a gummy thing that he could scarcely work the lever to close the sluice gate.

Late in the morning Noah went up the road to the rope walk. Thomas Grevel, the spinner, had such a mass of fiber around his waist that he looked like a porcupine and such another pile beside him that it looked as though he had accumulated a hummock of dead animals. At the other end was his oldest son Peter, the walker and the twister. And in the middle were the smaller boys with spikes to keep the growing rope from kinking, because until it was set it was like a live thing that desired mightily to buck and unravel. Already it was over a hundred feel long. Noah guessed that if all the fibers were used it would grow to three or four times that. But he did not go forward to speak with the rope-makers as he had planned, for there sauntering down the road, arms around each other's waist, oblivious, were Simms and Martha. Noah slipped off into the woods and crouched behind a tree trunk from which he could safely peek out through the bramble.

When the couple reached the rope, Martha touched it and did not shy away from it as if it were a huge serpent, but slid her hand along the hairy surface and along the sleeve of cotton cord that the boys had whipped around the rope to keep the strands from separating. Then she returned to Simms, and presently they sauntered by Noah's hiding place, arms still about each other's waist, walking thigh to thigh despite the growing heat of the July sun. When they reached the end of the inter-mittent shadow of the near woods and entered upon the unbroken sunway of the South road, Simms bonneted Martha. The bonnet had been hanging down her back from a blue ribbon around her throat. Simms smiled and pressed the bonnet onto Martha's wild hair. The sun pierced the wide weave of the straw and speckled Martha's face with jewels of light. Noah's heart was divided between love and anger.

᠊ᢍ᠊

Summer waned. The honeysuckle browned and fell. The hummingbirds disappeared. The August cicadas emerged from earth, climbed the trees, swarmed, snapped their thoraxes like drumheads, shed, and died. On a sled Ben dragged Lemuel's forge to the mill house, where the new firebox and the mechanical bellows waited. The next day Tess grew wildly angry with the sour odors of the cellar and threw half of its contents onto the compost pile—old dried fruits, the scummed remainder of the pickle urns, a bucket of buttermilk, armloads of moldy straw, and so on.

And then one breathless night on the verge of September Ben died, with no comforter, no witness to his dying but Gertha, who stood well apart with a heavy nervousness when Noah came into the barn that morning. Ben had first fallen down on his front knees and then tumbled over onto his side. That was what Lemuel surmised from the position of the animal's legs. At Noah's call he had come to the barn, Tess not far behind. Ben's eyes, half open, were soft and lightless, docile to death.

"He died peacefully," said Lemuel. Noah nodded, but to his great shame tears welled up in his eyes, hot and blurry, so that he had no choice but to wipe them away in the presence of his parents.

"In this weather," said Lemuel, "we must deal with him quickly. I'll do it."

"Do what?" said Tess.

"Do what has to be done with the hide, the tallow fat, the meat, and the bones. What else?" Lemuel was obviously annoyed with Tess that she had required him to be particular in front of Noah.

"You will do no such thing," said Tess.

"What do you mean?"

"I mean that we're not so pauperous we must dismember an animal that has worked for us a dozen years."

"The animal is dead."

"And will receive due rites."

"There are no due rites for animals," said Lemuel, firmly but gently, for it was obvious that Tess's feeling ran deep. "Do whatever ceremony pleases you and Noah and then I'll do the rest."

"The animal will be buried, whole."

"Here, under the barn floor?"

"Of course not."

"Then how do you propose we three remove the carcass to a proper burial site? Have you any idea of the dead weight of the animal?" Lemuel did not pause for Tess to answer. "And I'll be damned before I'll get up a party of neighbors to drag an ox to a grave. They all have better occupations than such folly."

Now it was Tess's turn to take into account the seriousness of her husband. Nevertheless she spoke with considerable intensity and even with a touch of taunting. "You have a mill that every day tries to uproot its house. Are you telling me it can't move a dead ox?"

"The mill is there. The ox is here."

"Mr. Grevel's rope will reach," said Noah.

In Lemuel's honest face was the tacit admission that it could be done. Tess said, "You're a good man, Lemuel. Go with Noah now to rent the rope."

They did. Simms came up from the creek and went with them, which was well, for it took the three of them to carry the rope, wearing heavy coils about their necks like yokes and stretching much between them as well. It was sweaty work. Back at the farm they rolled Ben onto the stone-sling, attached the rope, ran it out the barn door, along the garden, and down to the mill. Then they brought the old stone-sled into the barn and positioned it so that with the first pull of the rope Ben would slide up onto it. Down at the mill house Lemuel opened the sluice gate and took a loose turn with the rope around the shaft, which would act as a winch when he tightened the coil. Noah stood by the knoll of the bank to relay messages between his father and Simms, who stayed in the barn with his mother. In this way, with some awkward delays in communication and with two bad but not catastrophic bumps, one at the barn door and one at the garden fence, they harnessed the power of the mill to pull Ben to his grave site on the creek bank some thirty feet above the mill house.

"I have work to do in the house," said Tess. "Call me when you have dug the grave."

"I will," said Lemuel, "but it'll be a while, for we'll return the rope first. I've paid only the half day's fee, and Grevel is a stickler."

So they walked the rope back under the mounting sun, and they sweated. The rough fibers gnawed Noah's neck. The rope was like a stubbly beast that meant to bear him down into the dust of the road and destroy him. And even when the rope was hung again in Grevel's barn, still his neck complained, skin and sinews. "Roll your head, Noah," said Lemuel, "and get the kinks out."

The digging of the grave was also sweaty work—not strenuous but tedious, indeed hypnotic. As Noah shoveled dirt out of the pit he began to imagine that they would discover ancient bones. He thought of the man in the valley of bones who asked if the bones could live. It was a story the preacher read from the Bible, but Noah could not remember the answer to the question.

At noon Tess came and called them to eat, but Lemuel said, "I shall take no food this noon." He said it without anger but with finality.

"Nor will I," said Noah.

Nevertheless Tess returned with a basket in which there were three mugs of milk, a loaf of bread, and a jar of syrup. She put it in the mill house and went back up into the garden. After another hour or so of digging Simms smiled and said, "It's no longer noon." He climbed out of the pit and went down to the mill house. At the door he said loudly, "Come along. Will you offend both the woman and your bodies? Life is for the living."

Lemuel leaned his pick against the side of the grave and lifted himself out. Noah set aside his spade and followed. And when he had finished his lunch he said, "How deep must the grave be?"

"Five feet," said Lemuel.

After a while Noah said, "When you find a deer's jaw in the ground, what's happened to the rest of the deer?"

When Lemuel said nothing, Simms said, "Why it's been eaten by foxes or other foragers. It's been tunneled by worms and roots, dissolved by sun and rain. All of these are merely ways of returning to earth what was always hers. But that says nothing of the life of the deer."

"What has happened to the life of the deer?"

"I don't know," said Simms, "but I know that it can't be destroyed. How can life be destroyed?"

Noah thought that Ben's life was destroyed but that his own could not be destroyed. If he were to break himself on the stones of the mill, still his life would go on somewhere, but he didn't know where.

When they had dug the pit five feet deep, Lemuel called Tess down and they rolled Ben into his grave with a heavy thump. "Well," said Lemuel to his wife, "will you speak something?"

"Bless, O Lord, Ben to thy keeping. He was a good ox."

"Amen."

Tess threw a spade of dirt onto the beast's body. Then she went to the mill house and got her basket and carried it up the hill. The sun was low before her and for some seconds she cast a long wavering shadow back over the grave. When she was gone, the two men and the boy rapidly filled the pit, tamped it down, and barrowed the remainder of the soil up to the garden, where it was added to the pile dug up from the floor of the house.

"Lemuel," said Simms as they were about to part.

"Yes?"

"What would you think if tomorrow Noah and I found a willow sapling and planted it over Ben's grave? It would be a fair thing to see and in years to come it would shade the mill house. It would be called Ben's Willow."

"I think it would be a fine thing."

That night Noah found in the last minute before sleep the bone he had not turned up in Ben's grave. It was a fine clean bone bleached white as the moon. Embedded in it here and there were tiny coronets of opalescent enameling, as of baby teeth. He was offering it. A hand was extended to receive it, a supple hand, the undernails stuffed prettily with garden green. From this he understood that he was on the ledge of an evil dream. He pulled himself back, shook his head, and went to sleep.

∽

One day shortly after Ben's burial the smoke from the chimney lolloped down like a windless flag, and that night the bats dove as low as the garden gate. A thunderous rain came and drenched the land. And the next day the sun rose pure gold. Summer was gone and it was autumn, just that quick. And Noah discovered that he was in an altered state. Summer had fanned up his desire so fierce and hot that it had half burned it out. Almost gone was his lurid sense of evil. He was no longer a demon who must keep himself distant from mother, father, and friend. In fact, he was not much more than a young thing of nature, rising to the touch, wilting after the pulse of slick, like a nightly season unto himself. All this was clearer to him now, just as the moon was clearer through the London pane than it had been through the five bottles.

One day he wandered up on the hill and heard the voice of Martha calling and laughing in the distance and losing itself with rich echoes in the woods. But he did not go on to spy, and thought that was a good sign. When his mother bathed, he went out of the house to see if Ben's Willow was thick enough yet to throw a shadow in the moonlight, and he thought that was a good sign. Another day a big fine covered wagon that had sides all honeycombed with lockers and drawers crossed the bridge. The young master gave Lemuel a rich coin and admired the bridge. The mistress stepped out to look at the pretty creek and showed her white-stockinged ankle. Noah looked aside, and that was a good sign.

That night at supper Lemuel chafed at his idleness. After the crop was in he must cover the bridge. All bridges of note were covered now. So must Parker Bridge be. Another ox, or a team of horses, must be obtained. There would be fall plowing. There would be sawn boards to haul to Conniston, where they would fetch a good price.

Tess laughed. "Do you want to become a rich man, Lemuel Parker?" But there was no asperity in her voice. Noah, in his mind's eye, saw the houses and the steeple of Conniston and the road beyond to Boston. The vision was furnished by the mill. The mill made everything possible. You used its force to bury an animal that old custom and need would other-wise have butchered. You made with it things to sell, and the coins you gained had a great force, capable of propelling you far down a road.

So Noah went out into harvesttime happier than he had been in months. Night after night dew formed on the earth and the sun rose clear. Tess began to fill her cellar with onions and potatoes. She brought in fresh straw and lined the stone shelves so that she would be ready for apple harvest. Noah, in a kind of dreamy state of warm satis-faction, helped.

Later Noah and his father and Simms scythed hay and packed it tight in ricks, and his mother adorned the tops of the thatched roofs with ornaments—a preening rooster, an open-mouthed fish, a star, an arrow-head, George Washington with a pigtail. The softer silage was packed in a long pit, covered with coarse straw, and buried under clayey soil. When that was done, Lemuel declared the old corn cratch unsuitable, and so they spent three days tearing it down and building a new crib with inverted pie pans on each of the four pillars to keep the mice out. "I'll buy you new pans," he promised Tess, "on our next trip into town."

"And when will that be?"

"When the word comes that the horse man is come from Pittston to Conniston."

"So it's horses, is it, and not an ox."

"Yes, it's time we had horses."

And then, all unexpected, it was apple time and Martha came down from the hill with her apple stick, a long oakling forked at the end, and just below the fork a little soft leather bucket. Noah was curious to know what would happen to him when this year he saw her again stretch up on tiptoe, her eyes and face shining under the sky and her breasts pressed tight against her blouse. But how different she was this time. Before, she was so flighty he thought she could hardly keep to the ground, and the apples often bobbled over the lip of the bucket and had to be caught in his mother's apron, or fell to the ground and had to be pressed. But this year she had more weight and balance and also great precision with her hands and arms. Even the rambos, tough on their stems, yielded to her expert thrust and twist and fell obediently into the bucket. So Noah did not lust after her much and did not envy Simms, for he reflected rather dolefully that Martha was growing up, surpassing him finally in emotional as well as in physical years.

Meanwhile, the two men and the boy carefully plucked the apples that could be reached from the ground, the three of them wearing on both hands soft white cotton gloves that Tess had sewn for them. This amused Simms and he laughed, but Tess took him up short. "What would be the use of cellaring apples bruised by such calloused paws as you three have?"

"The callousness comes from honest labor," said Simms, still smiling.

"It doesn't matter where it comes from," said Tess. "It matters only what it does to the apples."

"Indeed," said Martha, atiptoe, "but he must needs talk, Tess. Talk, talk, talk."

"Nor must the apples touch each other," said Tess emphatically, repositioning a russet that Lemuel had carelessly placed against another in the straw-box. And he only sighed.

When all the perfect apples—rambos, russets, goldens, ribstons—were cellared, then the slightly bruised fruit were washed, sliced thin, and set out in the sun on drying trays made of woven grass. Tess said to Martha, "There will be others, I warrant, that will have to be brought up from the cellar and dried by winter fire, judging from the heavy-handedness of our pluckers."

"Enough," said Lemuel, out of patience at last with work that was not to his liking and with his wife's taunting. But already Martha was whispering to Tess, "His are tough but gentle," and added when Tess looked at her sharply, "He has held my hand and held me about the waist and even touched my cheek." And then she laughed gaily and seized Tess's hand, saying, "Oh, what did you think I meant, Tess?"

"I think you're a naughty woman, to trifle with your friend's worry."

"Worry not, dear friend," said the jolly Martha.

The day came inevitably when the apples that were badly bruised or rusty or warted or wormy or bird-pecked must go to the press, with some crabs and rennets thrown in for tartness. And the five of them, having worked carefully for many days, were jolly and carefree now, taking irregular turns dumping the apples, screwing down the press, drawing off the fiber, bottling the juice, and carrying the pulp off to compost. And when all was done, they took a mug and toasted the fine harvest and the sun, the king of apples. And Simms said, "At the harvest festival next Saturday we may have something to announce."

Martha looked up from her mug and boldly surveyed the faces of the Parkers, stopping on Noah's and laughing. "It's not the sentence to the gallows, Noah Parker, though to look at you, you must think so."

Noah said nothing. His mother said, "Noah and Mr. Simms have worked cheek by jowl these days and have drawn close and become great friends. Noah will be sad to lose his friend."

Martha's face shadowed for once. "I'm sorry," she said.

Simms said, "Noah knows better than to think he can lose our friendship. We're knit up together tighter than the wood of the mill wheel. Our friendship has a life of its own and can never die. Let us drink to that."

They lifted their mugs, but on the surface of his cider Noah saw the dark reflection of his face crossed and almost tearful.

Harvest Day dawned so bright that the dew fled among the grasses before Noah's very eyes as he gazed down from his loft through the clear London pane. "Get dressed up there, drowsy head, and come down for breakfast," Tess called. Noah heard in his mother's voice the lilt of excite-ment—betrothals would be announced. He put on his meeting clothes: low shoes, white leggings, knee pants, and a white shirt. Lemuel was already at table, also in a white shirt, his black hair slicked down. "Gertha has been milked and fed," he said matter-of-factly, but his voice, too, brimmed with excitement. Noah knew why—because all the neighbors would speak with admiration of the improvements at the Parker place, and his father would talk with them all day of bridges and roads and the future. And what of Noah himself? Was he excited? He examined himself and discovered that, yes, deep down there was indeed a low throb of excitement. But what could it be? Neither marriages nor bridges. His mother set before him a bowl of hot oats and honey. Was it his mother's beauty, which would be on display this day? Indeed, she did not wear her severe dark meeting clothes but a light flowered frock that flew up about her white-stockinged ankles whenever she moved and that, despite the underskirt, let the light through and created a shadow of legs. At the neck of the frock a small square dipped down and revealed a hint of cleavage. Below the square was a loosely laced bodice of blue. Noah looked at his father, who from time to time stole an admiring glance at his wife. He *wanted* her on display. This was new. Noah felt the current of change. He felt the bindings of his own clothes loosen their hold on his body. It was the mill, the water in the wheel. The mill was freeing their bodies.

The long harvest table was set up in the shade of a patchwork cotton awning that ran between Thomas Grevel's two biggest ricks. Beyond lay the broad expanse of Grevel's stubble field, and beyond that the rolling green forest all streaked with red and yellow, and beyond that the shaded flank of Placket Mountain, and beyond that the blue sky with a few fleecy clouds. Old man Claylock sat in the center of the table with a dead pipe hanging in his crooked fingers. To all who would listen he described the old valley. "It was only man's country, then," he said, "and Indians. I remember when the first soldier's wife came to Conniston in seventy-eight, Iona Marston. And then some brave ones came out to farm, like this lass's brave mother." The old man pointed with the stem of his pipe to Martha Tewkes. And all eyes turned to her, as well they might have before that, for she was a brilliant thing. Her hair, ribboned but finally untameable, was shot through with light, as though the sun itself had walked in with her under the awning. But Noah turned his eyes back to the old man and listened to the rest of the recitation of laborious clearing and road-building.

"And now Parker has a mill away out here on Crowfoot Creek. And look ye," he said, squinting, "at these cloths." A woman from Conniston had set out a display of linens and silks—some plain, some satiny. "What do you call that?" said the old man, touching lightly a napkin of reversible flowered design.

"Damask," said the woman.

"Damask," repeated the old man. He paused to revolve the word in his mind before he went on. "When the women come to the valley there soon are children and then linen and then many marriages. How many marriages are to be announced today? Seven. Who ever heard of such a thing?" Lost in wonder, the old man ceased to speak.

"This is made of worm spit," said one farmer to another, poking his finger into the silk like a child despoiling a pudding.

"Then if my apple worms was the right kind," said his companion, "I would be rich." They laughed.

Noah did not wish to dazzle his eyes again gazing at Martha, so he looked about for Simms, who, it turned out, was hard to identify because he was not dressed in his usual assortment of hides but wore a pair of black trousers and a billowy white shirt. He smiled at Noah and came to sit beside him. Noah said, "Did you send back to Boston for your clothes?"

"No. They appeared this morning draped over Martha's arm, but I think your mother had a hand in it." And Simms' odor was much subdued, Noah noted. They sat together for a while silently, watching the women set out the food. Besides all the fruits and vegetables of the harvest, there was much prepared food also—cornbread and corn pudding, meat pies and fruit pies, and sweetbread and syrup and honey; and to drink, mead, sassafras, cider, and milk. The children swarmed in from the field and were shooed away for the nonce with only the concession of an apple apiece.

Once Noah stole a glance at his mother working in her blue and white among the women, and there was none like her unless it was the fabric dealer from Conniston. This woman's hair was a gorgeous red and the blue ribbons in it were like a clear sky in foliage time, and her flesh was ivory, but she had a thick neck and cheeks too plump. Oh, there was Martha, of course, but this day so augmented her beauty that she must

be compared apart. And, in fact, Noah might have picked out the other
young women betrothed if he had taken the trouble, but at that moment
the two old Indian traders came by and stopped on the road and looked
at the harvest crowd. "They'll know our houses are unguarded," said one
woman. But the preacher went out to the road and brought the Indians
to table. Fortuitously, they had with them baskets, which the women
loaded up with fruits and vegetables.

Then the Indians looked at Tess, and she made signs with them
and said, "They will be sorry to leave without tasting the white man's
special food." So they were given mead to drink and slices of cornbread
and pie which they could eat or take away as they pleased. They chose
the latter. And during all this the chief in his snake fillet and moccasins
stood with great dignity and allowed his assistant in white man's hat and
boots to do the signing. And even the children, who had gathered
around now, did not laugh or smile. The Indians went back to the road,
where they stopped and ate for a while before they picked up their
baskets again and went on.

At this time wheelbarrows appeared and the children partnered
and ran races over the rough furrows of the field, and there were great
collisions and many tippings and much laughter. Meanwhile, the two
oldest Grevel boys began constructing the mazes with sheaves of wheat
that had been specially set aside for the purpose. There would be two—
Julian's Bower, which was round and had one entry, and Rosamond's
Bower, which was rectangular and had two entries. And now all the children had to stay behind the ricks so that they could not study the
patterns before it was time for the prizes to be set in the middle and the
contestants to make their run against the preacher's watch.

Simms rose from his seat next to Noah and went out into the
field, where he spoke to the eldest Grevel boy, who nodded agreeably.
And then out beyond the two mazes Simms made a pile of sheaves and
began to construct his own maze. Perhaps, thought Noah, it was a
maze he had learned out west. At any rate, he worked with great
purpose, stepping back from time to time to measure with his eye the
perimeter and the convolutions of the maze as it progressed.

Noah got up and walked apart. Up on the rick top the vane was making a creeky noise in the shifting breezes. Its shaft, Noah thought, must be stuck in a bottle. The sound, however, was not unpleasant but was like the call of a faraway bird broken by the wind. He looked back at the harvest table where the women and the older girls were still gathered, putting the final decorative touches to the food—garlands of dried herbs, striped gourds, motley corn, and the like. He passed his eye from face to face, but the only ones that ignited his interest were his mother and Martha. From this he understood that if ever he was to find a wife he would have to leave the valley. He tried to imagine what she would be like. He could not conjure her face, but he could picture her standing before a door which had its own little gable. She was not a farm wife. Her eye was more inquiring and looked not at the expanse of field but at the works of man.

Two grasshoppers bumped against Noah's britches and fell back into the thick grass, where they struggled weakly among the stalks. They and a few hatches of gnats down by the creek were all that was left of the pestilential swarms of early summer. Time buzzed in Noah's ear, time which had until now been merely a benign conveyance of days and seasons. It was the discovery of his own sex that had thrust Noah into time, that and the mill, the alternate throbs of the same force. And yet all around him were things of timeless return—harvest and marriage, the bones of deer that kept their secret record in the bowels of earth, the great carcass of Ben giving itself up to earth, and the slow thickening of the willow, which would also fall back into the earth, and the odor of a turned field. Yet he would not stay among such things. He would go away with a few coins to seek his fortune beyond Conniston, which would be a great sorrow to his father, but it could not be helped. Perhaps he would apprentice himself to a printer and perhaps someday write his own book in black ink that would, though by an inconstant son, stand as an enduring record of the life of the valley.

Noah walked out onto the field, to the place where his friend Simms was hard at work on his maze, his black britches now more flaxen than black, his shirt wet with sweat, and his powerful odors rising to the surface again. "Why are you making another maze?" said Noah.

Simms looked up, brow and beard bristling with sweat. "For

Martha," he said, "for a little ceremony we shall have. Look." He put his
hand on Noah's shoulder and led him to a certain point on the perimeter of the maze. "What shape do you see?"

"It's like a thin egg."

"Do you see the way into the middle?"

"No."

Simms led Noah a quarter way around the maze. "Now what do
you see, my son?" His voice lilted with inner laughter.

"A perfect circle."

"And do you see the way to the middle?"

"Yes." Noah smiled. "So, what does it mean?"

Simms laughed. "The wise man never glosses his parables, but lets
them work deep upon the mind."

But there was not time for Noah to ponder design or words, for
the other two bowers were done, prizes were set in the middle, and the
children commenced to run the mazes against the preacher's watch. And
what wild whoops and frenzied clapping attended. Oh what a demon it
was to run down a long blind alley and oh how tempting to leap low
wall upon wall of sheaves to the treasured center. But always the grown-
ups were there to cry foul. And tick-tock tick-tock went the preacher's
watch like an instrument of doom. This continued for a great while until
by contrivance of gentle hints and the stretching of time, every child,
even the least apt, had mastered both labyrinths and won two prizes.

And now it was noticed that a third maze had been built and that
Simms stood in the center of it. And, as will generally happen in an
assemblage when a strange presence enters, the crowd slowly became
quiet and all turned their attention to Simms, who presently called out
gaily, "Is there a woman among you that goes by the name of Martha
Tewkes?"

Martha blushed and laughed low, but did not answer.

Simms called again. "If there be such a one among you, tell her she
must come and free her poor beast from the labyrinth of his pining."

"Go!" whispered Tess.

Noah, who had drifted back toward the harvest table during the
running of the mazes, stood aside now to let Martha pass. Her hair
glowed in the sun, the bonnet hanging forgotten on her back, the deep

violet ribbon on her throat a harbinger of sweet night. In her hands she carried a necklace of clover, which Tess had given her. But she entered Simms' bower by the wrong gate, as Noah guessed she would, because Simms had made the false start closest to the harvest table. In and out of the cul-de-sacs of sheaves she went.

"I always thought he was a queer one," said a stout woman. "He has made a false maze."

"No he hasn't," said Tess.

Noah looked at his mother. Her face was crossed by fear and hope. Why should she suffer such tension, he wondered. And then he understood. Martha must find the way. She must not come to Simms by leaping the sheaves. But Martha was frustrated and all aquiver, her face flushed with excitement. That was plain to see. Nevertheless she retraced her steps and came back out of the maze and went around looking for another gate, which soon enough she found and saw the circle whole and the way through and ran to her beloved and threw the garland over his head. And he put one arm about her waist and the other under her thighs and lifted her up to him. "Can you hear me out there?" he shouted.

"Aye, we can hear you!" It was Lemuel who had come forward with great interest and stood now by his wife.

"Then hear ye this!" How strange Simms' voice seemed to Noah, as though it were coming all the way down the hill through the woods and yet was clear as a cowbell, as though the trunks of the trees had passed it swiftly from one to the next.

"Hear what?" said Lemuel eagerly, humorously.

"We are to be married, Martha Tewkes and the poor old bear Simms, whom she has converted into a gentle man." And Martha lowered her head from where he held her up high like a great prize and kissed him full on the mouth. And Tess ran out to them with her arms open, kicking through the bowers of wheat as if it were all so much chaff, at which point Lemuel led a great cheer from the crowd. And after that the other betrothals were announced and a great feast was consumed.

Law

Pittsburgh, 1911

The historian stood on the brow of the high hill. It was dusk. A pall of smoke partially hid the monstrous city, which was sectored by two tarnished rivers and bathed in the volcanic light of furnaces. The historian gazed down at the darkening streets and buildings. Just now furnace fire and lamplight were overbearing the last tepid rose of sunset. Smoke contaminated clouds that might otherwise have been prettily pink. Indulging his old inclination toward metaphor, the historian discerned there two incompatible calligraphies—behind the erasures and soot-script of man a palimpsest of nature's perpetual beauty. He smiled wryly. The moon was rising east of the city—impaled on the unholy pinnacles of the smeltery, he might have written in the old days. Still smiling, the historian paced the promontory, felt a curious ruckle underfoot, stooped, and held up a piece of slag. What a wretched thing was slag—porous, weightless, deprived of all in it that was of value. It made the historian think of the punky bones of immemorial skeletons—heaped in catacombs, mounted on walls in Guanajuato, pitched about the desert of Ezekiel's lamentation, strewn over all the earth in fact. He brought the slag to his nose. Just as he had expected, it still breathed a faint redolence of the sulphurous fires that had eviscerated it.

The historian chunked it idly down the talus of the hill, where it made brief report of its plunge and then caught among briars. Law. The historian meditated. All proceeded according to law—the separations of smelting, the rate and inertia of the slag's fall, the friction of the thorn.

He redirected his gaze to the smoky city and nodded resolutely. It was his, because he understood that it was just as lawful as the fall of slag. Oh, there was veil upon veil of human contrivance that seemed utterly unlawful, outside the realm of science and mathematics. He had once called it corruption. But he knew now that vice and graft were merely manifestations of immutable law. His task was to document and quantify that truth. The historian descended the hill.

∽

The historian went to the newspaper and saw the editor. He was recognized immediately of course, and a dozen or more of the staff gathered outside the office to gape and listen. But the editor, a gray-headed Nestor, merely slid the unlit butt of his cigar into the corner of his mouth, folded his hands on his vest, and said, "Have you come to rake muck or do portraits?"

"Tsk," said the historian. "I haven't done any muckracking for over five years. The evil that men do lives after them while the good is often interred with their bones."

The editor grunted good-naturedly. "You made the right choice. There ain't much muck to rake around here."

"It's that well lidded, eh?"

The editor didn't respond to that but instead leaned out past the historian and said, "Boys, this is none other than the author of *Three Americans*. At one time he was the greatest muckraker in America—John Tenace's boy and trainer of the notorious Red, Charlie Derwood."

The assembly in the hall, obviously already in possession of this information, laughed and greeted the historian, who gave them a smile and a wave. "He's come to do portraits. Who would you recommend?"

"Gorham!" piped a staff wag and set off a volley of laughter.

The historian understood the joke. Gorham, the industrialist, one of the richest men in America and virtual dictator of the city, was reputed to be absolutely unapproachable. "Laugh away, friends, but I'll get to know J. Gorham intimately. The portrait I intend to do, however, is not of Gorham but of the city itself."

"Forget the city," said the editor while the boys closed in around the door and several slid in. "Do J. Gorham, the mystery man in his tower." The boys nodded. "Not the way you and Tenace done up Tweed and Crocker, but the way you yourself did Duncan, Cody, and Moody in *Three Americans*, only the whole book on just him."

The historian nodded. "I suppose it would be quite a thing, but I can't do it. I have another mission. First I was a raker, then a biographer. Now I'm a city analyst."

The editor shook his head, paying little attention to the distinctions, it appeared. "I don't get it. You and Charlie Derwood had it going. You were the scourge of the cities, bigger even than Tenace. How come you busted up? And where is Derwood now?"

"Nobody knows," said the historian. "Can't get a whiff of him."

"Well, why did you bust up? Why did you let him go red?"

"There wasn't as much to bust up as you might think," said the historian. "To begin with, Charlie didn't admire me. Can you believe that?" The historian laughed.

"Naw!" said one of the boys.

The historian went on. "Charlie admired Tenace and old Riis because they were men of gentle anger. But me, I was hard and unfeeling. One time he said 'What's your philosophy, boss?' I obliged him. I said, 'I don't have one, and that's what makes me so mean.' But Charlie and I had a good working relationship. I set down the outline of what you boys call corruption. Charlie wrote the textures and the glow. Everything I did was black on white. Everything Charlie did was brassy, blue, red. Charlie was the best color writer in the business."

"So why did you bust up?"

"It was inevitable," said the historian. "One night we were sitting in a grand saloon in a city, never mind what city. And Charlie said, 'It's all over, boss.' And I said, 'That's right, Charlie. It's all over.'

" 'Why is it all over, boss?' says he.

" 'Because it's too easy, Charlie,' says I. 'We don't even have to try any more. The birds sing before we prime 'em. The cities fall into our hands like overripe peaches.'

"Charlie nodded. 'Reform is dead, boss.'

" 'You're right, Charlie,' says I. 'The writers pretend to be morally vexed by the exposures they make. The readers pretend to gasp with horror. The exposed make noises of penitence and rectification. It's all show biz. It doesn't mean a damned thing.'

"Charlie nodded. 'You going to become a Red, boss?'

" 'Not me,' says I. 'I think I'll become an historian. You're the color man, Charlie. You be the Red.' That's the way we left it."

The room was quiet. After a moment the historian slapped his hands down on his knees and leaned toward the editor. "I want you to do me a favor—newspaperman to newspaperman."

"What's that?"

"I want you to set me up a lecture and give it a big splash."

"What's the lecture?"

" 'In Memoriam: John Tenace.' "

"You could give it in the Paulson Rotunda," offered one of the staffers.

The editor held his hand up cautiously. "What will the lecture say?"

"It will say farewell to a great American."

"What else?"

"Oh, it'll be a little salutation to your great city, a chance to say hello and tell the public I'll be working here a while."

"You picked the wrong city, friend. This ain't Tweed's New York. We're pretty quiet here. Anything you want to know about this city, me and the boys can tell you."

"I don't think I've made myself clear." The historian paused. "Put it this way. Everywhere there's three cities. There's the newspaper city, which is half puffery and half scandal. There's the muckraker's city, which is melodrama. And there's my city, which is order and number—law. It's this last I'm going to write up. Can you give me a hand?"

"I can't give you a hand because I don't know what you're talking about."

"Just help me set up the lecture."

The editor slowly unfolded his hands from his belly, took the cigar butt out of his mouth, and dropped it into a brass spittoon, where it made a soft cloacal plop. "All right," he said, "I'll set you up in the

Rotunda, friend, and put a good man on the story. It's trouble. I know it. Bad trouble. But I might as well be hung for a goat as a sheep."

The boys murmured approval.

∽

It was a pleasant if decidedly autumnal Sunday afternoon. The Rotunda was not packed, but a goodly crowd of perhaps four hundred created a stir of animated anticipation under the allegorical paintings of the dome: sheaves of wheat and overflowing granaries, wide vistas of grazing sheep and kine, onrushing trains, ore-laden barges, and, of course, the vaunting stacks and fires of the smelteries. Presently a large woman led the historian out of the wings and sat him down off to the side of the raised lectern. She was one of the leading matrons of the city, wife of a railroad man, and a singer of no mean talent. In a strong but mellifluous voice she announced the cosponsors of the afternoon's lecture, The *Gazette* and the Quill Club, and introduced the historian as one of American's greatest journalists and biographers: ". . . a westerner who reversed our national movement and came East to make his mark, to our great good fortune. In this way he followed in the footsteps of his great mentor, John Tenace, who is the topic of his talk this evening. But I have also urged our sometimes too modest guest to focus for a while on himself and his work . . ."

The historian received handsome applause and then dived immediately into his talk. "Madam, you have been too kind, and promised more than I can deliver, but I will try to provide something of value.

"Ladies and gentlemen of this great city of steel, I hope you will indulge me while I recall John Tenace, America's greatest journalist. My topic is his legacy to you and me, and the charge he has left with us. In making this matter clear I have to talk about the strange destiny that seems to have joined me to John Tenace. I hope you won't think me egotistical. It's the only way I know of saying what I have to say. So think of my voice tonight and my work in progress as essentially an extension of John Tenace."

The historian paused to give weight to his declaration of purpose and to give himself a chance to survey his audience. Actually he cared very little for its general character though he could see at a glance that it was essentially middle-class with a scattering of crust and workers. What he was looking for was a particular face, of a man or a woman who would prove to be of great importance to him in his work in the city of steel. How did he know that such a person was in the audience? It was inevitable. In all of his travels with Charlie Derwood to America's cities of sin there was always such a person. You went to a meeting, you received a delegation, you gave a talk—and there was the face shining up from the crowd, as bright as Edison's bulb. But this night he didn't see the face immediately. He went on with his talk.

"Let us begin in evil old Gotham, where I went as a youth to seek my fortune, journeying from west to east. John Tenace was there, the man with a pen mightier than the sword. I presented myself to him as brazenly as a stage-door Johnny with a bouquet of red roses. My bouquet was adulation, effusive youthful adulation. It amused Tenace. He picked me for his boy. I was in seventh heaven. Little did I know that he was going to work me ragged and whip me into a bona fide news-paperman if it killed me. Pretty soon he sent me out to do a story on King McCartney, the legendary poker player, said to be the best big mitt man in the country. Oh, I wrote a probing account, but my informants withheld from me the episode of the shark from Cincinnati who one night stripped McCartney bare and picked him clean. But McCartney's backers called in some pug-uglies to deal with the shark and his men. Within an hour they had the visitors trussed up and entrained for the West and the money safely back in the pockets of the investors.

"Well, Tenace came down on me like a wolf on the fold. 'You might expect a new man to miss a detail here and there,' said he, 'but to miss the whole story, the feature itself—why that takes a special gift, boy.' And more along that line until I was almost in tears. Finally I said, 'Why did you pick me for your boy in the first place then?'

"Tenace laughed and said, 'Because your ignorance was so monu-mental and trashed over with book-learning that I knew I couldn't fail. Ignorance as fresh and profound as yours, boy, don't come along once in a decade, even out of the West. So naturally I pounced on it.' "

The audience laughed and the historian laughed with them. But while he laughed, his eye was busy passing among the aldermen, the educators, the businessmen, the clergymen, and their wives. Where was the face? It didn't glow up at him yet. He plunged on just as the last chuckle was subsiding. "So my education in New York was a little rougher than my earlier studies in Berkeley and Germany. But Tenace's training eventually began to penetrate my thick skull. Then he could let up on me, and in rare moments of leisure he would tell me something about his boyhood in old California."

The historian paused and brought to his face a look of renewed wonder. "Ladies and gentlemen, it was downright uncanny. Tenace would tell me, for instance, about riding the plains on his pony—'a tough little cayuse,' he said, 'that could go from sunup to sundown on half a flake of timothy and a sup of ditch water.' It seemed to me that was the very same pony I rode daylong up the American River. Tenace also told me about a crazed widow he ran across on the plains. She had lost her husband in the Texas Campaign. She spoke a kind of riddling poetry and sang him songs of lamentation and wanted to take him in her arms and mother him. And all of this gave him goose bumps so that he would ride wide around her place as if it was one of the Devil's Paint Pots. And this reminded me of old Widow Hutchins, who was a mysterious presence in my boyhood. In earlier days she would have been condemned as a witch, for she spoke prophetically. One day she crooned to me, 'Stay free, my boy, and single foot it down the flaming road.' And I pretty much have."

"And there were even more of these uncanny parallels between Tenace's youth and mine. But I never told him about them, then or later. They frightened me. I began to fear that I was not merely Tenace's boy but his Döppelgänger."

The historian punctuated the strangeness of all this with a sizable silence. "Ladies and gentlemen, even to this very day I am sometimes seized by a preternatural conviction that destiny, knowing that Tenace would die early, had fashioned me out of the clay of old Sacramento to finish his work."

The historian looked out over his attentive audience. And at that moment he saw the inevitable flaring face, a man with red hair, a fractional stab of sharp features. In the moment before he began to speak again he noted that the light of the face seemed more reflected than inherent. Was the face familiar? He had no time to think about it.

"In Gotham, therefore, ladies and gentlemen, I learned to view the city through Tenace's all-seeing eyes. And here I must touch on unsavory matters—the raw underside below the fair shows of Fifth Avenue and Central Park. For instance, Tenace took me to lunch at Lyons and pointed out to me a number of famous dips, second-story men, confidence men, porch climbers, boodlers, and other vicious types. He took me to many saloons, including a famous fairy bar, the most exclusive place in town, according to Tenace. I wondered that toughs didn't come and beat them up. 'The police protect 'em, boy,' said he, 'same as they protect all the saloon clientele.'

" 'The police!' I was shocked.

" 'Certainly, boy—in the interest of Tammany Hall and the upright citizenry of the city.'

"I was confused. Hadn't the Reverend Parkhurst shown that the saloons were corrupting the workers and breaking up families? 'These questions,' Tenace said, 'get us into the area of social paradox, and you ain't ready for that yet, boy.'

"Tenace took me on a ride in the back of a fly-by-night hawk. We pretended to be coming inebriated from one of the grand saloons off Park Avenue. We lurched up with our hats down. Tenace slurred a swell address on the east side, and away we went at a trot through the park. Presently, just as Tenace predicted, we were stopped and the doors flung open. A rumbling voice said, 'Let's see if the ladies have left anything in your pockets, lads.'

"Tenace snatched his hat off and stepped down into the street. 'Begorra!' said he. 'Is it Michael the Lifter and his lads? We've come to write you up, mister—me and me boy, a grand sketcher. Take out your pad, boy, and limn the features of that noble countenance.'

"I did as Tenace directed, but I could hardly look into that face, for it was a hideously cratered chronicle of the black pox and who knew what other diseases and brawls. I had only made a mark or two with my pencil when the park terror slapped the pad out of my hand.

" 'Tsk,' said Tenace, 'we'll have to paint him with words, boy.'

" 'Don't paint me with nothing,' said the terror.

"Tenace said, 'The next thing I write about you will be your obituary, Michael, if your hawks don't look to their fares more carefully.' That turned out to be prophetic. One night Michael robbed two choleric young gentlemen of means and they hired gunmen and planted them with a hawk. Down went Michael the Lifter like his nefarious mentor Duke Davies before him—Michael, who until that fatal night was as rich as Croesus and could buy all the stout he wanted and any saleable woman in town. Yes, even with that face."

The historian paused. "Well, I wanted to talk to Tenace about the meaning of Michael the Lifter because he seemed to me the emblem of everything that I'd been learning. But Tenace would have none of it. 'Nothing,' he said, 'gets in the way of good reporting more than philoso-phizing.' Later we did talk a great deal about meaning, as I will come to. But not then.

"One day I was with Tenace when he shook loose from the Police Benevolent Fund some money for an old Jewish granny who kept three orphans alive down on the lower East Side. I complimented him on his eloquence and power. 'The pen is mightier than the sword,' I said. He got angry. 'The pen is a straw in the wind,' he said. I must've shown disbelief because he grabbed me by the lapel of my jacket and pulled my face down to his. 'Listen to what I'm saying, boy. This is important. You're learning to be a newspaperman, a reporter, a recorder. If you want to change things, go be a preacher.' "

The historian let silence descend on the Rotunda. He found again the face of the flame-haired man. He knew that, as always before, the man would come up after the talk and announce himself. He went on with his speech.

"Perhaps you're wondering, ladies and gentlemen, what kind of mixed portrait I'm painting here—cynicism, altruism, pragmatism. I share your wonder. Tenace's mind was too rich for me to encompass." The historian paused. "And now in the interest of brevity I will rush ahead several years to the time of Tenace's dying, which was terrible. A wen came on his neck, was lanced, but spread. It suppurated and suppu-rated. Nothing could stop it. It spread and bent his head down painfully. It clouded his eyes and eventually shrank his whole body. And then it rendered him unconscious and killed him. Why do I burden you with these terrible images? Only to tell you that never once did Tenace complain. On the contrary, he kept up with me a lively if fevered conversation until the very end. When he understood that the disease was irreversible he said, 'Now is the time to talk about meaning, boy.'

"I was saddened. Nevertheless I warmed to the subject. 'I wondered,' I said, 'when you were going to unlock the secrets of the universe for me.'

"You can imagine my alarm when Tenace said, 'I'm not going to unlock 'em for you, boy. You're going to unlock 'em for me. You're the one with the philosophical education.'

"I laughed, no doubt nervously. 'Well, you've got to give me a little time if you want a disquisition on teleology.'

"Tenace said, 'Time is what I don't have, boy. So why don't you start now telling me what you learned back before we met.' I couldn't put him off. He was dying. The great reporter of all things human in Gotham, the master of the American city, did not have the big picture. He yearned for it, and time was running out on him. You must know how I felt. Like a swimmer with no hope of reaching the shore, but with an absolute command to start stroking. I began. I told him that in Berkeley everything was Hegel—philosophy, art, and history. And that was true. I told him that the great cloudy German lured me to Heidelberg, where I studied with Kuns Fischer, his devoted interpreter. From there Hegel propelled me to Munich, where I hung around the old cafe Blüthe to listen to the intellectuals tell how he was going to unify all art and history just as he had unified Germany. And how, Tenace wanted to know, had Hegel unified Germany? 'Well,' I said, 'by putting his countrymen in touch with the Zeitgeist.'

" 'Zeitgeist,' said Tenace. 'Never met him. Who is he?' " The historian had made his voice gravelly. The audience laughed heartily, glad to be released for a moment from the images of encroaching death. " 'Well,' I said, 'the Zeitgeist is the Time Spirit that directs the general flow of history. At that time it required the unification of Germany and the ascendance of the Teutonic spirit—as part of the ongoing unification and evolution of the modern state.'

"Tenace shook his head. 'Sounds like a big day for the pols and wise bulls, boy, and a bad day for the little man.'

" 'You bet,' said I. 'The apotheosis of the state inevitably involves the trampling of the commoners by men of high destiny. But don't worry. The suffering of the people is suffused with significance.'

"Tenace cackled evilly, as only he could. But alas, ladies and gentlemen, it must be all too clear to you—this miserable farrago of undigested experiences and ideas of mine. Oh, I went on with it, desperate swimmer, went into the famous Hegelian thesis, antithesis, synthesis business. But what did it all mean to me then? Tenace was dying. Where was the antithesis to that thesis? Apparently the world spirit hadn't taught it to the doctors yet. The world spirit hadn't even taught the nurse to keep the blackness of annihilation out of her eyes."

Again the historian paused, as if to gain strength before pushing on against the memory of bafflement and death. "The next day when I came back to the hospital I could see that Tenace had been mulling all this in his fevered mind. 'I've spent the night with Hegel, boy.'

" 'Alas,' I said.

" 'No, actually he wasn't the worst company I've ever had,' said he.

" 'Oh well,' I said, 'in a checkered career like yours he could hardly be the worst.'

" 'Sit down, boy, and help me think this through. Here's the question I started with. What have all our muckrakings in the cities of this great republic taught us?'

"I let him answer his own question. 'They have taught us that the pattern of corruption is everywhere the same.' I nodded. 'And what have we two cynical inkhorns learned about corruption's alleged antithesis, morality?' Again I let him answer his own question. 'That the more morally upright the citizenry is, the better things go for the wise bulls. Because your moral populace demands strict laws about liquor, gambling, and prostitution—all unenforceable. So the bulls run everything for a handsome return and keep it all out of sight, which is what Tammany and the polite citizenry want—a sump for the lower elements.'

"I said, 'I agree with everything so far.'

" 'All right then,' said he. 'We have our thesis, this universal pattern of corruption. But where the hell is the antithesis?' He fixed his eyes on me so fiercely that I thought somehow I was responsible for this

deficiency. 'Well,' I said, 'how about Parkhurst and the reformers?'

"Tenace waved his hand impatiently. 'Oh, they'll knock Tammany out. Then, four years later, sick to death of reform and moral exertion, the people will vote Tammany back in, in a landslide. So where's the antithesis in that? The antithesis has to change things, create a new thesis, don't it?'

" 'Yes,' I said. And you know, of course, ladies and gentlemen, that Tenace was prophetic. The Parkhurst people were in and out in four years.

" 'Well then,' he said, 'Parkhurst ain't the antithesis of nothing.'

" 'All right,' I said. 'Then he ain't.'

" 'Let's try old Hegel another way, boy.'

" 'All right.'

" 'I'm remembering the unification of the state, men of high destiny, all that. And I'm thinking that this stuff we call corruption—vice, bribery, graft—is just the way nature takes power out of the hands of the ineffectual and puts it in the hands of privilege—from democracy to plutocracy and on up. Nature hates democracy. That's Hegel, ain't it? Look for an American emperor before long. What do you think, boy?'

"What I thought was that the encroachment of death was finally darkening his spirit. I hated to see it. What I said was 'Well, it's plausible, but I doubt that you believe it. If so, why did you take up the cause of the Jews, the whores, the Negroes? You've explained the system and the Parkhurst people. But you haven't explained yourself.'

" 'Myself!' He smiled. 'By God, you're a clever one, boy.' He seemed genuinely amused, but he was exhausted by pain.

" 'Sure I am,' I said. 'You knew I studied philosophy. So I'm going to tell you where the antithesis is. It's right here.' I touched his forehead ever so gently. I wished I hadn't. It was on fire. I couldn't prevent myself from drawing my hand back in the most cowardly alarm—worse than the fatalistic nurse. But he chose not to notice. 'All right,' he said, 'tonight I, John Tenace, will cogitate my own philosophy—a novel prospect, though I doubt it'll keep me awake long.'

"I don't know if it kept him awake long or not, ladies and gentlemen. I know it kept me awake. I resolved to tell him what I wished I'd already told him—that he, John Tenace, principle of uncompromising honesty and clear-eyed compassion, was the only worthy opponent of the machine, was the antithesis. But when I went to the hospital the next day he was gone. His brilliant dark eyes were mattered over like an old dog's. When he tried to speak, black bubbles covered his lips, blood and bile."

The historian bowed his head. After a while he lifted it. The audience was rapt. "I've been left, ladies and gentlemen, with a lifelong burden. You know what it is—the obligation to discover the thing that transcends the corruption of Tammany and the impotent reformism of Parkhurst. And for a time I tried to discharge my obligation with the extraordinary assistance of Charlie Derwood, the greatest color writer of our times. My idea was this. Though I was uncertain of the antithesis, I could help it by flaying the machine in every city in the land. But nothing happened. Nothing changed. I lost faith in muckraking. I turned to biography. I thought I could discover the antithesis in extraordinary individuals. And I was much honored for my attempt, beyond my deserts, but I didn't find what John Tenace and I were looking for. So I've come here, to your great city of steel. I believe that in its bosom beats the very heart of the age. I mean to listen, and then to represent."

The historian stopped and seemed to cast about for adequate words. "You understand, ladies and gentleman, that I'm not speaking of scandal or exposé. And I'm not speaking of portraiture. I'm speaking of attempting an absolutely unbiased trueness of representation, of the very essence of our life. The truth, it is said, will make you free. Well, you may be thinking, didn't John Tenace write the truth, and after him Charlie Derwood and I? No, we did not. We tried to write the truth. But a veil of emotion and story got in the way." Again the historian paused and revealed his struggle for words. "I know, ladies and gentlemen, that this must seem riddling to you because I haven't been able to give you a clear image of my work. But it'll become clearer if only you'll speak to me and let me listen to you. Write to me at my office in the Monongahela. Speak to me when we meet. Speak to those who aren't here and who ought to speak to me."

The historian let his words settle on the audience, some of his burden falling on their shoulders now. Then he said, "I must let you go now—to your homes and your appointed work. And I must go to my work. But we're intimately connected. So I shall not bid you farewell, but simply say thank you and good evening." The historian bowed amid a loud and spirited applause and went to the chair beside the influential matron, whose beaming face gave him added assurance of the success of his talk.

∽

At the end of the long line of well-wishers was the flame-haired man patiently waiting his turn. And now as the historian shook hands, acknowledged praise with humility, and routinely issued thanks for promises of support, it suddenly came to him who this was, though he couldn't summon up the name: he'd run against Bodman for mayor but his stance was so leftist that he was beaten soundly even though he was riding the crest of the national reform movement. The historian was disappointed. It seemed improbable that this was the revelatory person-age he'd expected to encounter here in the Rotunda. But then he remembered and saw again the reflected quality of light in the man's face, which renewed the intuition that he was really the surrogate for someone else, someone perhaps vastly more important.

"My name is Jacob Arondel." The man wore a turtleneck sweater of undyed wool. The historian took his hand with genuine warmth and looked up into his pale blue eyes with interest. "Of course. The worthy opponent of Bodman."

Arondel smiled, but didn't register the epithet, indeed seemed not to have heard it at all. "My wife and I are great admirers of *Three Americans.* We want you to visit us in our home. My wife would've been here this afternoon but she had to attend a meeting."

What a curious voice, thought the historian. It rose and fell with a rhythm that seemed scarcely to register the natural emphasis of the phrasing. The historian said, "Well, as I tried to make clear, you're scarcely speaking to the author of *Three Americans.*"

Arondel nodded. "Yes. I understand. When I tell my wife what you said about trueness of representation, she'll want to show you aspects of the city you wouldn't otherwise see."

So it was his wife Arondel was standing in for. It was she who had rescued him from the wages of defeat, breathed new life into him, and plunged him into novel occupations—some kind of work among the

needy perhaps. The light in his face was hers therefore. But it was inter-
mittent, raising the question of whether the rescue was completely
successful. Even now, as Arondel's eyes roved over the historian's person,
they were without luster and penetration. And there were also the peculiar rhythms of the voice. Maybe Mrs. Arondel was a kind of female
Coppelius. That would be fascinating. "Certainly I'll come, and with
pleasure," said the historian. "Where shall I find you?"

"At 387 Rilton Street. May I tell my wife that your visit is a
certainty? Otherwise I'm afraid she'll chide me."

The historian decided to seize the moment. "Do you suppose your
wife is free now?"

"Yes, or certainly will be by the time we reach the house."

"Then I'd be honored to be introduced to her."

⁌

It was a brisk half hour's walk to the house on Rilton Street.
Arondel was companionable but not talkative, only occasionally pointing
out a notable building here and there, obviously leaving for his wife all
conversation of real substance. As they approached the door, a working-
man came out, nodded to Arondel, and went on his way, preoccupied, it
seemed, by matters of moment.

Mrs. Arondel greeted them in the entryway.

"This is my wife, Hannah." Arondel gave the name with exagger-
ated syllabification—to signify foreign extraction, the historian
assumed, and had this confirmed immediately when Mrs. Arondel said
with a strong accent, "Well come to our home."

The historian was not disappointed. Mrs. Arondel was an extraordinary woman. Her voice was wondrously accented and musical, and her
face was powerful — round and olive and ringed with black bushy hair.
And her eyes, too, were black but characterized by a striking scintillance,
as if flecked with pyrope. She wore a long dark dress that emphasized
her considerable stature and the fullness of her breasts and of her body
in general. Leading them from the entryway to chairs in the parlor, she
said, "We admire your writing because you use the words and the
rhythm new." Her voice was richly larded and songful.

"Thank you," said the historian.

"And now the paper says you will work a new kind."

"Yes, I hope to."

"You were well to leave the muckraking, which raises only the old reform delusion."

Arondel nodded. "We have all at one time thought we could defeat the machine inchmeal."

The historian said, "I take it you have hopes that extend beyond reform." During this brief exchange he had unobtrusively taken in the parlor. It was full of the redolence of tobacco and crowded with chairs whose nicks and worn seats announced their constant use. "Yes," Mrs. Arondel said, "a thing that flies above corruption and reformism."

Arondel said, "Our guest himself spoke this afternoon of the true antithesis of the machine, which is not reform."

"Yes," said the historian with alacrity, "but I confessed that I'm uncertain what it is. You seem already to know. Please tell me." He smiled good-naturedly.

Mrs. Arondel returned the smile but held her hand up as a mild disclaimer. "I can tell you some thing, but first you tell us a hint of your work."

The historian laughed modestly. "Well, let's see. You can compare me to the old Babylonian numerologists who believed that statecraft advanced along secants and sines."

Mrs. Arondel didn't ask for an explanation, as the historian thought she might. Rather, she smiled a curious smile that animated the scintillance in her eyes. "Numbers and statecraft we don't take in our view."

"But we're not anarchists," said Arondel, "are we, Hannah?"

Mrs. Arondel arose from her chair, fetched a green sheet of paper from a sideboard and gave it to the historian, who was struck at once by its tactile quality—a rich vellum that felt like kid.

"You want more light."

"No, this is fine." The historian concentrated on the script, a thick, powerful calligraphy enclosed between two living trunks—of trees, presumably, whose branchings were lost in the sky.

> Illumination of farest star, even you raise dreams in our soul and harmonize us with our Time and our Socius. So do moonbeams mingle the

secret suspirations of Earth and make the foxfire that lights the meadow. So are the Socius and the Work blessed by the most distant light in the heavens.

These words had a strange effect on the historian. He seemed to hear them from the edge of a misted meadow. They evoked the wild cry of the nightjar, heralding perhaps the distant hoofing of the goat god. He handed the sheet back to Mrs. Arondel, whose fingers, he noted, were as powerful and fleshy as the script. "I think," said the historian, "that this is new indeed."

"I took it from Juarés. Jacob helped me English it because that is not my tongue."

"I would need time to consider the implications," said the historian. The name of Juarés had reared in his mind's eye the image of flambeaux lighting a mob of wild sans-culottes.

Mrs. Arondel held the sheet, but didn't take it away, so it continued to jut out urgently toward the historian from her fleshy fingers. The historian lifted his eyes. Mrs. Arondel's dark dress, spreading down and out from her swart neck, might have been a velveteen effluence of her melodious voice. And with it came a rich odor of natural musk and perfumed oil. He was grateful therefore when at last she returned to her chair. He took a long breath, as unobtrusively as he could.

"Well then, we will show you one other thing, and to return you can tell us more of your work." She rose and led the way down a dim hall that presently opened into the bright sunburst of a solarium. The historian's eyes were immediately drawn upward to vaulting ribs that supported panes of glass through which could be seen clouds and patchy blue. It was some time before he lowered his eyes to take in the profusion of flowers that ringed the solarium, recognizing among others impatiens, tiny lilies of the valley, and the red hearts of cyclamen. Then, after a surprising delay, caused by what obtuseness of eye or impulse of avoidance he didn't know, he focused on the large central object in the solarium, a loom. It was to this that Mrs. Arondel was clearly referring as she now said, "This is a thing of work," giving the word work something of the numinous accent of the name of a god.

Arondel added, "It's not only a machine. It's a symbol of modern history."

The historian nodded. Not far from the loom was a spinning wheel and a carding table heaped with combed wool. "What's the age of this loom?"

"Of the seventeenth hundred." Mrs. Arondel led the historian to the loom. "My husband says history. You think of history as writing down. But history is doing. For history you don't put down words— dead black, even the finest handmade ones I show you, unless there is somebody to suspire it. Sit here." The historian sat down in a bare wooden chair at the foot of the loom. Mrs. Arondel helped him slide in close under the cloth beam, which held already a roll of perhaps a dozen feet of cross-weave wool, almost as tightly spun as worsted but with a frail nap that caught the sun intermittently like the first ephemeral green of winter grass. Out beyond that stretched the silvery heddles of the harness along which ran the warp of strong wool. And again, the historian was aware of the pungent mixture of odors pouring down from behind him—body and perfumed oil.

"Now you are going to do a work of history. Hit down the treadle with your foot and keep it down."

The historian did as he was told. The heddles separated. "Now take this." Mrs. Arondel handed the historian the shuttle. It was like a little boat that streamed from its stern a bright wake of yarn. "Pass it through."

The historian's fingers with surprising quickness slid the shuttle through and pulled the weft taut. "Now," said Mrs. Arondel, "you pull the weave to you hard to get it close." The historian drew the comblike frame tight against the thread he had just laid and tamped it twice for good measure.

"Good," said Mrs. Arondel. "Now you have battened the pick. That is history—a need, for clothes, and a way to do it. Not words on paper."

The historian looked at his fingers and flexed them, surprised by the nimbleness with which they had passed the shuttle through the partible sets of heddles. He saw that they were perfectly spaced and jointed for the task. Mrs. Arondel smiled and said, "You are asking which came first, your fingers or the work—the warp and the woof."

The historian nodded. "But that's a question for evolutionary science, not history."

"Nevertheless," said Arondel, "if you want a capsule history of the modern era, you work your way from this machine to the automatic fly shuttle, the multiple drop box, and so on."

"Until," said Mrs. Arondel, "you come to the women in the mills, with the thunder and lint and ammoniac of sheep's urine. Then remember the light and the flowers and the little tick-tack sound in this loom and then you know the history of work."

"I know the Jews of the garment district well, madam," said the historian. He started to push his chair back from the loom, but Hannah Arondel impeded him, a soft but impermeable barrier. In his mind's eye he saw the flesh within the dark dress making a warm convexity between the slats of the ladder-back chair. So he was imprisoned between the machine and the woman, and knew he could not escape without her commutation.

"See this. Suppose you could not get up now, no matter what your requirement. You are imprisoned in this chair. That is the way of our work now."

And again, as when she stood above him with the green vellum and poured down on him her dark fragrance, the historian felt dizzy, and was greatly relieved when presently she moved. He arose from the chair, and the three of them returned to the parlor. There the historian said, "You have a beautiful oasis of light here, out of the hurly-burly, out of time. But I have no idea what your work is." Placing special emphasis on the word work, the historian echoed something of Mrs. Arondel's peculiar ictus.

She took him up sharply. "It is not out of time, as you say. It is the very time when work must be sanctified. But enough this day."

The historian nodded. "Yes. Well, I thank you. You've given me much to think about."

"Please come again, soon," said Arondel. Was there a note of urgency in his voice? It was hard for the historian to tell, overborne as all the man's tonalities were by the peculiar sing-song. And now Mrs. Arondel was speaking. "Yes, next time you tell us more of your real work, which you only tease us about the Babylonian, and we can tell you more of our work."

"It'll be a pleasure, madam." The historian didn't stop then to consider whether he would actually return or not. At the door he found the ordinariness of Arondel's handshake a relief—fingers and knuckles responding with a commonplace hardness.

∽

On Monday afternoon the historian went to the tower to see Gorham, ruler of the city, reputed to be a brilliant mathematician, aloof, brutal when necessary. Boldly dispensing with formality, he strode past the secretary through the open door to Gorham's office. The sun shone in through long, soot-stained windows behind Gorham and threw his image into silhouette. Before him, on his desk, was a ledger over which the great man bent motionlessly.

"Good afternoon, Mr. Gorham."

Gorham looked up. "Who are you?" The voice, slightly guttural, brimmed with irritation.

The historian offered his card. When it was not taken, he set it down precisely in the center of the sheet of ciphers.

"You're a journalist?"

"No, sir, an historian."

The great man looked at the card. "The American portrait fellow?"

"Not anymore, sir. I'm the first of a new breed. I'm a cliometrician."

"What do you want?"

"It's not what I want, sir. It's what I'm directed to produce, a scientific model of the city."

Gorham made a gruff noise of half-amused incredulity. "Is that what you fellows call muckraking nowadays?"

"This has nothing to do with muckracking, sir. It has to do with discovering the pattern of your city."

"Go back and tell your boss it's a wild goose chase. Tell him J. Gorham said so. Go on now."

"I can't do that, sir."

"Why not?"

"Because my boss is the Zeitgeist."

"Well then, do his bidding, but not here, where I have my own work to do." The great man bent over his ciphers again, flicking the historian's card aside.

"Your work is my work, sir. The Zeitgeist informs me that you are the distributive principle."

"What in the devil do you mean by that?"

"I mean that what you do here is transposable to all other cities."

Gorham wrinkled his brows. "A city's not a formula, man."

The historian heard within the contradiction a crossrip of interest. "Not one, of course, but a whole galaxy of elegant polynomials. But you know that, sir. If the city weren't lawful you couldn't predict that your officers and the populace would always behave the same. You couldn't direct the city."

"They don't always behave the same, damn their eyes."

The historian smiled. "In the aggregate they do, sir. They keep strictly within the bounds of your calculations or your command would bleed off into mere anarchy."

"Anarchy," growled Gorham. "Sit down. I want to look at you. I want to see what an historian gone mad looks like." The historian sat in a chair off to one side of the great man's desk. "Oh yes," said Gorham, "I know you now. Your picture was in *The Gazette*. You gave a talk at the Rotunda, scared the devil out of some aldermen."

"Yes, sir. I'm glad the word got to you. I went to a lot of trouble to attract your attention." Gorham grunted and studied the historian. The historian studied the great man, whose quintessential characteristic, he perceived, was striation. Several images conspired: pin-striped suit, regimental tie, black hair swept back in sharply individuated lanks, and black brows straight as hyphens. Deep down, the historian judged, the great man was as precisely railed as his locomotives—will and act perfectly parallel. He said, "I'm not sure the audience knew what I was talking about and you can't blame them. They've never seen a work of scientific history."

"Neither have I."

"But you grasp the potentiality of it, sir. And there was one man at the talk who seemed to understand what I was getting at——Jacob

Arondel. You know him?" The historian withheld the fact that he'd already visited the Arondels.

"I know him. Stay away from him. If you're not crazy, he is."

The historian's mention of Arondel was not innocent of course, and now, on evidence of disturbance, he pressed. "Crazy? He was well-spoken and even perceptive. Why do you say he's crazy, sir?"

A darkness came into Gorham's face. "He's an anarchist, and that means he's crazy. You as a cliometrician see that immediately, don't you?"

"Yes, sir." The historian paused. "Well, I promised to visit him and his wife, who he hints is an extraordinary person. But I'll be careful, sir." It seemed to the historian that the mention of Arondel's wife aggravated the disturbance, but it was hard to tell. The great man merely nodded and then said, "What in the devil gave you the idea that cities are lawful?"

"Seized on the road to Dasmascus by a book, sir. It set forth in vivid graphs and tables the immutable laws behind the brute savagery of teeth, talons, and claws— I mean the great ethologist's study of the armored crabs, jinnies, and lampreys on Gilman Reef."

Gorham nodded, obviously familiar with the work. "So you decided that we in the city are like eels, snipes, and crabs."

"Yes. And not only that, sir. Immediately after I read the book, Mnemosyne, the goddess of us historians, crowded my head with other improbable instances of law, mostly from my youth."

"Like what?"

"Like my father's house with its antic balustrades, bays, wild cornices, half mansards, turrets, widow's walk, lightning rod, weather cock, and God knows what else—which I'd always thought of as merely a wild farrago of pure fantasy and which I suddenly saw was a treasure trove of architectural laws."

"Go on."

"I also remembered my first big story for John Tenace, a bank scandal in Queens. I remembered that the manager told me he should have expected it, and when I asked him why, he said there was a defalcation there every six months. So I saw that crime, too, follows certain laws of periodicity."

"Give me another example," said Gorham.

The historian probed his memory, then said, "All right. There was the case of Clubber Williams. When I was a greenhorn in the city, Tenace got the Clubber to take us to the park and give us a demonstration of the art of the billy stick, which was preceded by a learnéd disquisition. Each stroke had its own special character and purpose. If the Clubber wanted the subject to skedaddle, he would strike either the foot or the apex of the skull, but very lightly. The stroke sent a galvanic current up or down the spine, as the case might be. If, on the other hand, the Clubber wanted the subject to lie down peacefully, he would tap the back of the skull, and that decisively." The historian paused and smiled, savoring the memory, as well as the great man's attentiveness to his somewhat antic retelling of it. "We found a bum asleep under a blanket of newspaper. The Clubber tapped the sole of a holey shoe and up jumped the bum like a jack-in-the-box and dashed through the dipping limbs of the park trees, which did not brain him. And I saw, sir, that there are many laws of physics and physiology at work in the Clubber's art."

Gorham grunted, amused. "Are you sure you're a cliometrician and not a spinner of yarns?"

"No doubt of it, sir. I'm a cliometrician. I've come to measure and model your great city of steel, because it's an archetype."

"Do you have any idea what you're getting into?"

"Yes, I do, sir. And I know I've sounded boastful, but I needed to get your attention because I can't succeed without your help."

"What do you want from me?"

"Two things. One is access."

"To what?"

"To all the details relevant to the functioning of the machine—names, records, modus operandi, and so forth." The historian smiled amicably.

"What's the second thing?"

"I want you to review my work, sir. You're the only man in the country who would know whether it's accurate."

The great man took a sheet of paper from his desk drawer, wrote a note on it, and gave it to the historian, who read it and said, "Will Mayor Bodman believe that this is a bona fide order?"

"No, because he's suspicious. He'll call on me, then he'll give you everything except some piddling little mystery he can't bear to part with, even on order from me." Gorham took up again his sheet of figures. Presently he said, "You'll find one visit to the Arondels enough."

"Probably so, sir, though you know how it is when an old news-paperman's nose begins to quiver and thrill to the scent of a story."

Gorham looked unsmilingly at the historian. "Stop up your nose."

The historian nodded.

"When you've got something worth looking at, bring it here and we'll talk about it."

"I am very grateful for your assistance, sir."

∽

The historian started with familiar things—the transactions in the tenderloin. The captain took $25,000 per month from the madams, the lieutenant $12,000 from the streetwalkers, the sergeant $8,000 from the pimps, a less powerful group here than in most cities due to tight police control and protection. The historian traced the flow of these collections to the mayor's office and from there down through the ranks all the way to the Benevolent Fund. He studied the conditions of the prostitutes—earnings, payoffs, living expenses, profit margin; recruitment, retirement, disease, mortality. He studied market fluctuations and the informal but tight guild system by which the women protected themselves from a flood of cheap workers.

In his hotel room the historian filled ledger sheets and charts and typed out the necessary glosses. Meanwhile, the city spilled its black smoke on the sky like a tormented ideograph, the furnaces flared demonically, and the rivers bore their burden of black alluvium, but the historian was not interested in allegories of hell. His formulas, diagrams, charts, and terse notes of explanation defied mere metaphor. And so, when he had the tenderloin worked out he went again to Gorham in his tower.

"Well," said the great man, "how is the cliometrician?" The light from the window, hazy and yellow, lay on all the surfaces of the office like an oily slick. "I'm fine, sir, but your empire is something malodorous."

"Filth and force go together. You get used to it. But tell me, Clio, have the mayor's boys and girls cooperated?"

"Oh yes, with the exception of one or two ladies of Damson Street who rendered their accounts somewhat reluctantly."

Gorham shrugged. "A small sample will do."

"Yes."

Gorham pitched his brows comically. "What was the mean and deviation in daily patronage?" The historian laughed. But Gorham frowned. "Do you think I'm interested in dirt for dirt's sake, Clio?"

"No indeed." The historian took from his valise a sheaf of charts, graphs, and tables. "You will find some anomalies, sir, but in the main the patterns are amazingly clear." Gorham grunted and began to scour the papers. After some moments the historian said, "Do you think, sir, that it was the enigmatic nature of God that led Pascal to the theory of probability?"

"Maybe," said Gorham absently, then added, "Pure mathematics is a thing of beauty, Clio. Statistics and probability are a mess. But it didn't take the enigmas of God to inspire them. Man will do." With that he dipped his head deeper into the papers. The historian kept silent. After some minutes, during which the noise of the street drifted up as a tiny screed of clatter, the great man stacked the papers and handed them back. "This is good work, Clio, but it lacks a topography."

"I'm not sure I understand what you mean, sir."

"I mean, what is the shape of the tenderloin? Is it a rectangle or a rhomboid? An epicenter with irradiants? Cellular? When you apply numbers to real things, Clio, they occupy a space. What is the space?"

"I will chart the space."

Gorham smiled mischievously. "Beware of space, Clio. It's not the uniform extension you historians think. It's treacherous. It has gaps, like a Mercator. It has edges and acute folds where all the numbers plunge into the pit, the catastrophe that Columbus feared."

"Are there such places in this city, sir?"

The great man looked sharply at the historian. "Two that I know of."

"Shall I ask where they are, sir, so that I'll be forewarned?"

"No you shall not. Stick to your business and you don't need to know anything about them."

The historian shrugged. "Well, I don't think I have to worry, sir. The mayor has a tail on me, who'll snatch me back from the precipice, I'm sure."

"That's because you've seen the Arondels."

"Yes, sir."

"In fact, you weren't straight with me, Clio. You'd already seen the Arondels when we first talked."

"Yes, sir, I'm afraid that's true."

"If I'd known you were lying to me, I would've thrown you out."

"But you won't now, I hope, sir."

"No, not now, but don't try to fool me again, Clio. It's my business to know what's going on."

"I understand." The historian paused. "But really, sir, is all this stir about the Arondels necessary? From what I could observe on short acquaintance, the Arondels are harmless otherworldly eccentrics."

The great man's face darkened. "Don't play games with me, Clio."

"I don't mean to, sir."

"Then don't test me with stupid statements. You know damned well that the Arondels are not harmless eccentrics."

The historian pulled back in his chair, struck by the force of the great man's contradiction. "Then the house of Arondel is one of the two precipitous places you spoke of."

Gorham nodded. "The other day you came here and declared that you are a cliometrician. You said you were going to describe the laws of the city, and in fact you're off to a good start with street vice. You're ready to move up higher in the machine. You've got a letter from me. So, do what you came here to do. Stay away from the Arondels. You can't measure them."

The historian nodded thoughtfully. "Do you think it would be useful, indeed prudent, sir, if I knew the location of the other precipitous place?"

"All you need to know is that it also has to do with the Arondels. Stay away from them and you'll avoid it." The great man leaned toward the historian, his face at once softer and darker. "These things you brought today, Clio, show a good eye for the way the city works. But the same eye won't do you a damned bit of good with the Arondels."

The historian shook his head almost sadly. "It's hard for me to concede, sir, that all my years as an observer of this republic, from its gutters to its pinnacles, have not equipped me to deal with the Arondels."

"And I have some experience too, Clio, but I don't deal firsthand with the Arondels myself. Go now and do your boss's work. The Zeitgeist, is that right?" The great man allowed himself a thin smile.

"Yes, sir."

"The Arondels have set themselves against the Zeitgeist. And you know what that means."

"Yes, I know what it means, sir."

∽

As Gorham suggested, the historian added a topography to his study of the machinery of vice and then moved on to investigate the higher echelons of graft. Here the facts would be harder to gather than those pertaining to vice, he predicted. Even under injunction from Gorham, aldermen and commissioners were not likely to be free with disclosures of bribery, peculation, sale of franchises, doctoring of contracts, etc. Nevertheless, the historian was confident of his ultimate success. His study of vice would stand him in good stead because, he was convinced, the two parts of the machine, lower and upper, would prove to be complementary, would in fact fit into the same mathematical envelope. Vice was the bedrock, graft the stonework of the plinth. They supported the columns, porticos, pediments, friezes, roofs, the whole phantasmagoric riot of the city's superstructure—skyscrapers, streams of traffic foot and wheel, Stoddard's fantastical Century Medallion, Philburn's centennial oration, Mrs. Adamson's Electrical Quadrille, everything. The investigator needed only a pure predatory eye to see amid the seeming miscellany the small scurrying creature of pattern and predictability. Then he stooped, seized, and soared back up on the grand pennons of law, commanding all the prospect and its inhabitants.

The historian lay in his hotel bed with his head propped up on two pillows. Weary, he had temporarily lost his grip on law and flown off among metaphors. Well, metaphor no doubt had its laws too, but it would be many generations before the genius was born who could codify that enchainment of word and image. The historian's mind drifted on, a feckless bird, until he came to a small gallery of wind-smeared faces— J. Gorham, Hannah Arondel, and his old mentor John Tenace. Tenace's face had a pitying look. The historian wondered what the object of its contemplation was. Probably it was not Gorham, though Tenace would understand perfectly that the great man was chained like Ixion to the cruel wheel of the machine, over which he only seemed to preside. Perhaps it was Hannah Arondel Tenace sympathized with, because she was lost in her impossible dream of sacramentalized work and burdened with a husband who was only a mechanical extension of her song. Or was it he himself that Tenace pitied, poor bird tossed between the clashing rocks of system and spirit? If so, Tenace didn't understand what a cliometrician was—a measurer of all things human, himself invulnerable to the vagaries of metaphor and spirit. A cliometrician sealed his heart off from pity. Thus self-reassured, the historian fell asleep.

When the historian awoke, he immediately experienced a gnawing curiosity. What exactly was it that Gorham and his minions so feared in Mrs. Arondel? Where was the second precipitous place? By mid-morning the historian was presenting his letter from the great man at the office of Chief Inspector Kern, who offered a hand at the end of an arm that bulged under his shirt sleeve, hard and knotted as a cudgel. The hand itself was hugely prehensile, the fingers more than three-jointed, it seemed to the historian. The inspector smiled his guest down into a chair. He had the outsize teeth of a carnivorous primate. He also had huge eyes, magnified by thick rimless glasses held tight against his nose neither by the springs of a pince-nez nor by arms but by a taut elastic band pressing against his temples and burrowing beneath his hair.

"That little note is famous in this city, friend, but it does not pass here."

"Really," said the historian. "Mr. Gorham didn't mention any exclusions." He failed to produce the exact minatory tone he intended because he was distracted by the inspector's speech, which was delivered through a smiling grimace, the chin lifting slowly, the teeth working autonomously, without regard for the necessities of diction, gnashing compulsively, as though to find some node of thickening in the insubstantial air.

"In this precise case, I mean," Kern was saying. The mouth went on working, as against some unmasticated cud of nuance.

"The Arondel case."

"Precisely."

"Then I think there's a misunderstanding. My work under the auspices of Mr. Gorham is statistical. Therefore I'm not interested in the sleuthing or political aspects of the Arondel case but in the organization of resources."

The inspector knobbed his fist under his chin and spoke. "X number of agents are dispatched by this office to points A, B, and C. Y number of agents are attached to personages D, E, and F. Therefore X plus Y equals the number of agents redeployed from other assignments within the force." The inspector smiled a gritty smile, working his teeth pleasurably, as if to dislodge some flavorful remnant. "If you want to know the actual values you must inquire of Mr. Gorham, the master mathematician."

The historian returned the inspector's smile. "Well, I'm personage D, E, or F, and there's one agent you might save."

"A mere apprentice, sir, unfit for other assignment." The inspector produced a great gust of brutal laughter. He folded his arms and kneaded his biceps pleasurably. "No offense, sir, but you aren't under heavy suspicion. Now if you was to continue steady with the Arondels or appear at the foundry . . . why then we could afford you a proper agent. But you won't do it, will you, sir?"

"Why won't I?"

"End your brilliant career entangled with mere anarchists? You won't do it, sir—out of respect for yourself and for those who admire your work, like Mr. Gorham."

"I am studying the Arondels, Mr. Kern, not entangling myself with them. And in any case, I don't think you can call them mere anarchists."

"I can, sir." The inspector gnashed this affirmation viciously.

"On what grounds?"

"On grounds of logic. There is law and there is anarchy."

"And nothing between?"

"Never mind between. The Arondels are anarchy pure and simple."

"And the center of anarchy is the foundry?"

"You might say so."

"And where is the foundry?"

"The foundry is point B, sir. The house is point A. The two are joined zigzag, as our streets do not go as the crow flies." The inspector made a smiling grimace.

"And point C?"

"Point C is outside this discussion, sir, which I must beg leave to terminate. Business calls me from pleasure. But come again, sir, and if you observe anything special at point A, we would appreciate a report."

"You know the place?"

"Secondhand. But very impressive, I take it, especially the solarium, the loom, and the cellar. You see, sir, one of their number is one of our number, which is the peculiar way numbers act in the presence of anarchy."

∽

So when the historian had gotten a start on his investigations into the higher echelons of the machine, he selected an afternoon and walked again to point A. A propitious wind blew the smoke away to the east, leaving a sky of scudding clouds too ragtag to dim the kindly if faded autumn sun. Behind the historian followed the faithful shadow, snap-brim hat pulled low to hide a face young and indistinct anyway.

The appearance of 387 Rilton brought him up short—not because he had arrived there more quickly than expected but because suddenly he was standing before the house of his childhood. Perhaps it was the rapidly moving sky that created the illusion, pulling his eyes up to the half-mansard roof, the triple-ball lightning rod, and the weather cock. Admittedly, there were no antic cornices or widow's walk—erased by the abrasions of time, as it were—but the silhouette was the same. And if you fixed your eye on the cock instead of on the sky, why then it was you and the house that were sailing the wobbly plains west of Sacramento, until you got dizzy and fell on your back and laughed, and your mother picked you up and said, "You silly thing!"

The historian lowered his gaze. Here was a noble project for some qualitative genius of the future: *The Affective Laws of Domiciliary Geometrics and Their Mnemonic Properties.* The historian went up the steps, knocked, and was admitted, leaving his faithful shadow the tedious task of watching the door.

Arondel, taking his coat and hat, said, "You have a new companion?"

"Yes," said the historian, in the parlor now, "an agent from Inspector Kern's office."

"Why?" said Mrs. Arondel, taking the historian's hand.

The historian smiled. "Why, because I'm visiting you."

Mrs. Arondel didn't smile. "I did not know we were to this yet."

"Oh yes. I don't know what dark deeds you have perpetrated, but I've heard of a foundry, nefarious to my informants, a zigzag way from here."

Mrs. Arondel made clear by a narrowing of her dark eyes that she didn't approve of this sally. "This is not fair, to press on our work. You promised this visit to tell us what stories you write."

"Stories, madam, are exactly what I will not write."

"I do not understand."

"I mean that the charm of stories veils the truth. Stories have prevented history from discovering the laws of society. Therefore I will write no more stories."

The pyrope flashed in the black of Mrs. Arondel's eyes. "It is not story against law," she said with great precision. "It is the writing down that is bad."

The historian nodded. "Yes, you said something like that the other day when I was at the loom. But one has to have some sort of notation if one is to represent. I use as few characters as possible, primarily numbers and charts."

"You are in the right direction," said Mrs. Arondel, "but you don't go far enough. Record in living, not on paper." She leaned toward the historian. "You put down these marks because you think you can make the things of living stand behind them in rank. But the things of living go their own way and leave the marks empty, only the men don't understand that. They worship the marks instead of life."

"What about the lovely marks you showed me on the green paper?"

"They say, go away from me back to the things of earth and body." She held her face close to his and poured on him her characteristic odor of body and perfumed oil. "In your hotel your pen scratches the air.

This is the historian's compulsive, to write instead of act, but the ink only goes into black silence."

Two images competed with each other in the historian's mind: one a drear waste of inert ink, the other the sensual black hair that rounded Mrs. Arondel's olive face. In speaking he hoped to free himself from these opposites. "And don't you use words in dealing with your colleagues here and at the foundry?"

"Living words in the throat with a song from one to the other, not silent marks on pages. Other ways we speak to each other you can see sometime."

The historian nodded slowly. "I knew my project wouldn't please you. Nevertheless I've told you what I'm doing. Now it's your turn to tell me what you're doing."

Arondel spoke. "We're trying to create a world in which the souls of our children, their bodies, and their work are all one." He never could have said that, the historian knew, if his wife hadn't taught him. And still the declaration fell short of final conviction. The voice went up and came back, scarcely displaced in its return, essentially stationary, the wave of his wife's energy having passed through a medium fundamentally inert.

The historian said, "You two who say that act is everything, keep telling me what you're thinking, not what you're doing."

"Because you are not yet one of us," said Mrs. Arondel.

The historian could not honestly say that he wished he were one of them, or that he actually was one of them in spirit if not in fact. So he let Mrs. Arondel's statement pass in silence.

Mrs. Arondel gazed at the historian with a curious look that mixed sternness and something like affectionate interest. Arondel was no longer beside her. He wasn't in the room. He'd vanished as quickly as if Hannah Arondel had snuffed the wavering flame of a candle. The historian looked at her and said, "Let me guess. You have planted a seed of radical change, and it has put out a shoot in this improbable city. And now you're gripped by fear."

"Why gripped by fear?"

"Because there never was a revolution without terror."

"That also is the historian's compulsive, to believe in the eternal repeat. It will change."

"Everything strives to protect its form. That's the morphological insight . . ." The historian interrupted himself with a peremptory wave of his hand, angry at his own pedantry. He began again. "Last night in a dream I saw a great host of ciphers marching down on you with picks and bayonets at the ready."

"It is a dream, not real."

"It's every bit as real as the billies and pistols Kern's men carry."

"What will they do?"

"They'll go to the foundry and tear down whatever you've built up there. They'll come here and root out whatever it is you have in the cellar." The historian looked frankly into Mrs. Arondel's eyes. A moment later she slowly rose up, went to a small secretary in the corner, and returned with a pad of paper and a thick pencil. She moved her chair and sat down beside him, the odor of her person very strong. "You can do something."

"What?"

"You can write."

"That's a sketching pad."

Mrs. Arondel didn't acknowledge the objection. "Once you wrote and changed cities, with John Tenace and Charlie Derwood."

"Ah yes, the pen is mightier than the sword," said the historian ironically, but found himself looking intently at Mrs. Arondel's lips, which were darker than ruby, moist and delicately striated except out in the shadowed corners where they seemed threatened with sanguineous lesions. The lesions startled the historian, awakening in him a sudden onset of pity and desire. He looked away, saying, "You don't believe in writing."

"You can write only to make us the time."

"The time?" The historian looked into Mrs. Arondel's eyes.

"Yes, the time when we will be too wide for Kern's men."

The historian shook his head sadly. "Even if I could write such a thing, I don't know what you're doing."

"You know much."

"Only hints from Kern and J. Gorham."

Mrs. Arondel's eyes flared. "You have talked to J. Gorham?"

"Yes, the great man himself."

"What did he say of us?"

"He said that you aren't harmless idealists, that you can't be measured, and that I should stay away from you." The historian thought that Mrs. Arondel would show anger, but she only nodded and dropped her eyes. His followed, to the sketching pad, which now rested on his knees. To his surprise the pencil was in the tripod of his thumb, index, and middle fingers, which were held firmly in place by Mrs. Arondel. "You can write something." It was almost as though he were sitting at the loom again. He felt an urgent pressure on his fingers. The pencil made a brief vibratile motion and then snaked out across the sheet, leaving a trail of loopless gray. "That is nothing," said Mrs. Arondel.

"As I predicted." But the pencil began to vibrate again, and after a short skate traced the outline of a crude triangle with its apex pointing out beyond the historian's knees.

"That is something," said Mrs. Arondel, so close that the sibilants titillated the historian's ear. "What is it?"

"Perhaps it's a delta."

"What is a delta?"

"A delta is a part of a thing that's always changing. You take it out of the stream for a little while to look at it."

"Ah ha!" said Mrs. Arondel. "I catch you contradicting. Before, you said the thing would not change, but destroy us."

The historian moved the pencil again. On the left side of the base he wrote the letter A, on the right B, and at the apex C. "Now it's a triangle," he said. "A is this house. B is the foundry. C is a place of mystery, unknown to me. Do you know where it is?"

"Perhaps I do."

The historian searched Mrs. Arondel's eyes. "Think," he said. "If you could tell me, it might make a difference."

"If I can think of it, will you write?" The historian felt the grip on his fingers tighten subtly. Hannah Arondel's face moved closer to his, the pyrope in her eyes swimming up into the black, and the lesions in the corners of her lips shining out from the shadows. "Could you write?"

The warmth of her breath filled his nostrils with a cinnamonish pungence. As at the loom, he felt imprisoned, and to free himself did the only thing he knew to do—suddenly splayed his fingers so that the pencil tumbled to the floor. A moment later Mrs. Arondel released his hand and stood up. "It is only because you don't know us yet." She studied him for some moments, seemed on the verge of making a dramatic revelation, and then thought better of it. "I will send to you and show you something."

The historian stood up. "I fear that I seem unobliging."

"I will send to you," said Mrs. Arondel, and before he could make reply, led him out into the entryway, where Arondel reappeared, his face betraying astonishment. Obviously he was amazed that his wife had not yet succeeded in her conquest of the benighted man of law.

∽

The historian took great pleasure in unveiling the higher echelons of the machine. And it was easy, because its operatives, whom the historian thought would be guarded, warbled like songbirds. Each integer, ignorant of all but its local functions, sang in its cage of circumscription as if those bars were the whole blue bowl of the sky—clerks of court, bureau chiefs, aldermen, commissioners. The historian threw himself passionately into the work of charting their activities. He even managed to push the Arondels out to the edge of his consciousness. His entries and exits from sleep were without image except when now and again a cadre of ciphers loomed behind the veil of unconsciousness and disappeared just as quickly, like a picket of lost soldiers in a misted forest.

It was the busyness and mercurial nature of these higher functions of the machine that made it so fascinating. By comparison the relationships among the operatives of the tenderloin were static. But here new contracts were written or old ones renegotiated daily. Increments of revenue suddenly widened or collapsed toward zero. Therefore the aggregate cash flow of the machine had to be rederived continuously from changed variables. The historian remembered with amusement how he and Tenace and Charlie had written indignantly about the way things were fixed down at city hall, but really nothing was fixed. The whole thing was dynamic and open. It was lawful of course, but what kept it lawful was not a set of fixed functions. Rather it was the limits of certain ratios of influx to egress—constraints which regulated the game of even the most daring speculators in land, transportation, and utilities, and made them all as law-abiding as the Puritan forefathers.

When the historian had his model pretty well worked out he took it up to the office in the high tower overlooking the confluence of the two rivers and laid it before the great man, who first scrutinized a chart or two almost dourly, then swept his own papers off his mammoth desktop and laid out graphs and formulas like a miser counting his gold. The historian grinned. It didn't matter to him that the great man already knew all this, that his fascination was only in seeing his own intuitions systematically arrayed. The historian at last laughed outright. "Your machine is a thing of beauty, sir."

The great man nodded. "Good work, Clio. A minor mistake here and there, but good work."

"Don't puff me up, sir. Already I've been dreaming of making the machine of machines, the ur-machine from which all others are derived."

Gorham grunted indulgently. "The ur-machine, eh?"

"Yes, sir. Equally applicable to a city or a waterfall, to the motions of a sidewinder or the drift of a galaxy. But you'd have to help me. What do you think, sir?"

Gorham meditated. And while he did, the historian studied the great man of lines, the black hair as perfectly striated as if it had been battened by the reed of Mrs. Arondel's loom, the narrow stripes of the suit falling parallel. Something, however, was different, but the historian couldn't tease it out. His eyes drifted to the window. Parallel rays of stained sunlight fell through the long panes. He thought that his gaze was idle, but in fact his subconscious was busy discovering in the yellow shafts of light a subtle convergence. He looked again at Gorham. The same barely detectable convergence was there too. He thought of the Russian mystic's parallels that in the extension of some unimaginable space crossed at a point, once and never more, the omphalos of geometry. Inspector Kern's point C.

Gorham said, "My answer is no. There's no ur-machine."

"Why do you say so, sir?"

"Because there's anarchy, which lies outside the machine."

"You're referring to the Arondels?"

"And all like them."

"I'm surprised to hear you say that, sir. It seems to me if law is law, it has to be everywhere. Otherwise we get back into those old heresies of dualism, Manichaeanism, whatever they called them. Which is what Kern believes, incidentally."

Gorham looked sharply at the historian. "Kern is a good man. Leave him out of this."

"Very well, sir."

"Anyway, I'm not interested in dualism, Clio—powers of darkness and light. I'm saying everybody's different. You can't predict what individuals will do, only the mass, and that roughly. Pascal. Probability. You said so yourself. So individuals do fall outside the machine and become ungovernable, anarchists. The Arondels." Gorham clamped his mouth down on the name like a vice.

The historian nodded. *"Individuum est ineffabile,* eh? But if individuals really were ineffable, the probabilities that make them governable wouldn't hold, would they? Any more than if a coin could go on willfully turning up heads every time. So, if the individual seems ineffable it's only because our instrumentation is crude."

"So, your friends the Arondels are lawful?"

"Yes, sir."

Gorham grunted. "You're a clever devil, Clio. But I'll tell you this. If the Arondels are acting according to some law, it's not our law. So they're not governable, not here and now. Therefore they're not tolerable."

"I would think, sir, that you would not only tolerate them but cherish them."

"Why the devil should I cherish them?"

"As a counterpoint, sir, that can keep the machine up to the mark; maybe even change it."

"Very noble, Clio. This is the antithesis of your beloved Hegel, I suppose."

"Yes, sir, I believe it is."

"Tell me. Have you seen the foundry?"

"No, sir."

"Go and see it." Gorham took a sheet of paper out of his desk drawer and wrote briefly with his pen. "Give this to Kern." Gorham handed the paper to the historian. A moment later he gathered up the historian's charts and graphs and gave them to him. "This is good work, Clio. It might even make you more famous, if anybody gives a damn anymore about these filthy cities."

The historian didn't like the valedictory tone. He wanted to pursue the Arondels, and point C. All his sleuthing instinct, which was considerable, told him that these were the cruxes and that Gorham knew it. He wanted to flush them out. He wanted them in his talons. "You'll help me with the corrections you mentioned, won't you, sir?"

"Of course. Send me a copy and I'll mark it—if necessary. But an eagle-eyed detail man like you will no doubt catch everything before it gets to me."

"Perhaps. And when that's done, I'll bring you another piece of work."

"What'll it be, Clio?"

"A model of the Arondel machine."

Gorham shook his head solemnly. "It can't be done."

"With all due respect, sir, I think it can be done. In fact, Inspector Kern has already given me important assistance."

"What are you talking about, Clio?"

"The inspector gave me a little lesson in triangulation. He said that the Arondel house was point A and the nefarious foundry point B. And then he spoke of a point C, which he wouldn't reveal. I had the distinct impression, however, that it was a place where the two systems meet, or at least once met—I mean the city system and the Arondel system, sir. So the machines are fundamentally analogous, instances of a bigger system, the ur-machine."

The great man leaned toward the historian, who could not remember his having done so before. "Never mind the antithesis, the ur-machine, and all that. Let me tell you something as a practical man. The two don't mesh, the Arondels and the city. They never will. Which means that the Arondels will give way, forcibly if necessary. And observers, in the heat of action, could be confused with the anarchists they're observing. In other words, stay away from the Arondels. Forget them."

"I can't forget them."

"Then remember them hereafter."

"Do you know, sir, what point C is?"

Gorham leaned slowly back into his chair. It seemed to the

historian a motion of massive patience. "You have my last word on the subject, Clio. Good day."

‿◠

There was the poor inept tail standing dutifully in the blue glow of a lamp at the corner, his eyes downcast, as though he were watching the darkness fall onto the chill street. The historian, pretending not to notice him, walked several blocks down the street and entered a restaurant. He wished he could have asked the tail to join him. He didn't want to sit alone now thinking about his meeting with Gorham. That was better done later. He was tired. He and the tail could have talked about police work, about all the wondrous forms and colors of vice and crime. But it was not to be. So he ate his beef and drank his coffee mindlessly, as old training had taught him.

Only once did a curious sequence deriving from his transactions with Gorham invade his mind. To begin, there was a photograph of Gorham's office—the two of them sitting there, the oily sunlight behind them, the massive furniture a composite of wood and shadow. Then a huge force had twisted and curled the photograph until it formed a catastrophe, a mathematical crease, and thus a cunning obverse. New inhabitants appeared. Who were they? The historian thought he discerned a man and a woman, large, nude, and in a space of different properties, one allowing of no angles or lines but only of curves. Before these mysteries could engage him, however, he deliberately darkened his mind. These images of exhaustion were not to be trusted.

A little later the historian mounted the stairs to his room, unlocked the door, turned on the pale ceiling light, and discovered a man sitting in the easy chair in the corner beyond the desk. For a moment he thought that his shadow had dashed ahead of him up the fire escape and climbed in through the window. But it wasn't the shadow. It was Charlie Derwood. He wore, as always, a red carnation in the lapel of his checkered coat.

"Hello, Clio," said Charlie Derwood. "I hear that's what they call you here." He didn't rise to offer his hand.

"Hello, Charlie. Where in radical-land have you been? East or west?"

"The revolution knows no east or west, Clio. In her no north or south." Charlie laughed, but it was not one of his old outbursts of irrepressible gaiety.

The historian threw coat, hat, and portfolio on the bed, turned on the low desk light, and said, "It's good to see you, Charlie. Suppose I found something in the desk here. Would you join me in a nip, for auld lang syne?"

"You bet I would. There's a touch o' autumn in the air."

The historian slid the drawer out, withdrew a bottle and two small glasses, poured two generous shots, gave one to Charlie, and sat in a swivel chair by the desk. "You should run your revolutions in the summer, Charlie, when everybody's hot and ready for action."

The two men touched glasses and sipped. "Revolution ain't seasonal."

"Revolution sounds like rough work to me, Charlie. Maybe you ought to go back to mucking. You're the best in the business."

Charlie shook his head. "Old Riis is still going strong. And anyway, my last stint with pen wasn't satisfactory."

"Where was it? I guess I haven't kept up."

"In *The Masses,* under a nom de plume, Mark Marcus." Charlie cackled cynically. "But now I have given up writing altogether, joined the ranks of the active. And I owe it all to you, Clio, for busting up the old mucking team and sending me off to the rads."

"I merely looked down into our two dark souls and prophesied."

"That you did," said Charlie meditatively and then went silent, which gave the historian a chance to reflect on the change in his old partner. He didn't like it. Gone was the dapper Charlie of their muckraking days. In his place was an unkempt radical with wild hair and fervid eyes. The familiar red carnation was no longer the badge of the bon vivant. It was an emblem of revolution. But it was the eyes, glazed with fever and exhaustion, that arrested the historian. They reminded him of Tenace's on his deathbed. Presently the historian broke the silence. "Tell me, Charlie, what's the most exciting thing about the rads?"

Charlie smiled. "The women, of course, old friend. Mabel and Victoria and Isadora and even Emma. They have a way of extracting from everything a sweet red ichor and dropping it on your tongue."

"And so they led you astray, you think, the lovely ladies of the left?"

Charlie gazed steadily at his old mentor. "No, not astray. I used to think so, but I know better now."

"What do you know now that you didn't know?"

"I know Hannah Arondel."

The historian nodded. "I know her too."

"No you don't. You've seen her but you don't know her. If you knew her you wouldn't still be a machine man, Clio."

"What would I be?"

"You'd be a member of the Socius."

"And they've sent you here to help me see that I must join the . . . say it again."

"The Socius." Charlie's face remained profoundly serious for some moments and then slowly relaxed into a smile. "Yes, I've crept through your casement like a moonbeam, Clio, to light your way to understanding."

"Like something Mrs. Arondel herself might have suspired, as she says."

"Exactly," said Charlie, the smile gone.

"And when I've understood, I'll write?"

"For a while. And something totally different from the old muck-rackings and the biographies and this new scientific stuff they say you're writing. And totally different from my red propaganda."

"What'll it be, Charlie?"

"Something that'll make people understand the Socius. It might be a kind of paean, like a song almost. I don't know. That's what you'll have to figure out."

The historian shook his head. "Not me. It sounds like a job for Charlie Derwood, the greatest color writer of them all."

"If I could have written it, I would have. But you're the only one that has the pen to write it and the name to make it stick."

"I can't do it, Charlie. I don't grasp it. You can't write what you don't grasp. You know that."

"That's my job, Clio, to see that you grasp it." Charlie's eyes flashed with something like the scintillance of Hannah Arondel's gaze, but with none of its depth. She was, the historian reflected, unfortunate in her selection of lieutenants. Charlie, meanwhile, was producing again his thin smile. "You'll be happy to know that I'm not going to make you grasp it by talking at you."

The historian shrugged affably. "You're a damned fine talker, Charlie."

"But I'm not going to talk. I'm going to give you the proof ocular." Charlie touched the corner of his eye. "Are you ready?"

"Ready."

Charlie drank off the last of his whiskey and rose. "Then don coat and hat, Clio, and prepare yourself to see what history has never seen before. And you'll be the one to record it."

The historian put on his coat. "Are we going to the foundry?"

"Yes."

"I could have saved you the trouble. I have an open-sesame from Gorham to Kern."

"No you don't. Gorham is a mechanic and Kern is a brute. Neither of them can show you what I'll show you." Charlie snugged a wool hat down to his ears and slid open the window. "We'll go down the back way so as not to disturb your shadow."

The gas lamps grew sparser and sparser as they made their way through the commercial area and out into the industrial district, until at last their steps were lit only by a speckled half-moon and the lurid underbelly of the thick sky that hung over the smelteries. Charlie set a brisk pace against a wind that pulled at their coats and bit their faces. The historian said, "Something there is, Charlie, that doesn't want us here."

"Bunk," said Charlie, pressing ahead. "You think the wind is one of Kern's agents?"

The historian had a vague image of cobbled streets, half-paved walkways, high fences, brick buildings, stone buildings, stacks, black windows, windows dimly lit, dogs prowling and growling in the obscurity. Presently they crossed a railroad track embedded in asphalt, shiny with use. The distant roar of the furnaces reached them, and the sudden whuff of a gas stack lighting off. The air was mildly sulphuric. "Charlie," said the historian, "are you taking your old friend to a place of vision or to the ultimate pit?"

"The scales will drop from your eyes, Clio. Now walk up."

The historian quickened his pace. His curiosity mounted, but also the feeling that he must be ready to guard himself against Charlie's monomaniacal energy. At a certain point, when the historian's feet were sorely wearied by the rubblous and slaggy walkways, Charlie took a sudden turn and they arrived at a pair of heavy gates hinged to two massive stone uprights. Beyond, against the pinkish glow of the sky, the historian could make out the silhouettes of turrets and bold castellations.

So this was one of those factories of character, the kind the architect, owners, and city fathers gather to christen, wreathed in smiles, having married industrialism and Arthurian romance. A guard appeared. Charlie announced himself and his visitor. The gates swung open and the two men proceeded down a long hedge-lined walk toward the entry, which turned out to be, appropriately, a pair of huge wooden doors arched at the top, with small square windows behind iron gratings. Charlie knocked authoritatively and distinctly, perhaps according to some code. One after the other, two heavy bolts slid back from within and the doors opened with a creak. In other circumstances the historian would have laughed, but here in the place of Hannah Arondel he didn't expect ersatz medieval romance. And so he entered seriously, but unprepared even so for what was there.

First was the simple magnitude and complexity of the machinery itself. Of course one had read, or heard in a dozen civic speeches, that there were fifty million tons of coal mined annually, and two million tons of pig smelted, that fifty thousand steam engines were in operation and fifty thousand waterwheels and ten thousand spindles, but one did not really understand from these raw numbers the actual effect of the force of the massed enterprise. One had to enter one of its domains, like this foundry. The air was crowded with force fields. The historian felt them like tentacles sliding along his limbs and torso, probing to see if he was malleable, fireable, or in any wise useful as an article of increase in the maw of the foundry.

The historian cast his eyes about but couldn't bring anything clearly into focus until, after some moments, the foundry began to brighten, slowly, in discrete pulses. Presently the historian discovered the source of light: electrical fixtures mounted high on the walls just beneath a tenting of large glass panes. These fixtures, human in shape, reminded him of those brave figureheads that under ambiguous moons pull the cutwaters of merchants through heavy seas to safe haven. And in fact what the figures bore aloft were milky glass moons, within which burned yellow-white filaments that washed the bronze of their bearers with a golden glow.

And now the historian made out two huge shapes looming up in the manmade moonlight. They were pots for molten metal, balanced within giant binnacles, lipped and spouted. In his mind's eye the historian saw the tipping and the brilliant flow into the big earthen molds below. And beyond these stood row on row of stout shelves crowded with metal molds for smaller castings. To the side of the shelves stood an army of forging hammers. Some were drop hammers, the historian supposed, powered merely by muscle and gravity. The bigger ones, he guessed, were driven by steam—or was it electricity? The thought made him aware of a hum that had intensified with the brightening of the lights, and this in turn led his eye to the far corner of the room, where a big drum was whirring and sparking the dynamo.

Charlie, who had disappeared during the switching on of the power, returned and said, "This is a complete foundry, Clio, a microcosm of the industrial era."

"I believe it, Charlie."

Charlie pointed to the machines and gave them names. "That's a rotary press. That's a ram . . . a header . . . a sizer . . . a coiner." His voice mixed in a peculiar way reverence and irony. To the historian the machines marching across his field of vision in the yellow-gold light were like the crepuscular soldiery of a Götterdämmerung.

At this point Charlie seized him by the arm and pointed to the whirring drum. "See the dynamo, Clio?"

"Yes."

"I'll tell you a parable about the dynamo." Charlie continued to hold the historian's arm. "Once there was a poor Persian who came here, before the Arondels, a Parsee. He saw the dynamo. He worshiped it. And one day when nobody was looking, he kissed it, reverently no doubt, thinking it was Zoroaster's messiah. And it kissed him back, fatally. What do you think the moral of the parable is, Clio?"

The historian smiled. "I think I get it, Charlie. Do not worship machines."

"Yea verily," said Charlie with a portentousness that was not entirely comic. "And that should tell you something about your current project."

"I don't worship anything, Charlie. I just try to describe everything accurately."

"There's no such thing as not worshiping anything, Clio." Charlie pulled the historian forward a step or two, then released his arm. "Follow me." They crossed the vast glass-domed room on a grated catwalk and stood beneath yet another catwalk, which was supported by a series of powerful stanchions. To the stanchions were welded thick pad-eyes, from which big blocks depended, several with as many as ten falls. Their hooks, partially hidden in shadow, were still now, but deceptively so, thought the historian, for they were creatures of pure intent merely waiting for a human servant to return to the work of their wills.

Charlie again urged the historian forward. They passed below the catwalk and approached the far wall, where the light was very sparse. Even so, the historian saw immediately that the wall was covered with an immense mural some fifteen feet high and three times that wide. They stood near the right edge of it. There was a sudden flare. From a sconce high on one of the stanchions Charlie had taken down a long-chimneyed oil lamp and lit it. A wavering light fell on the mural. For some moments the historian perceived only a tumbling of cereals and fruit, with domestic animals standing among them as in a stream of inexorable fecundity. Off to the left in the shadows, he surmised, was a cornucopia disgorging this plethora. But when Charlie led him to the far panel of the mural, it proved otherwise. Here was a huge girl-child holding at leashes' end a brace of fierce tigers whose eyes were jewels, whose teeth were steel cogs, joints rotary differentials, claws die punches, and whose stripes were the geometrical flames of a furnace. The child was at once innocent and sensuous. She had sky blue eyes and tassels of blond hair but pectorals and a mons veneris that heaved out like hummocks. It was from her that the superabundance flowed, propelled after its issuance by the straining tigers—earth, animal, and machine joined in a single creative act.

"Mrs. Arondel's work, I take it."

"She designed it. Many hands executed it. Every worker painted some part."

The historian nodded. That helped explain the bold and sharply defined panels of primary color that characterized the mural. "Very impressive," he said, "and no doubt an inspiration for those who have to work here among the din and the fires."

Charlie was displeased with this comment. The backwash of the lamp's yellow light accentuated his frown. "You still don't understand. Follow me." He led the historian out of the main room of the foundry and down a long dark corridor. He opened and shut behind them two thick doors and finally a third. With each thud the historian imagined he heard the daytime clamor of the foundry recede further and further behind until, with the shutting of the last door, it faded altogether.

"This is the nursery," said Charlie, making a wide arc with the lamp so that the historian could see a spacious room furnished with small chairs and diminutive workbenches. A large area was left open, for exercise or dancing perhaps, and there were also plump floor pads for resting. "This is for the children who don't go to school yet. All the workers here are couples. The man and the woman both work in the foundry. If there's a small child, they take their turn caring for the children here in the nursery. All are paid equally." Charlie led the historian out of the nursery and down the corridor to another door. "This is the room where the workers come during their rest periods. In this foundry they're not driven like oxen from sunup to sundown."

"Very humane."

Charlie fished in his pocket for a key. On the door the historian saw the inscription, "Socius." Charlie unlocked and opened the door. The room beyond, larger than the nursery, presented to the historian's eye a soft sea of cushions strewn about the floor but somehow not in disarray. Charlie took him by the arm and led him across the room. "This is the other mural." Charlie's grip was insistent, as though he feared the historian might bolt. He held the light up to the top of his reach. It illumined a huge face wreathed about with garlands of immortelles—green and russet plants the historian could not identify. The style of painting was like that of the mural in the foundry, composed of bright bravura swatches, but not all the colors were primary. There were subtler hues. And the figure wasn't seen entirely under the aspect of a single frontal light, like those in the main room of the foundry, but admitted of shadings. The expression of the face was one of both transport and calm. Similarly, the eyes looked inward and outward with equal joy. But unlike the figures on the wall of the foundry, this one didn't immediately suggest to the historian its identity or meaning. Nor could he determine its sex, which was still not revealed as Charlie lowered the light. The breasts, massive but muscular, were tipped with small rose teats and aureoles, not clearly male or female. The light passed down along a belly so muscular that it seemed almost plated, and then descended to the pubes, but there were no genitals to solve the mystery. The pubes were grass. The whole figure in fact grew up out of soil, the base of its torso rooted deep in earth rich with worms and water. Overall, the flesh of the figure was a rich brown, as of vegetable essences. The arms of the figure were thrown open in a wide but soft arc clearly meant to embrace everything.

And now the historian began to experience an almost dizzying complexity of feelings about the painting. Had he been able to make a purely aesthetic judgment, he probably would have rejected the mural as crude and pretentiously primitive. But its context complicated things enormously—its designer, its execution by many hands, its placement in the inner sanctum of a revolutionary plant. And there was also Charlie, who stood rapt before the painting, his grip on the historian's arm as infrangible as if it had been forged of steel there in the foundry. For some minutes they stood there together. The historian would have preferred to turn away, but he went on dutifully looking at the figure, as he had been brought to do. He couldn't penetrate it. He couldn't analyze it. It remained what it was from the first moments of his viewing—huge, earthy, androgynous, immortal. It didn't unfold. Its surfaces were obdurate. It promised much. Indeed, it tunneled to dreams. But it asked in return nothing less than everything, the total commitment represented by the rapture that Charlie was now obviously experiencing. So the historian remained silent until there came a moment of relaxation, caused by what he didn't know, when Charlie loosened his grip, turned away from the mural, and led with the oil lamp back out of the Socius. In the corridor Charlie said, "Don't say anything."

"I would have expressed admiration."

"Be quiet."

In the huge vaulted room of the foundry Charlie stepped aside briefly. The historian heard the snapping sound of a switch. The dynamo whirred down. The yellow-white light of the moon-bearers dimmed. A moment later Charlie smothered the oil lamp and replaced it on its sconce under the high catwalk. Slowly the historian's eyes began to grow accustomed to the dark, but it wasn't necessary for him to see. Charlie led the way out of the foundry. Behind them, the heavy bolts slid back into place, moved by hands the historian had never seen. At the end of the hedged walkway the massive gates opened and closed behind them. Charlie made brief exchange with the guard, but the historian didn't hear their words.

They walked in silence through a thickening mist that rose up from the rivers. When they had passed several lamplit intersections, Charlie stopped and said, "Do you know where you are now?"

The historian surveyed the skyline and looked at the street sign. "Yes."

"You're in Cain's city, Clio. Don't you smell it?"

"Is there another kind, Charlie?"

"I just showed you. And now you've got a choice, Clio. You can't avoid it—the Socius or Gorham, Kern, the prostitutes, the machine. Think about it."

"I'll think about it, Charlie," said the historian, but his guide disappeared even as he spoke, swallowed up by the fog.

∽

Walking carefully, as along a misted battlement, the historian at last came to the corner across from his hotel. There in the shallow portico of a storefront, the shadow drooped shapelessly. The historian approached, detected no animation, gave the hunched shoulder a gentle shove, and watched the lifeless body sprawl out onto the sidewalk. The wide-brimmed hat flopped off to reveal the fixed glister of half-opened eyes. Beneath the throat blossomed a black stain of blood. The historian shook his head ruefully. The end of the inept apprentice. And a provocation for Kern, who would look to the Arondels, and that would have evil consequence. The historian went no further with it. He was tired, his mind resistant to thought, his legs numb. He trudged across to the hotel, passed the sleepy night clerk, and climbed to his room.

There he found his second visitor of the evening, Hannah Arondel, who must have come in through the same window as her legate. A brief image came to the historian's mind, her powerful body moving swiftly and silently up the steel rungs of the fire escape, skirts lifted carefully. Mrs. Arondel sat just within the yellowish glow of the desk lamp, in the same easy chair where Charlie Derwood had appeared. The historian closed the door softly behind him, laid his coat and hat on the bed, and sat down in the desk chair, giving Mrs. Arondel a cordial but quizzical look, his alertness restored.

"I am sorry to intrude myself," said Mrs. Arondel, "but we have little time."

"Very little, I'd say."

"You have seen the Socius."

"Yes, Charlie took me to the foundry."

The fire flecks in Mrs. Arondel's eyes flashed at the historian. "In all the factories they wait. The police know it."

"And now there's the dead man."

"What dead man?"

The historian didn't doubt the genuineness of the surprise in Mrs. Arondel's voice. "The young man Kern assigned to follow me."

Mrs. Arondel's eyes darkened. "They will set the blame on us, because they know in all the factories they wait."

"Who is it exactly that waits?"

"Members of the body of the Socius."

"And what do they wait for?"

"For the sign to welcome their fellow workers into the Socius."

"When will you give the sign?"

"When we are wide enough. Soon, not yet. But now Kern has the dead boy."

The historian looked closely at his visitor. Perhaps in this different setting he could get a truer image of her. He took in anew the olive face surmounted by its ring of dense black hair lit as by a nimbus of painterly light. On her shoulders lay the fibrous whorl of the woolen shawl. And down from her neck flowed the dark fabric of her dress, over the large bosoms, down into the rich folds of her lap. Breathing out from the dress was the powerful mixed odor of body and perfumed oil. The scintillance, as of pyrope, flecked the eyes. Yes, the historian saw her truer. She was mad, dizzyingly, hypnotically mad. Now she was saying, "That is why you must write for us, for the time. We only need time."

And that also was a part of her madness, the historian saw—the unshakable belief that he could produce something with this pen that would throw up between her and the wrath of the machine an unbreachable battlement. The fact that in her cosmology writing was evil only served to strengthen her conviction that it would be effective against Kern and his bosses.

"Only you can hold them away with writing and give us the time." She looked at him steadily with her black eyes. "You have seen the child and the Socius." She reached out and touched his hand. "Your mind hides, but in your heart you love us." She increased the pressure on his hand. "Write for us." It was at this moment, the historian knew, that he was supposed to succumb, as Arondel had and Charlie had and all the sub-lieutenants in the factories of the city. The touch of her hand and the warmth of her breath were to conspire with the immense power of the child and the earthwide embrace of the Socius to bring down the defenses of the socially corrupted newspaperman cum historian. And why not, thought the historian. Why cling to the sullied operatives of the machine when one could repose one's trust in the immense warmth of Hannah Arondel's mystic communion? The historian looked away. He didn't want to see again the subtle lesions in the corners of her mouth. But she made him look at her, pressing his hand and saying, "Your mind holds back, but your heart sees and loves us. Write for us."

The historian shook his head regretfully. "You would only have a part of me, and that the baser part." He saw Mrs. Arondel's eyes dilate momentarily, against her will. Obviously she was amazed that he didn't come over to her. The historian said, "I can't write for you, but I'll make a call."

"Will the call give us the time?"

"Time enough to withdraw."

"Withdraw?"

"Yes, because they're not ready for your experiment, no matter how noble it is."

Mrs. Arondel rose and stood over the historian, her dress pouring down over him a deep pungent shadow. "We don't have experiment," she said, her voice husky. "We have only what must be." She reached out and gently laid hold of his throat. Under her hand he felt the yielding of the soft flanks of his neck and the little wattle under his chin. "You will make us the time for the Socius," she said. "You will write for us. The next time we will begin." Then, by a gentle pressure the historian could never have described exactly, she caused him to rise to his feet. And while he stood there swaying toward her, she kissed him on the lips. And then she was gone, leaving him unsteady and confused. He sat down. He pressed his lips together. They had been signed, and though he didn't know the exact meaning of the sign, he knew that it contained a promise and a fatality. He looked at the darkness in the open window. The mist outside took from the desk lamp a barely perceptible glow, but it was altogether too faint to relieve the primary aspect of the night, which was one of pure absence.

∽

In the morning an officer came and escorted the historian to Kern's office. The inspector's eyes, owlish behind thick glass, glowered at the historian, who sat in a chair while his host paced. "You know that the man we assigned to you is dead."

"I'm sorry to hear it, but it's no great surprise."

"What do you mean by that, sir?"

"I mean that he was lackadaisical and inept. I hope he had no wife."

The inspector stopped and bent toward the historian. The bands of his spectacles caused the hair on his temples to tuft and flair up like little horns. "There're many inept on the streets who don't end up in pools of blood. This is the work of your friends the Arondels."

"Psh! Whatever the Arondels are, they aren't murderers."

"What are they then?" For once there was a hint of uncertainty in the inspector's gnashing speech.

"Mystics, harmless mystics."

"Harmless, you say."

"Yes, harmless because their ideals are so overblown they can never come to anything."

"I don't consider obscenity, the hoarding of arms, and murder harmless."

"Do you have any proof of the murder?"

"Not yet."

"Have they used any arms to illegal purpose?"

"Not yet."

"Has the obscenity, by which I assume you mean the murals, caused any public immorality?"

"Public? Not yet."

"What's this 'not yet,' inspector? The law answers simply no, because law acts on deeds, not prophecy."

"Not so, sir." The inspector kneaded his massive arms. "The law is preventive, or else it would be forever chasing down stolen goods and mopping up blood, and the citizens would hate our stupidity. No, sir, we must detect violence before it reaches the streets."

"This time you're tilting at windmills, inspector. But you have a spy in their midst. Does he report that they are planning violence?"

"Had a man, sir. Had." The inspector bit the d's off fiercely.

"Ah," said the historian after a short pause. "And he went over?"

"Hypnotized. And he did have a wife."

"In that case she's no doubt still with him, unharmed. They're very monogamous."

"Perhaps for the time being, sir." And now Kern bore down so penetratingly with his owlish eyes that the historian feared he might actually spy out some vestige of Mrs. Arondel's visit, a finger mark on his throat, the bruise of her kiss. "For the time being, but you know the same as I know."

"What?"

"That out of anarchy comes license." The inspector made a toothy hiss.

The historian sighed, as with strained patience. "Well then, what do you plan to do?"

"Make my report, take my orders, and execute them."

"Well, that's that then, inspector." The historian slapped his thighs as with a regretful finality and made as if to rise. But the inspector held him, employing unexpectedly a tone of shrewd camaraderie. "You're a man of the world, sir. What do you make of the murals?"

"You've seen them?"

"Only through the eyes of my man."

"And those perhaps already hypnotically infected."

"Yes." Kern worked his teeth. What a burden this Arondel affair was to the inspector, the historian thought—ambiguous and insubstantial, unamenable to firm seizure by tooth or claw. "Well, what do you make of them, sir? Are you captivated too?"

"One represents the fertility of the earth, the other peaceful communion with the earth," said the historian matter-of-factly. "They hardly seem to me a threat to the state, inspector, but you'll make your report and take your orders."

The inspector popped his owlish eyes and worked his teeth. "My man said it was a threat, sir, and went on to prove his point in the most unfortunate way."

The historian kept a long meditative silence before he spoke again. "Do you remember once, inspector, speaking to me of a triangle made of house, foundry, and a third unidentified point C? Would it be possible to speak of that again?"

"No, sir. I'm not at liberty." The inspector's reply was abrupt and final. So the historian rose and extended his hand. "Until that happy hour, inspector, when both of us can make full and frank disclosures."

"Very well, sir." Kern wrung the historian's hand and quickly dropped it, as though it might propel the unquiet sensations of his brute body toward some violent plunge. The historian departed.

∽

"What are you doing here?" said Gorham. In the slant yellow light from the window the face of the great man was forbidding.

"I won't keep you long, sir. I've only come to make a plea in behalf of the doomed."

"I'm not interested. I told you to stay away from them. I also asked you not to come back here." It seemed that Gorham might rise and force his visitor out of the office. The historian said, "Give me just one minute, sir, please. It's pitiful. She asked me to take up my pen in their

cause. I have come instead to you, the master of the machine, to ask you
to stop it from crushing her."

"Take up your pen, Clio, by all means. It's the best in the land,
isn't it?"

"Please don't insult me, sir. You know it's too late for that, if there
ever was a time. You're the only one with the power in this case."

"And now you are insulting me, Clio, on two counts. First, I don't
give a damn. Second, you of all people should know I don't control the
machine. It goes its own way."

"You can at least keep it from destroying them."

Gorham's face was hard. "No I can't. I might hold it back for a
little while. But that would only make things worse in the long run, more
violent." He paused briefly. "You know all this, Clio. But go on. Stick
with them to the end. Nothing I've said has sunk in."

"Give them a week, sir."

"For what?"

"To disband."

"They don't need a week to disband."

"What will you give them, sir?"

"Three days. And I mean for a complete withdrawal—the cadres
broken up, the walls scrubbed, the rooms fixed, the men and women
sorted, and the stores at the house disposed of."

"Do you know, sir, in any detail what things you're speaking of?"

"I know the effects on the machine. That's all I need to know."

The historian shrugged. "Very well then, sir. I'll convey to them
your terms." After a momentary pause he went on. "It's something of a
mystery to me, sir, why the machine has delayed so long in dealing with
the Arondels. Kern, I warrant, has been raging for weeks to have at them."

"What's the mystery, Clio? The machine isn't brutal. It rattles
along doing its job until some deviants threaten to throw a monkey
wrench in it."

"Like the rearranging of factory labor."

"Yes."

Out beyond the window a cloud came and went, changing the
light, making the historian aware again of the striation of the great
man—the hair isometric, the brows hyphenated, the pinstripes of the

coat a methodical moiré. There was nothing here to suggest the operations of a clumsy machine. But there was, as before, a hint of convergence. "I think there's more to it than that, sir."

"What?"

"You, sir."

"Me?"

"Yes, you sir. I begin to appreciate your amplitude better. I see that you're rich, like a tapestry of the city. I see in you many scenes. One of them is the foundry. I think the foundry is yours. Is that true, sir?"

"It may be," said Gorham flatly. "You've studied our holding companies. It's likely I have an interest."

"But I think that you know, sir, that the foundry is yours."

"Suppose I do. Then what?"

"Then you have known from the beginning about the activities there."

"Be logical, Clio. Do you think that I go around poking in every nook and cranny of my properties?" The great man grunted. "From the beginning, you say? Tell me what a beginning is, cliometrician."

The historian nodded. "You're right, sir. There's no such thing as a beginning. Everything streams endlessly backward and forward." He stopped, as though confounded by complexity and indeterminancy, but then started up with animation. "What we can know are intersections, like point C."

"Point C again. You've found it, haven't you, Clio? The foundry, where the plots of the Arondels intersect the interests of the machine."

"No, sir, that's not an intersection. It's a carom. The foundry is point B. Point C is where the two worlds once actually mingled briefly, and having mingled are now joined, never to be parted." The historian looked sharply into Gorham's face, where he thought he detected, as on his last visit, a furtive disturbance. But suddenly Gorham made a triumphant smile, perhaps genuine. "Then point C is you, Clio. It's your initial."

"Very ingenious, sir."

"Not ingenious, Clio. Where else but in your head are the machine and the Arondels married?"

The historian leaned back and cogitated. "In my head, eh? Let me tell you something that came into my mind the other night just as I was dropping off to sleep. It was at the end of a strenuous day. I'd seen Kern, always a trial—for both of us. I'd been to the foundry. I'd had an unexpected visit with an old friend. I'd had a seance with Hannah Arondel. So my mind was pregnant, sir."

"No doubt."

"Have you ever been to the foundry, sir?"

"No, but I've heard that it's impressive."

"Why don't you go there, sir?"

"Because I have to captain the ship of state, Clio." There was humor in the great man's voice.

"Ah! Then you too have heard the siren call, and having heard it lashed yourself to the mast. Isn't that true, sir?"

Gorham didn't answer.

"I'll finish my story, sir. I was lying there in the Monongahela thinking, as often, about point C, and suddenly I was in a room, very much like this one, and in the presence of a personage very much like you, sir. And then suddenly the entire stage of my mind was folded over and two other persons appeared, a man and a woman." The historian stopped and searched the great man's face, but found nothing.

"I told you, Clio, space is treacherous."

"Yes, sir. I know you did. It makes me wonder if C is on the obverse of our reality, created by one of your catastrophic folds."

"It's the Arondels, not me, Clio, that created the catastrophic fold."

The historian cogitated. "Imagine," he said. "If the optic nerve didn't right our image of the world, we'd worship gravity instead of the sky gods. The good would go to her above, in the bowels of earth. The evil would fall down into the pit of the heavens." The historian arose slowly from his chair and walked into the right wing of the room. In front of him stood a towering glass-front bookcase. On his left were the tall windows flanked by heavy drapes. On his right was another set of bookcases. He turned slowly, as one tantalized by an elusive recognition. He let his eye fall here and there. He breathed deeply. He tilted his head upward, as if opening himself fully to the ambience of the space. Gorham watched him silently as he crossed with meditative step in front of the desk and went to the other side of the room, which was symmetrical with the first except that the bookcases were less extensive, to make room for an ample leather couch and a wing-back chair also upholstered in leather. Again the historian turned slowly and took in the aura of the room. At last he spoke. "I owe you a great debt, sir."

"What's that?"

"The lesson you taught me about the importance of space. You remember when I brought in my first draft on the tenderloin, you pointed out that I had no topography. You were certainly right, sir. An apprehension of space is indispensable." Gorham nodded silently, his face too deeply shadowed for the historian to see what moved in it, if anything. "Do you think, sir, that space is so completely defined by activity, like the tenderloin, that a percipient geographer can tell its functions and its occupants present and past?"

Gorham didn't answer, or move. The historian came back to his chair, sat down, and looked intently at the great man. At last Gorham spoke. "Have we come to the end, Clio?"

"I suppose so, sir. But I would be eternally grateful if you would favor me with an answer to the following question. When she was here, did you warn her that this was how it would end?" Gorham didn't answer. After a while the historian said, "What if she's the spirit of the time and we are the party of regression?"

"Then she'll win out in the end." The great man paused and then spoke again, this time with finality. "Send me the book, Clio. Don't come here again. We have raveled each other out." He didn't rise to offer his hand. So, after a slight hesitation, the historian arose and left the great man as he'd found him, seated dark and unmoving against the soiled sky.

∽

Outside, the brittle chill of winter's approach contended with a pall of dull smoke. Darkness began to fall, and the lamp man came along globing the dusk with pale blue. Foot traffic thinned and became more hurried. The historian went into a restaurant and ate. When he came out he was still tired. He thought of the hotel, of his room and bed. But when a cab rattled up, he seized his purpose, boarded, and directed the driver to 387 Rilton Street.

It was about eight when the cab pulled up in front of the Arondel house. Light seeped out around the parlor drapes. Along the street the horses of workingmen's carts were tethered to the fence. A meeting was in progress. "Park over there," said the historian to the driver, "and we'll wait."

"Wait, sir?"

"Yes, wait dammit. You'll be well paid."

The historian settled into the rough leather cushion. He thought that now he would rehearse arguments to persuade Mrs. Arondel to withdraw. The cab was cold. The horse snorted and stamped from time to time. The cabbie hunched dejectedly under a heavy blanket. It was a propitious time for crisp thought. But the construction of arguments eluded him. Instead, as he shut his eyes against the glum interior of the cab, there floated into his mind a dark shape rooted in the old heartland and pushing upward to a cold sea. Though there was no crest of crowned black bird, he recognized the entity. It was Germany, Hegel's Germany, the Germany of his school years—bad tobacco, fine beer, and inspired talk. But how dark and looming it was tonight. The cold sea beat against its embankments, and across the snowy ground fell barbed shadows, sharper than the fatal machines of the foundry, soldiery of the Götterdämmerung.

The historian opened his eyes. Across the way a cart horse backed to the end of its tether and neighed impatiently. The meeting was still in progress. The historian closed his eyes again. Germany did not reappear. Instead, there drifted along the dark curtain of his mind the face of his old mentor Tenace. What would he have to say about all this? The historian imagined him cocking his eye in that half-cynical, half-heartfelt way of his and saying, "You and me can't deal with the likes of her, boy—maimed as we are by the crazy widows of our youth, wifeless, worshipers of the word. She's not in Hegel's philosophy. Leave her to heaven, boy." He cackled and disappeared.

The cabbie turned with a huge and lugubrious effort. "What was that, sir?"

"Nothing." The historian stared dully across the way until his field of vision blurred and into it fell an imaginary snow, covering everything— ground, foundry, house, tower. And under the innocence of cold whiteness the fever of revolution and repression broke softly with a gentle suspiration and left its hosts calm and disburdened. And then he must have dozed off because the next time he opened his eyes the workers were coming out of the house. Some in fact had already reached the street and were loading up, four and five to the cart—men with caps and coats and good leather work boots, and women with serviceable skirts and shawls. They were sturdy people, purposeful in their movements. The historian watched until they were all gone. Then he saw a conveyance he hadn't noticed before, a coupe behind a gray horse, police observers inevitably. But it was the workers that occupied his thoughts. They weren't what he'd anticipated. Without explicitly acknowledging it to himself, he'd expected them to be fevered by an extravagant cultism. Well, and why shouldn't he? There were the murals and there was the exotic person of Hannah Arondel. There was Charlie Derwood's feverishness, and Jacob Arondel's hypnotic state. But the workers seemed to belie all that. They'd come out of the house not bursting with conspiratorial excitement, but walking together firmly, their voices pitched modestly to the tenor of their common purpose. It was no longer possible to think of them as subversive proselytizers, despite the talk of germ cells in factories throughout the city. But still there were the murals. The historian couldn't harmonize these contradictions. And he didn't have time now to think about them. He stepped out of the cab. "Wait." He proceeded to the door of the house. Behind him, the driver, locked in cold and misery, didn't bother to protest.

Jacob Arondel answered. Under the entry lamp his blue eyes shone brightly, but with an entirely external light. He hesitated momentarily and then swung the door open. "Come in."

"Thank you." The historian took off his coat and hat and hung them up, grateful for the warmth and the fragrance of pipe tobacco. "May I have a word with you and Mrs. Arondel? I'll be brief."

Arondel turned at the sound of steps, but it wasn't his wife who appeared at the end of the hall. It was Charlie Derwood, still wearing in the lapel of his checkered coat his badge of red flower, and on his face the flush of revolutionary fever. "Hello, Clio."

"Hello, Charlie."

Arondel stepped past Charlie and led the way into the parlor, where the chairs were arranged in a circle, some two dozen perhaps—a meeting of only the cadre leaders, the historian assumed. "Sit down," said Arondel. The three men sat apart. Presently Charlie said, "What news?" his voice betraying an unwholesome excitement.

"I'd hoped to speak to Mrs. Arondel."

"She'll be down momentarily," said Arondel. "She's changing."

"I am here," said Hannah Arondel, entering the room. She wore a long black housecoat and below its hem embroidered slippers, silver against black, a series of trifoil apertures within which were revealed miniature cleavages between the toes. The historian started to rise, but she motioned him down. "I heard you. I knew you would come back to us."

"Things have come to a head."

"Because of the murder of the young man?"

"I told you, the murder's only a pretext."

"Pah!" said Charlie disgustedly. "A nighthawk, and an accident at that. Not everybody has mastered the constabulary's art of nonlethal clubbing."

"It was a stabbing." The historian looked closely at Charlie, but found there nothing but the constant glaze of radical fever.

"What do you believe?" said Arondel.

"It doesn't matter what I believe," said the historian. "What I've come to tell you is that I've seen J. Gorham."

"What did he say?" asked Mrs. Arondel, sitting down near the historian and fixing him with her fire-flecked eyes.

"That he won't call Kern off."

"Kern is a brute," said Charlie with a hatred so pure and elemental that the historian had to admire it.

"So, fear him," the historian said. But it was clear that Charlie did not fear Kern. In his imagination, the historian guessed, he was already rushing ahead to some gorgeous conflagration, the apex of the colorist's career. The historian looked at Arondel. He was a similar case, gazing fixedly into the middle distance, on some fiery image perhaps of ultimate fidelity and doom. Only Mrs. Arondel seemed to attend to the historian. "We fear him," she said.

Was it possible, thought the historian, that she was at last beginning to consider their situation realistically? He said, "Then you see what has to be done."

"Yes," said Mrs. Arondel. "Now you will write for us."

The historian was stunned, not so much by the repetition of this old demand as by the confidence in Mrs. Arondel's voice. He shook his head slowly. "Whether I write for you or not is of no consequence, I assure you."

"He's telling the truth," said Charlie with a grim flatness. "The city is sealed tight as a drum. Even if McClure's rushed out a feature on the humane work we're doing and the horrors of police repression, it wouldn't have any effect downtown."

The historian nodded and gave Mrs. Arondel what he hoped would be a sympathetic but firm look. "You must withdraw."

"Withdraw! How?"

"Take down the murals. Send the women and children home. Hold no more meetings. Gorham will restrain Kern for three days."

Mrs. Arondel looked at the historian for some moments, her black eyes large, stippled with red, yet not incredulous or angry. She stood up, went to the mantel, and lighted an oil lamp. "Come with me," she said to the historian.

"Hannah . . ."

"No," said Mrs. Arondel, cutting her husband short. "He will see." The historian arose and followed Mrs. Arondel down the hallway to the cellar door. They passed the entry to the solarium, which was closed. Even so, the historian felt the force of the loom curling out through the frail fragrance of the blossoms that bloomed below the arching glass.

At the head of the cellar stairs, Mrs. Arondel said, "Even you believe we are people of violence. You believe we have a cellar of bombs. Come with me."

"I never said so," said the historian, descending the stairs in the backwash of Mrs. Arondel's lamp. The mixed odors of soil and coal rose up to meet them, and presently the historian felt the fading warmth of the furnace. When they reached the basement floor, Mrs. Arondel lifted her lamp to display the space. The historian had feared a cramped and oppressive cellar, but in fact it was spacious, almost airy, with a high ceiling and windows up at ground level along the east wall. These were dark now, but in the morning, he supposed, they would glow with sunlight.

"You see our great store of guns and bombs," said Mrs. Arondel, slowly turning full circle with her lamp lifted. But the historian only saw the woman herself, her hair a paradoxical halo of light and darkness, her black gown a counterpoint of sheen and shadow. His eyes fell to her feet, to the proliferative clefts revealed through the silver trifoils. What were the feet doing? They were not merely turning. They seemed to the historian to be engaged in some ritual act of communion with the earth of the cellar floor, tamping something into it, receiving from it in turn a pulse of energy.

"Come." Mrs. Arondel stopped turning and led the historian to the far wall of the basement, where she showed him a deep rack that reached from floor to ceiling, stretching some twenty feet wide and containing dozens of very large cubbyholes, almost every one of which held a scroll of thick paper. Mrs. Arondel handed the historian the lamp. "You hold it. I show you now our guns." Almost fiercely she pulled a scroll from the rack, unfurled it, and held it up to the light. It was a drawing of an ear. "This is our weapon."

In the first moment the ear startled the historian because it was so huge, a giant's ear. But a moment later he saw that it was quite beautiful, the conchlike concavity whorling slowly inward to the delicate dark canal that led down to the soft tympanum. Mrs. Arondel rolled the drawing back up, replaced it, and pulled out another. For some moments the historian couldn't identify it — a series of lines unwoven but shaped and held together by some implied force of purpose. His mind rushed off to Gorham, the man of lines, then to the loom, then back to the drawing itself. At last he saw. It was muscle. What had concealed its identity from him was its massive enlargement, its disproportion with everything around it, including the hands that had made it. Mrs. Arondel continued to hold the drawing under the light, obviously aware that the historian was arrested by it. And what exactly was the source of the thing's power, the historian wanted to understand. Was it simply the immense magnification of the musculature? Was it the privilege or the voyeuristic pleasure of seeing an interiority usually protected by integument? Some of that, thought the historian, but not principally. And then he began to perceive why his experience of the drawing was so charged. It began with an uncanny sense of collusion. His eye changed to meet the demands of the eye that had made the tissue. As a result, his sense of his own body began to change and vivify. He found that he could send his perception down into his thigh, in fact to a precise bundle of muscle in his thigh, and feel exactly its contraction and elongation, and thus feel microcosmically the pitch of his whole body and by extension the slope of the plain on which it stood and the force of the wind in its face. He felt himself teetering on the edge of a wholly transformed sense of his body. Disturbed, he looked away.

Mrs. Arondel rolled up the drawing of muscle and took out another scroll, and another, and another. There was a long bone luminous and strong. There was a section of elaborately reticulated tissue, perhaps a hugely enlarged retina. There was a finely ridged thumbnail, its forward edge pared to a thin cusp, the arc of lighter tissue rising up under the cuticle like an auroral bloom.

In each case the historian was careful to look away before his eye could be lured like a tranced voyager into those interior vistas of miraculous light. He said, his voice thick with wonder, "These are extraordinary."

"Because the men have put the body away under the machine. And now we take it out again. And earth too. Come." She took the lamp from the historian and led him to a long platform under the windows. On the platform lay a tapestry. Mrs. Arondel held the light over it. The historian ran his eyes back and forth in search of a central design. He couldn't find it, and so let his eyes settle into the details of the fabric, which turned out to be an amazingly dense and varied skein of grasses of all kinds—low and high grass, grass as erect as palings, grass so soft that it bent under the mere pressure of air, grass knotted thicker than hair, grass as wispy as fox fires, grass deep rooted in earth, grass afloat in the sea on bulbous islands, and all of it devouring the sun, sucking earth's sweetwater.

Mrs. Arondel took the historian's hand and sat them both down on the bed of grass. She set the lamp at their feet where its soft glow highlighted the cleavage of her toes and washed upward into their faces. She smiled, almost mischievously. The historian had never seen this expression on her face before. "See how the lamp pugs our nose and makes horns? You think we are two demons amidst our arms?"

"No, I don't think that."

"You think you are in an evil dream?"

"No, I don't think that either."

"You do not know what to think, do you?"

"Not precisely."

Mrs. Arondel put her hand on the historian's shoulder and pressed gently. "You are tired. Lie down in the grass." The historian resisted for a moment but then allowed himself to settle into the soft fabric. It didn't seem a perilous yielding. The hand that held his was soft and benign. The wide face in the wash of the lamp was smiling and kind. But then Mrs. Arondel bent over him, her housecoat parted at the neck and the powerful fragrance of her bosom pouring down. He breathed carefully. "Tell me. What did you plan to do with the drawings?"

"They will go up," said Mrs. Arondel lifting her free hand. "From the hands of the workers they will go up on the walls. So the work and the body are always one. You understand?"

"Yes, I understand."

"Then why are the men so afraid? They do not understand?"

"I think they understand. If the pictures go up, they come down."

"But they will have better."

"They can't believe that."

"But you believe it." As if for emphasis Mrs. Arondel increased the pressure on his hand and leaned closer to him. He thought maybe he saw the perfumed oil shining in her cleavage, but her bending had diminished the light. He said, "It doesn't matter what I believe."

"Yes, because if you are with us, we cannot lose."

This frightened the historian. Against the heat and fragrance of her body, powerful as it was, he felt he could fight successfully. But her proclamation of his virtual omnipotence filled him with a strange excitement. To combat it he said, "I can't do anything. Charlie told you so."

"Charlie's wrong." She brought her face close to his. "Don't say more. Gather up your strength." She put her finger on his lips, and then a moment later in a deepening dark and in a confusion of sensations she replaced the finger with her own lips.

Though the historian had allowed himself to slip down into a place from which no act of will could retrieve him, still he didn't succumb. And although only later would he fully understand his resistance, he knew intuitively even then it was pity that defeated her, his pity for this noble, mad, immense woman who must go about the man-chained world offering her body to free it and who encountered everywhere the maimed—Arondel, Charlie, himself, and yes, Gorham, too. The thought made the historian's mind swing wildly and angrily off to the tower. He took Mrs. Arondel's shoulders in his hands, thrust her away, and sat up, all with a strength far greater than he thought he had. He slipped his hands down onto her arms and held them firmly. "You don't want me. I have no power." He looked into her half-lit face. It registered the rebuff, but its pride was unbroken.

"So you always say and never try."

"Hannah, listen to me." The historian gave the arms a gentle shake. "Don't waste your time with me. Go back to Gorham. Make your own case with him."

"He will give me nothing." Mrs. Arondel registered no surprise at the historian's knowledge of her congress with the great man. He hadn't predicted that she would. But he also hadn't foreseen that her tone would preclude all possibility of contradiction. The historian dropped his hands. "I admire you greatly."

Mrs. Arondel said nothing. She continued to look at the historian, but with diminished interest. "Will you lead me back?" he said.

After some moments Mrs. Arondel took up the lamp, and slowly ascended the stairs.

In the parlor the historian had the distinct impression that Charlie and Arondel hadn't spoken, hadn't moved, hadn't even exchanged glances. Now they looked up and saw immediately from Mrs. Arondel's face that the historian had remained intractable despite his introduction to the mysteries of the basement. She set the lamp on the mantel and extinguished it. Arondel looked at the historian, obviously amazed again that he had once more resisted. Charlie showed neither surprise nor anger, but only disdain.

"I'm sorry," said the historian, "that I didn't have the power you thought I had."

"Go," said Mrs. Arondel. "They can strike us down. But the Socius will live and come back stronger."

"You are brave people," said the historian, but the words had no effect. He understood that he was dismissed. In fact, Charlie rose and made a very precise pantomime of a slap, his hand moving swiftly through the air, stopping sharply, and then drawing back. "Get thee behind us, Clio."

The historian looked one last time at his old partner, but the colorist's eyes brimmed with bitterness and fever. A moment later the historian went alone into the foyer. Alone he put on his coat and hat and alone stepped out into the night. On the other side of the street, before climbing into the cab, he stopped and looked back at the doomed house of Arondel. It was to have been the house of the Socius, full of images of the unity of all things, chanting the univocal chant of machine, earth, and humankind. But it was not to be. Could any house be? He thought of the house of his childhood with its bravely flying mansards and turrets and its high-leaping fish. And all around it the wind blew as it listed, and the voices of the plain—owl, coyote, cow—rose up in a great and wondrous cacophony.

Individuum est ineffabile, Gorham believed. He was wrong, of course. And yet who could ever know the immense weft of law that governed each of the everchanging moments of even the quietest night of the plain, much less the daylight moments of a teeming city? The historian looked up. Something was falling from the sky, pricking his face. He rubbed his fingers across his cheek and examined them in the dim light. They were streaked with moisture. It was cold. The police coupe suddenly came into view, globed in a tear that the wind had brought to his eye. A moment later his eyes were filled with tears—caused by the cold, by exhaustion, by sorrow. He couldn't separate them. He climbed into the cab and directed the driver to his hotel.

∽

That night, lying in the bed of his hotel room, the historian had a dream-vision that swung wildly back and forth between the familiar and the irreal, the profound and the cartoonish. It arose from a roiled mixture of jaundiced clouds and black smoke that darkened the windows of the tower. At his desk sat the man of lines. Between two lamps, in the

double pool of light, the hand that held the pen was twice imaged in
shadow on the paper. The pricks of the pen were quick and precise, a
cipher here, another there, the ledger balanced, the idiosyncrasies of the
populace called to account, marshalled in the ranks of law.

Now came the woman Hannah Arondel, not Arondel really of
course, but some name a poet of old Persia might have written, with an
impossible Q in the beginning and a final syllable that echoed in the ear
like the lament of a mateless nightsinger. The two began to talk to each
other, or to sing to each other. And when it became clear that this wooing
would continue for a time, the historian, his eye mounted in the skull of
an accipiter, went swooping up and down the city. There he saw heat
shimmering above roofs like the remnant of a bereaved spirit, saw the
spume from stacks dimming countenance and carriage along the street,
saw the blue light from gas lamps creating on patrician faces a shadow
that jutted forehead and crooked nose demonically, saw the rote of smoke
in stone doing its devilish work. Meanwhile, the woman's voice rose up to
the high ceiling and insinuated itself into the deepest shadow, even into
the close grain of the oak beams so that the whole room began to swell
and reverberate with the name of the king of the city. And all the while,
of course, the striped suit of the man of lines unraveled, and the black
effluence of the woman's gown poured down from her breasts. The regimental stripes of the man's tie fell bravely in rank, and his starched shirt
withered and evaporated as in a fire. The woman's skirt loosened and
rustled away into the corner, where it was consumed by hungry shadow.
Thus, presently the two stood naked in the limited light of the two
lamps—stood so, in fact, for a long time before they moved off into the
shadow. But the historian never saw them embrace, because from outside
the window there came a cynical laugh, a jackal's laugh. The historian
rushed to the glass. "Tenace!" he shouted angrily. "Tenace!"

But the laughter only deepened and grew blowsy with beer and
German bumptiousness—the mad belching laughter of old München.
From this it took up a more regular rhythm and purified itself into a
laughing mantra, then dilated again into a cosmic Buddha's laugh, and
finally became Rabelaisian, Brobdingnagian, deafening. From his high
perch on the windowsill the historian saw a cannonade of spittle, huge
and deadly laden with garlic and ale, batter smeltries and factories and

topple stacks. And then the laughter declined to a chuckling fusillade of grapeshot, which nevertheless terrified the populace with its doomsday rattle against house and shop, and then the laughter stopped altogether with an unaccountable benignity. And the people came out under a new sky and marveled that the gods of time had spared them yet a while longer.

And when the laughter stopped, the dramatis personae of the historian's mind quickly exited—the trysters of point C and the amazed populace of the city of steel. Even the backdrop of the ruined and rubblous metropolis had no tenancy or salience beyond the surface of the eye and fled the moment the lights were dimmed.

And so the historian slept, too exhausted to undress, lying in an uneasy sprawl on the rented bedspread of ersatz Indian diagonals.

Yesterday at three-thirty in the afternoon, special squadrons of crack riot police made simultaneous raids on anarchist elements at 387 Rilton Street and at the Pitcairn Foundry.

At the latter location, although the Force under the able direction of Inspector Russell Kern struck swiftly and efficiently, their approach was alarumed to the anarchists within, who formed a human clot horrible to behold. On the outer rings men linked arms with men. Within, women clasped each other as well as a clutch of bawling infants. Readers who are confounded to learn of the presence of women and children in a foundry must understand that in the cadres of this especially perfidious sect of anarchy a sort of indiscriminate community of sexes and ages, to the confusion of their natural functions, went forward under the aegis of a chimerical egalitarianism.

Upon the entrance of the officers of law this aforesaid human clot set up a horrid chant that sounded in this reporter's ears—and by later testimony similarly in the ears of others—like nothing so much as the veritable banshee cry of a lost libertinism. In short, the mass wailed and keened so horribly because it knew it must now lose the black prizes and pleasures of a thoroughgoing lawlessness. In fact, this massing and moaning so astounded eye and ear that for some moments our sturdy constabulary hardly knew how to proceed against the conglomerate— not out of fear for their own safety but out of humane concern for the welfare of the benighted souls who must if possible be returned to the order and succor of normal society.

Inspector Kern, ever resourceful in these grim matters, on this occasion worked out an especially ingenious stratagem, which was simply to break down the tenacious organism cell by cell, removing one man and then the next. Thus were the arrests made without harm to the misguided wretches of the foundry, and most particularly the infants, whose tender age was assurance against the infections of their elders and who, we trust, will now be safely placed in the hands of loving foster parents until such day, if ever it happily come, that those who begot them are thoroughly cleansed and reclaimed.

Unfortunately, two fatalities marred this gallant work. Neither, however, was due to a flaw in the well-designed and executed police procedures, which will ever remain testamentary proof of the humanity of Inspector Kern and the Force. One involved a former police agent who, subverted by the wild visions and excesses of the anarchists, had attached himself to their perverse community. He, seeing that the eventual dismemberment of the body anarchic was inevitable, as well as his own arrest by the very powers of law from which he had defected, broke loose from his still chanting comrades, raced across the foundry floor, and before the police could stop him, took the steel casing of the factory's dynamo in a fatal embrace. At this point the electric lamps were almost totally extinguished, leaving the foundry to be illuminated principally by a pale glow from the skylight above. And just then, had it not been for their fanatical self-enchainment, some several of the inmates of perdition might well have made good their escape through the darksome confusion within the confines. Meanwhile, the dynamo first fastened and charged its suicidal victim, then charred, stiffened, and discarded him, resuming its appointed task of sending current to the wall lamps. Thus was the foundry once again illuminated—and thus, alas, was it once again demonstrated that too often our machines are more dependable than their keepers.

The other fatality was a more ordinary case of mad-dog violence. An improbable personage wearing a checkered jacket mounted by a red carnation and sporting a cocky hat, an apparition from the theatrical districts of New York City, threw himself at the officers most frenziedly, wielding a billy club. Such was the fury of his attack that every effort to control him manually was defeated so that in the end the officers had to resort to use of their own sticks. One blow proved fatal unfortunately. Blood ran from the criminal's ear and he was some time later officially pronounced dead by the coroner, who also issued a statement to the effect that it was very likely that the dead man suffered a congenital defect of the brain or one of the social diseases so common among such libertine groups. Thus was the violence of the attack explained, the restraint of the police affirmed, and their behavior vindicated without the smallest exception.

Once the police had disengaged the male members of the cadre and carried them away in wagons provided for the purpose, the females were somewhat easier to disentangle, though even among them there was a frantic and almost piteous tenacity which attached itself to the central member of the mad circle. This personage is a certain Hannah Arondel, married to Jacob Arondel or at least cohabitating with him. Readers will recall Mr. Arondel's extravagant reformist idealism, his misguided campaign for the mayoralty some years ago, and after that his abrupt disappearance from public life. More will be reported of him in a moment. What remains to be said here is that Hannah Arondel (née we know not what) functioned as a kind of queen bee of the foundry hive, a very large woman stuffed no doubt with unspeakable sweets fetched by her innumerable drones. There can be no doubt that she has been the evil genius of the cadre and that the law will fall most heavily on her. Even as the officers escorted her away, last of the host, she continued her inces-sant chant, like an automaton. Of foreign extraction, though precisely what strain or strains is not known, she may or may not be a citizen. Her face was fixed and her hair frizzled as though electrified. She seemed quite mad.

Once the cadre had been removed, there remained the murals to be dealt with. These Inspector Kern ordered obliterated immediately. One of his lieutenants suggested the simpler expedient of merely painting over them, but Inspector Kern wisely chose the course of complete extirpation, for if these monstrosities were left as a kind of palimpsest, who knows what message future generations might read there to our disgrace and their own moral peril. In short, then, there were two large paintings, the work, we are told, of diverse hands, so that many have been infected not only by the sight of them but also by their execution. As for their content, let the upright reader of these pages be satisfied to understand that upon first glance they seemed merely crude and bizarre, but closer scrutiny revealed their devilish purpose, which was to confound in the ostensible images of child and woman not only the sexes, but even the basic functions of the bodies which they so nakedly and forwardly presented. This corruption, not in the least attenuated by certain fantastical idealizations of machine and nature, was their essence. Enough said. This reporter did not wish to expose himself longer than was necessary to give an accurate account as required by his profession. It was with great satisfaction that he noted before his departure the considerable progress in effacement that Inspector Kern's men were making with the abrasives with which they had so percipiently been provided.

Of the raid at 387 Rilton there is less to be said. This reporter, taken up with events at the foundry, was, of course, not present. His assistant, however, gives the following account.

Only the proprietor of the house, Jacob Arondel, was present. He was discovered in the cellar, where he was burning papers in the furnace. These no doubt included records of the nefarious cadre. It is also certain that he had burned some fabrics or weavings, for when the officers arrived under the command of Captain Wirtz, Inspector Kern's chief assistant, they smelled the distinct odor of scorched wool. All that remained intact, however, in the pile that Arondel had prepared for conflagration were several drawings of the same ilk as the murals at the foundry. These were unfurled, examined briefly by the officers, and seized as material evidence. My assistant, perceptive but youthful I might add, got only a brief glimpse. He was galvanized, he reports, by their obscene imagery of androgyny, fleshiness, and pullulation.

Elsewhere, the house was ordinary in its appointments, though it has long been known by the police that it was used for meetings of the cult. There was, however, in a solarium recently added to the premises, a large loom of ancient provenance, rather stately withal. Whatever had been in progress on its bed was brutally cut away, however. Frayed ends of weft and warp still hung about the machine, and fragments of cloth lay about the floor.

Arondel himself was described as being in a state of demented purposefulness. He hardly seemed aware of the advent of the Law, even up to the moment the officers seized from him the remaining drawings and shut the furnace door. Thereafter he said nothing, but remained in an agitated state. He offered no resistance when the officers led him away to be taken to the jail, where he will find numerous company of his own kind. Our reporter speculates that though Arondel's primary motive was no doubt to destroy evidence, there was also in his extraordinary willfulness something of an act of renunciation. No doubt the upcoming investigations and trial will clarify all this.

Post Scriptum. There is just time before going to press to offer the following two additions to the story above.

First. Inspector Kern reports that there are the seedlings of anarchistic cadres in several other factories of the city, offshoots of the Arondel conspiracy, but that these shall be quickly uprooted. All the deeper grows our gratitude to the inspector for his tireless vigilance.

Second. The man who died in his violent assault on the police is reported to be Mark Marcus, a former contributor to the now defunct leftist organ, *The Masses.* It is believed that this same man may be connected with the recent murder of Paul Sommes, a young member of Inspector Kern's corps of plainclothes detectives. His exact relationship to Mrs. Arondel and to the erotic and cultist aspects of the cadre is also under investigation.

This paper will, of course, report in the timeliest possible fashion all sequels to these bizarre and shocking events.

∽

The historian set the newspaper aside. He had no intention of mulling over this tawdry narrative of the end of the Socius. In three days he would leave the city. He would read no further accounts of charges, arraignments, trials, or the like, whatever their notoriety. He was deeply sorry for the Arondels and Charlie and the workers, but he intended to wash the whole affair from memory. He would put out of mind all images of Hannah Arondel at her loom or drawing table fashioning the mystic representations of the new order. He would refuse to

hear again the low rolling cadence of Arondel's voice playing to his
wife's descants of enchantment. He would not think of Charlie
Derwood, alias Mark Marcus, into whose ear the fatal flights entered
as song and issued as blood.

So the historian pushed the Socius from his mind and returned to
his work. By the time he left the city he would have completed the book,
had it copied and sent for commentary to Gorham—whom he would
never see again, but that was all right because he wanted now only the
product, and not the presence, of that extraordinary mind. Gorham
would write a preface, and the historian would write an acknowledge-
ment setting forth most graciously his debt to the great man.

The historian could feel the book in his hand. It was, though
scarcely two hundred pages, weighty. It was stoutly stitched and bound
between thick covers, the pages deeply recessed. It was made to last.
What would the title be? The historian smiled. He would like to call it
A Prolegomenon to the End of History, but of course they couldn't permit that
title. Let it, then, have an innocent title: *An Introduction to Urban Structures
and Dynamics.* In any case there certainly would be no fetching frontis-
piece, no photograph of vaunting stacks and towering buildings, or the
like—only the title page printed in a strong blocky sans serif. And then
would come Gorham's brief preface. First there would be a word about
the author, his nativity near old Sacramento, his boyhood on the plains,
his student days in Berkeley and later in Germany, where he studied
under Kuns Fischer and Wilhelm Wundt and roistered with the young
Hegelians of the Blüthe, a good man fallen among metaphysicians . . .
"Thereafter, initially under the tutelage of John Tenace, he became a
journalist, an investigator and inspector of the problematical aspects of
city life, rising to the first rank among those known as 'muckrackers.'
Then, seven years later, he extracted himself from the journalistic field
and became a notable portraitist of prototypical personages, winning the
highest awards in the field of interpretive biography. Then, through the
action of a catalyst not fully understood by the author himself, he
became the first 'cliometrician' if we may introduce a new term into an
old field of inquiry. By this we mean that he found a way, through
mathematical dynamics, into the inner sanctum of the American city.
Unlike the Empiricists, he avoided the fallacious rearing of abstractions

on so-called fixed facts, the familiar inductive method. Unlike the Idealists, he avoided the imposition of spirit on matter, despite his youthful Hegelianism. Instead, depending on extraordinarily keen intuitions, both material and mathematical, and on an unfaltering faith in law, he entered the difficult circuit of structure and detail, mind and substance. The result is that this work marks the end of history as we have known it, which was actually a prehistory of old stories. Consequently, we are now liberated from the old contentions between pattern and narrative. We enter an era of almost pure dynamism. It will be the task of coming generations to set forth with ever finer precision the kinetics of all our sociopsychological processes. And all future investigators will owe a considerable debt to this brave pioneer."

The historian was well satisfied.

On his last afternoon in the city the historian hired a cab and directed the driver to take him to the top of the hill above the confluence of the two rivers. It was no great surprise that he had brought Tenace along with him. The two old newspapermen debouched from the cab and stood together looking over the city. It was cold and damp, but the first real snow was yet to come. Below, mist and low-lying smoke obscured the streets and stacks of the city. Tenace swept his hand over the soupy spectacle. "Whatever possessed you to come to a burg like this, boy?"

"It's the pure essence of the American city."

"Phoo! It looks like the goop the Irish and the Jews ate, and smells like it too." The old newspaperman shook his head and then pointed down to the river. "What's that?"

"A tug with a string of ore barges. It reminds me of my old *Schlepper.*"

"It looks like a sludge-eating eel to me. This is an awful place, boy."

"I don't remember that the New York you showed me was any garden spot."

Tenace chuckled, then stopped abruptly. "What did you think of the article on the raids?"

"There was a lot of bunkum in it."

"Yep, but without bunkum you don't have news. You know that, boy." Tenace spoke decisively and without expectation of reply, so the historian remained silent while his old mentor continued to scan the city. "They can't stop 'em though."

"Who can't stop who?"

"The police can't stop the revolutionaries, what's their name?"

"Arondel. But they did stop them."

"You know better than that, boy. The business of America is revolution. That's what makes us different from the rest. The business of the British, for instance, is custom and law. The business of the French is to show that an idea still lives after it is severed from the head that conceived it. The business of the Germans, as you know, is to convert law into metaphysics. But watch out for the Russians. Winter and vodka and sheer distance have made them mad and there's no telling what they'll do." The historian laughed, but Tenace was sober. "That's old stuff, boy. Tell me what's new. What did you learn here? Because you were ever a learner."

"I learned to look through cold clear eyes—what you tried to teach me in the first place."

"And what I never learned myself, but then neither did Riis—a couple of incorrigible old sentimentalists."

"The two greatest hearts of the profession."

Tenace waved off the compliment and turned his attention to the city again. "Something's writing a message in that filthy sky down there."

"What does it say?"

Tenace shook his head. "I don't know. We got a bad angle. You spend all your life trying to get the right angle. You never do. But you already knew that, boy, because you're a newspaperman at heart."

No, the historian doubted that he was. But anyway, at that moment, almost involuntarily, the historian took leave of his old mentor sailed out in his imagination like a godhawk and peered down on the design below. Clean of appetency he was, and clear of eye. And this is what he saw there in the city at the confluence of the two rivers: point A, a once-brave house that flew its mansard across the rolling skies of old Sacramento, huddled now below the heavy smog; point B, a stone foundry, its stack mysteriously smokeless; point C, a tower, the fatal tryst of the man of lines and the nightsinger. His eyes remained fixed on the facade of the building, where the lighted windows inscribed a sort of hieroglyph, the kind that rings ancient obelisks. It seemed intended to augment the script that Tenace had tried to read in the clouds and smoke. Perhaps it represented an old narrative of the city's birthing and subsequent travails. But the godhawk would have no traffic with it, for to such an eye one thing is clear above all else: the fatality of writing, which leads to story, which leads to death. Imprisoned below, in fact, was another hawk-faced man and his wildly singing wife, who had not only tried to fly the nets of story but had even dreamed of soaring above language itself into the realm of pure song, which proved a vaunting and unwise aspiration, for now they were hopelessly trammeled in a most vulgar and public plot. Alas.

The historian tipped his wings and sailed back to the hill. He would tell his old mentor that what he had learned in this infernal city was the falsity and fatality of story. But even as he dropped his talons and folded his wings he saw that Tenace had lost color and was rapidly fading into the gray afternoon.

The Robbery

The Great Plains, 1912

So once again they were headed west, this time in the private car of
Alfred P_____. The car had been transferred from the New York City-
Adirondack line, where it was used to convey Mr. P, family, and guests to
and from Bantry House on the shore of Comsequah Lake. Beautifully
appointed in golden oak and dark mahogany, the car contained sleeping
accommodations for four, bath, salon, study, diner, and compact
kitchen. The salon and diner lamps had frosted chimneys and floral
flanks, the sleeper and study lamps damask shades in pink and rose. On
this occasion Portney, the cook, wasn't on the train, so meals were
brought in by special arrangement from the common diner. The historian and his cousin Simms would have the car to themselves until the
train reached Grand Junction, where Mr. and Mrs. P would board,
having taken a private conveyance down from Cashcou, Mr. P being an
amateur naturalist and Mrs. P a landscape painter. Indeed, there was a
notable example of her art on the salon wall—Lake Champlain at dusk,
a swirl of vast dying fire, the shoreline's ordinary marge of blue and green
consumed by the tawny flare of the setting sun, all in thick bravura
strokes that dazzled the historian's eye in the bright light that shone in
from the streaming September prairie. "It's half Turner and half Hudson
River School," the historian said, "but also entirely her own."

Simms looked at the painting, nodded assent, and returned to the
occupation of watching the wheat speed by. There was nothing impolite
in his rather cursory glance at the painting or aggressively antisocial in
his preoccupation with the prairie. He was genuinely fascinated. The

historian saw that and waited until his cousin should choose to break the silence again, which he did some minutes later. "Does it seem strange to you that a machine can change the face of a nation?"

"The train?"

"Well, the train will do, dotting and spurring its lines with people. But actually I was thinking of the thresher, which has made possible these vast golden fields innocent of the unsightly habitations of man." Simms stirred in his shapeless sack of woolen suit and grunted like an old bear. He was grizzled on top and about the muzzle. The historian smiled and nodded.

Simms said, "Tell me, coz, as the most brilliant historian of our era, what will happen when the machines no longer need many men for their operation? Won't we have a dangerous mixture of superabundance and unemployment?"

"No. Your question is based on two false premises—one having to do with my attainments, which is more or less incidental. But the other is germane. You assume that meaningful employment is devoted to production, whereas even subsistence cultures have always provided a livelihood for bards, shamans, healers, bead-makers, and the like."

Simms grunted and smiled. "Even historians."

"Oh yes. Lawyers, judges, and politicians, too. And don't forget warriors."

"They're going to have another war in Europe, aren't they?" Simms looked closely at his cousin.

"I don't see how it's to be avoided. And this time we'll get into it." Simms looked away in disgust. But the wheat fields were gone. In their place sprang up a low dry scrabble dotted here and there with clumps of stunted, wind-bent trees. The sun itself seemed to take less interest in this scene and began to race out in front of the train, leaving the vegetation with long shadows of indifferent definition.

After a while Simms said, "The sun is below the yard arm, coz. In fact, in our native Boston it's already night, the commons and the old church and the other scenes of our youthful triumphs all dark. Therefore it's time to comfort ourselves with whiskey. Will you pour? I don't trust my paws on that crystal decanter."

The historian found some elegant goblets and poured from crystal

to crystal. The cousins touched glasses and drank—"To the West,"
they said almost simultaneously, and talked a bit about the great salt lake
to come and the mountains and San Francisco. But presently Simms
grew restless. "Let's go back to the club car," he said, "and listen to the
voices of America."

The car was crowded, but a small gentleman motioned them to his
booth and they pushed in gratefully.

"Very kind of you, my friend," said Simms, introducing himself
and his cousin and discovering in turn that their benefactor was one Carl
Durban of Pittsburgh, an agent for manufacturers. But to the historian
he had rather the appearance of a professional gambler or spielman, his
hair slick, his shirt pearl-buttoned, and his checkered jacket decorated
upon the lapel with a red carnation. "The pleasure is mine," said
Durban.

"But the drinks are on us," said Simms. "My cousin will pay."

"With joy," said the historian. And when they had them in hand,
Simms said again, "To the West," and then presently, "What propels
you across these vast plains, Mr. Durban?"

"Money," said the little man with a sharp, toothy smile that
seemed to the historian mirthless and even mischievous. But since the
answer didn't seem to interest Simms much, the historian felt obliged to
pursue the matter. "And what do you sell, Mr. Durban?"

"Physics," said Durban, giving them again his mordacious smile.

This rekindled Simms' interest. "In what form, Mr. Durban?"

"In the material embodiment of the laws."

"Such as?"

"The laws governing the forces created when magnetic poles are
reversed, as in dynamos; the laws of cams that convert rotary to linear
motion, as in die works, mills, and looms. That kind of thing, sir."
Durban looked firmly into Simms' eye. "I never sell merely a machine,
Mr. Simms. That's criminal. The client doesn't understand the chain of
forces that stamps out the nail he wishes to sell to his customers. And
failing to understand that, he can't understand his opportunities for
expansion. In short, I'm basically an educator."

Simms held out his glass. "To you, Mr. Durban. I don't think
Justice Holmes himself could've given a nobler account of his profession."

The historian drank along with his cousin. And yet he couldn't suppress the distinct image he had of Durban as a sort of rodent, sub-social, perhaps even criminal. Something of this came out in Durban's next words to Simms. "I thank you for the compliment, Mr. Simms, but I'm not warmed by the comparison."

"Why's that?"

"Because your judge is of a profession built on sand."

"Why do you say so?"

"I mean that the whole idea of the legal system is erected on a false analogy, sir. In nature there are indeed laws. And if one doesn't adhere to them, he'll be pitched out, crushed. But the so-called laws of society are a subterfuge, an arrangement of forces that hampers the dynamism of men in natural relationships."

Simms stroked his beard. In this gesture the historian perceived a mixture of playfulness and genuine cogitation. "I'm surprised to hear this, Mr. Durban. Hasn't it been pretty well established that these very railroads have acted outside the restraints of law and that the result of this lawlessness has been to line the pockets of a very few, who have acquired yachts and castles and other things perfectly useless to society as a whole?"

Durban smiled a sharp smile of triumph. "Precisely my point, sir. The reason the railroads are able to plunder us is that there are laws preventing retaliation. And that's the way it always is. When this is perceived, a new law is passed which attempts to recompense the enfeebled by lifting them up beyond parity. And then a law must be passed in behalf of the original group, and on and on until our relationships are not based on interest and ability but on a huge heap of worthless laws. And if Justice Holmes bestrides this heap with more style than others, it's still a stinking meddlesome rubble."

Simms turned to his cousin. "Mr. Durban is a man of conviction."

"He is indeed," said the historian. "I take it, sir, that you find much to admire in Darwin."

"Much, sir, but we humans aren't quite so simple as your black and white jinnies."

It had been the historian's intention, whatever Durban's reply, to point out that lawfulness was a principal characteristic of Darwin's theory and that Durban's own theory of open relationships really presupposed some system of social law. But the contradictions in the little ratman's position failed to secure his interest. Instead, his mind drifted out into the dark moonless sky above the rolling plains. Momentarily, his imagination converted the plains, however improbably, to Boston. He was there walking on new snow, which seemed to have a luminosity of its own, as though falling down the winter sky it had captured in its crystalline structure small essences of star light. Simms was tramping beside him. In any deep shadow the Irish might be lurking in wait for them, but they plunged on, invincible, immortal in their youth. How painful it was, then, to see the whited head of hair and the grizzled beard of his cousin, who had gone on talking to Durban with good show of interest and purpose.

Presently, the historian took out his grandfather's watch, snapped open the golden lid, and announced that it was time he and his cousin retired for supper. Durban's eye affixed the shine of the timepiece as a predator will its darting quarry, but this caused no hitch in his valediction. "I trust you gentlemen will enjoy your journey in Mr. P's car."

"We will," said Simms, rising beside his cousin, "but we're a little isolated and may well see you here again."

"I hope so." Durban offered his hand and gave them each a quick energetic shake.

∽

The dinner served to them was roasted chicken, twice-baked potatoes, julienne beans, and apple pie. The steward also produced from the kitchen icebox a splendid bottle of Meursault. Both men ate with gusto, Simms consuming his potato skins and gnawing the joints of the chicken as if they and not the flesh were the pièces de résistance. He looked at the historian and smiled. "I'd be ashamed of my gourmandizing, coz, if you weren't wallowing the wine around on your tongue like a decadent duke of Burgundy."

The historian laughed. And after the steward came and cleared everything away, he said, "If I hadn't sworn abjuration, I'd sit down and write, there on the lovely little greensward of the desk, under those pretty pink lights, and with broad strokes so that they'd be less affected by the sway of the train."

"What would you write, coz?"

"Oh, just a little sketch of our friend Durban. He seems too good to lose."

"Why then, go to it, man. It'll ease your heart and aid your digestion." Simms got up and went into the little study. "Come in now and sit down."

The historian entered and took the small chair before the writing desk, almost shyly.

"Now write," said Simms. "And I'll sit here and gaze out into the night and listen to the mellifluous scratch of your pen. And if perchance you care to mumble now and again a snatch of your composition, it'll drone in my ear like a golden bee."

The historian nodded. From his pocket he took a pignut and set it on the writing table. "My god," said Simms, "the same?"

The historian laughed. "No, this is the third. The first two grew punky. But I think that this one will last the duration." He took a sheet of paper from the little shelf above and a pen from the tray. He unstoppered the inkwell, dipped his nib, and after a brief moment's pause wrote a few words.

"What color is the ink?" said Simms.

"Midnight blue."

"Good."

The historian wrote. "I am writing," he said, "that Durban is one of a new breed of Americans, a creature of machines and speed. His molecules are much agitated by speed. We would not, of course, want them absolutely motionless, for then they would decay into a kind of zero dust. But his are entirely too frenetic."

The scratch of the pen and the historian's voice paused simultaneously. The train hit a ragged section of track, rattled and yawed, and then smoothed out again. The historian went on. "Somebody in Germany has said that there is no matter, only motion and fields of force."

"You'd expect the Germans to say something like that, and then try to prove it with war machines."

"Such speed," continued the historian, "destroys all sense of collectivity. Every individual is hurtled off into his own orbit and imagines himself absolute, a law unto himself. And so you have Durbans."

"It's a damned fool thing to do," said Simms. "If a man wants to cross a continent, he should walk it, get the feel of it in his legs. What otherwise could be the point of it?" He rose up angrily. "I'm going to walk up and down this blasphemous hurtling piece of steel a little bit. Maybe it'll settle my nerves. You go on writing. It's good. See that it gets published in every paper in America."

∽

The next morning the historian awoke to discover Simms squatting naked on his haunches in the salon. Shafts of sunlight from behind the train sliced through the pane, lay along the rich wainscoting, and touched the rug at Simms' feet. In the clear pane itself there shone a faint whorl of minuscule scratches, the patina of city soot and Adirondack winds. But Simms was oblivious to all these wonders of light, his eyes closed, his mouth open slightly, and his breathing deep and slower even than the long sway of the train. He seemed scarcely animate, his cullions swinging almost imperceptibly with the roll of the locomotive. The historian didn't disturb him, and when the steward came, he told the astonished Negro that Simms had a back condition that required very specific morning exercises, but that he should bring breakfast along in a half hour or so, at which time he could also make the beds.

At table the two men were unusually quiet, Simms grinding up his bacon and rusk with great gusto but leaving his eggs to stare cold and congealed up from the white plate, which was gilt-edged and monogrammed with a fantastical calligraphic P so complex and brilliantly aureate as to be virtually indecipherable. It made Simms smile. But presently, cupping his tea in the palms of both hands, he stared out the window, where the sun was beginning to flame on butte and mesa. The historian allowed him some moments before speaking. "What are you thinking?"

"I'm thinking," said Simms, "that if we were hawks hovering in the wind out there and looking down, we'd see a pattern composed of canyons and arroyos, each with its own little system of rivulets and windrows. And it wouldn't be to us, if we were hawks, something titanic and hopelessly labyrinthine but merely a convenient run for our quarry, because the quarry, no matter how agilely it twists and turns, must sooner or later come under the shadow of our descent." Simms took a swallow of tea. "Is that how you were thinking of it, coz?" He smiled broadly.

"No, not exactly. I was thinking of this train track with its rails and cross-ties and ballast as a battlement. And we're the sentinels of the lord of the castle, guarding against an uprising."

"Of Indians?"

"No, of nature."

"And who's the lord of the castle?"

"I don't know."

"Is it history?"

The historian frowned comically. "How contracted you must think my soul, cousin."

"Not at all. Many think of history as conquest."

"I suppose so. And I myself may have once thought something like that, but now I think that evolution is deeper than history and more in tune with nature. It's down in the body, molecular, like the changes in Durban."

"Well, you, a historian, were writing about Durban just last night."

"Yes, but probably I wasn't writing history at that moment."

"What was it?"

"Speculation, I suppose—metaphysical portraiture."

"You're clever, coz." Simms twiddled his beard. "I hope you'll continue so when our fellow travelers join us, for I've lost the knack of conversation."

"You needn't worry about that. Alfred is a great naturalist and will extract from you accounts of your trampings about the continent. And then I can hear them, for you've never considered me an appropriate receptacle."

"I most certainly have," said Simms with comic hurt and insistence. "I've told you that I went out into the forest and found birds and animals there and streams there. And I was there. That was the miracle of it. We were there, together. I'm still there. It's endless. But you, you churlish historian, you expect some wondrous tale, I suppose, of being borne aloft by an eagle and dropped on the edge of a pit of vipers and then being saved and suckled by wolves and so forth. And I suppose Mr. P will expect the same. More's the pity."

The historian laughed heartily while Simms looked glumly out the window. "There are a million million things to see out there, historian, but we won't see a fraction of them, too busy whizzing along to San Francisco, whoever he was."

Again the historian laughed. "Well perhaps Mrs. P'll be able to tease some scraps of conversation out of you. I understand she's quite fetching."

"You mean you don't know her?"

"No. I know Alfred well but not his wife."

"A recent acquisition is she?"

"Or he is." The historian smiled. "I understand she comes from an obscure and improbable background."

"I thought from the way you were talking she was a famous painter."

"There is at the moment unfortunately no such thing as a famous woman painter."

∽

In fact, when the train stopped in Grand Junction, only Mrs. P appeared, sans husband. After the bustle of stowing her trunks had subsided, she explained to her guests, "You'll have to forgive my husband, gentlemen. He's with an Indian named La Flecha. They're searching for a rare kind of bird that never flies but always runs along the ground." This was reported entirely factually and without any implication that the lady thought it folly. And in any case, sarcasm would have ill become her. She was a beautiful woman in her late thirties, with hair that glowed between honey and maple and with the frankest green-brown eyes the historian had ever seen.

"We're sorry to miss Alfred. I hope you haven't inconvenienced yourself on our account."

"Call me Celia. Not at all. The country is grand but finally over-powering and wearying. I have enough in my sketchbook and in my memory to keep me busy for years. Now, if you gentlemen will excuse me, I itch for a bath. I absolutely crave a bath."

"Certainly. The steward has just been through to clean, so I trust you won't be troubled by snippets of my cousin's beard."

Mrs. P smiled. "I hope not, or they'll surely make me sneeze." So saying, she left them, snapping shut behind her the curtain that sepa-rated the salon from the sleeping quarters. Presently there was the sound of trunk tops and dresser drawers opening and shutting purposefully, and the mixed fragrance of fields, toilet preparations, and a woman's body. The two gentlemen, who had removed themselves to the study, were nevertheless silent until the sound of running water could be heard over the rhythm of the train. Then Simms said, "Do you know where he got her?"

"In San Francisco, I understand. A girl of the golden west."

"A Pygmalion case?"

"I don't know, but I wouldn't think so. She doesn't appear to me transmuted, or even transmutable, do you think?"

"No, she doesn't."

Some further light was shed on these matters when Mrs. P reap-peared in a long housecoat, her wet hair in a turban of towel. She smelled pleasantly of bath oil. "Excuse my informality," she said, "but it's necessary even in this limited space to be comfortable."

"By all means, madam," said the historian, "but you mustn't encourage my cousin Simms too far. He's accustomed to living in the forest in a loincloth."

Mrs. P laughed. "And eating wild honey and locusts and prophesy-ing. Then do spare us that, Mr. Simms. I've had quite enough of the primitive this trip." Simms smiled good-naturedly. Mrs. P went on. "So we have here a historian and a man of nature, neither of whom seems to be the least interested in what I am. It's disconcerting." Mrs. P pretended to pout.

"Oh, we're very interested, madam," said the historian, "but in congress with ladies we're both somewhat backward, I'm afraid."

"Ah. Then let me tell you straight out. I'm called Celia, a name that's easily within the retentive powers of all of my friends but seems troublesome for you gentlemen. I used to be Celia Bryan, but now I'm Celia P."

"Celia," said Simms laconically. "I shall never forget it."

"Will you carve it on a tree in the forest, Mr. Simms?"

"That won't be necessary," said the historian. "And besides, my cousin doesn't like to scar his friends."

"Would that the companions of my youth had been as delicate," said Mrs. P, swiftly rolling the left sleeve of her housecoat up well above the elbow and displaying to her two auditors an interesting scar that circled her arm, returning upon itself but not meeting exactly, as though a serpent armlet of old Egypt had dropped its tail from its teeth. Simms took a great interest in the cicatrix, leaning forward intently. "Would you like to examine it closer?" said Mrs. P.

"Not necessarily, but I'd be curious to know how you got it."

"Let's just say that a primitive thought to brand me for his very own."

"Which bands of steel couldn't have done, but only a tiny band of gold." The historian gave his voice a gallant lilt. But Mrs. P disagreed. "By no band at all, sir. None of us own each other. We're only lent to each other for certain periods of time."

The historian willingly nodded assent.

"Well," said Mrs. P, softening her voice, "perhaps that was my Irishness speaking. We've been a people long in bondage."

"Indeed."

"And as you have no doubt heard, I was a dancer. And though dance is the primordial, the greatest art, it's also in bondage."

"How is dance in bondage?" Simms asked. His attitude toward the woman had changed, the historian saw, ever since she revealed the scar, which shone ghastly white against the pink skin of her naked upper arm.

"It's in bondage to a set of beautiful but worn-out conventions called classic ballet. When I danced, I shook those loose, but was immediately caught up in other bonds, namely the stupidity and even lasciviousness of a great part of my audience."

"So you've given up dance?" said Simms.

"Yes, I converted my aesthetic impulses to painting."

The historian was just about to comment on the happy results as

seen from the painting on the wall, but he never had a chance. There was
a sudden jolt, followed by a horrible hissing. The train ground to a stop.
Mrs. P was thrown full-length across the couch where she was sitting.
Simms was pitched face down onto the rug of the salon. The historian
was luckily ejected upright from his chair and pressed safely into the
forward corner where the salon was walled from the sleeping quarters. It
was a miracle that the train wasn't derailed.

Simms, the first to regain his composure, leaped to his feet and
looked out the window over Mrs. P's still supine body. "By God," he
said. "We're being robbed!"

Mrs. P rose up and looked out. The historian crowded in beside
them. Along the track on the south side of the train were some ten
mounted bandits who, though masked, were variously identifiable as
whites, Mexicans, and Indians—a motley and frightening lot. But Mrs.
P was more angry than frightened. "How ridiculous!" she cried. "Trains
aren't robbed in the twentieth century."

At this point the bandits began to dismount and climb aboard, all
but two, who stayed behind to keep the horses. And one of the horse-
keepers, it turned out, was a woman. Her black hair swelled from
beneath her hat. "Well!" Mrs. P was shocked. But at that moment
Simms said, "Go back to the bath, Mrs. P, and lock yourself in."

"I shall do nothing of the sort. Do you suppose all the other
women on the train are provided with baths to lock themselves into?"

"None of the other women are as rich and ransomable as you.
Now please do as I ask, or you leave to those who are unarmed the duty
of trying to protect you."

That seemed to pierce Mrs. P's anger and pride. She went through
the sleeping room and into the bath, locking the door behind her. Not a
minute later two masked bandits entered the car carrying a gunnysack.
One of them, wielding a revolver, the historian recognized immediately
as their companion of the club car, Durban, alias who knew what. The
other was a Mexican. Durban snatched the historian's watch out of his
vest and stuck it into his own pants pocket, and then he directed the two
victims to sit quietly on the window seat, after which the bandits began
methodically ransacking the car. Durban opened cabinets and drawers
and pointed out to the Mexican what was to be taken. When, some

moments later, he saw the Mexican dumping silver haphazardly into the sack, he said harshly, "*Cuidado!*" At another point Durban looked longingly at the crystal decanter, but quickly shoved it aside. "*No podemos llevarlo.*"

"*Es verdad,*" replied the Mexican, also lingering a moment sadly by the cabinet of crystal.

In the salon there was nothing to take but the wallets of the two captives, Simms' almost empty. To be double sure there were no secret pockets, the Mexican patted their coats expertly, then twitched his mustache comically at Simms. "*Qué animal!*"

Durban nodded and chuckled evilly.

In the sleeper they found two small gilt-framed pictures, Alfred's studs and cuff links, a silver-handled brush, and the like. But Durban was not satisfied. Shrewdly, he tapped on the bath door. "Madam, where is your jewelry?"

No answer. Durban tried the door, found it locked. "I would hate to have to shoot my way in, Mrs. P."

The door snapped open and Mrs. P stepped forth, still robed and turbaned. Without a word she went directly to the built-in dresser, removed a false bottom from the top drawer, and delivered a box to Durban, who nodded curtly, then turned to the Mexican. "*Vamonos. Es todo.*"

When the bandits had gone, the historian said, "I'm sorry, Celia."

"They were nothing but garnets. The Adirondacks are full of them."

For some minutes after this brief exchange the three occupied themselves watching the bandits climb down from the train with the loot and secure it to their saddles. So thick were the walls and panes of Alfred P's luxury car that the stir and cries of the other passengers came to them only distantly. But the minute the bandit gang mounted and rode off, firing a few shots in the air to discourage any retaliation from the train, Simms jumped up and ran forward, the historian and Mrs. P close behind.

From the engineer, who was furious and voluble, they quickly got the essentials. A mass of pine poles lay across the track and surely would have derailed the train, with potentially grievous injury to all, if he'd tried to plow through it. The wireless was inoperative, having been tampered with by "that goddam little weasel in the checky coat—excuse me, ma'am—" who'd also disarmed, bound, and gagged the mail guard. "And now it'll take us half the day to roll them timbers away while the varmints ride off to who knows where."

When they were back in Alfred's car, free from the agitation of the other passengers, Simms said to the historian, "Well, coz, your little molecular man was even more frenetic than you thought."

"Yes."

"Speed, individualism, criminality—it's all too much for me, coz. This is where I get off."

"Yes, I thought you might."

"Get off!" said Mrs. P, quite surprised.

"Yes, let him go, Celia," said the historian. "You and I will have to try to amuse each other until we reach San Francisco."

"Let him go where?" said Mrs. P, already reconciled perhaps, but still showing a surface of consternation.

By this time Simms had disappeared into the bath, taking with him an amorphous duffle that he'd stowed somewhere in the sleeping compartment. The historian said, "I don't know just where he'll go— somewhere out into the countryside here. Eventually he'll find some people, and eventually show up in Boston again, I hope."

"Will he be tracking the bandits?"

The historian smiled. "I hope you won't be offended if I say that I doubt Simms has much interest in the recovery of the booty."

"What is he interested in?"

The historian didn't answer for some time and then he said, "I think he's interested in the arrangement of things in nature."

"Does nature include us?"

"I'm not certain of the answer to that," said the historian. "To some extent, I suppose." Simms himself, it turned out, was the best answer, emerging from the bath wearing a buckskin jerkin, leather britches, and moccasins. He said, "I've left the suit hanging by your bag, coz. I trust you'll get it back to Boston, or dispose of it in any way you like."

"Yes."

"Mrs. P, I hope your husband finds his bird and that you find San Francisco pleasant."

Mrs. P smiled. "Oh, I shall, Mr. Simms. And I hope you find the wilds less comfortless than these manmade quarters."

Simms returned the smile. "If at this moment I were seeking human companionship I would look no further than you two. But the train ride has unsettled my molecules and I must have a little quiet. Take care of her, coz." With that he was gone. From the window the historian and Mrs. P watched him shamble like a bear off into the scraggly brush and disappear from sight—at which moment they commented on the vigorous shouting that came back to them from the head of the train, where a company of passengers and crewmen were rolling away the timbers.

∽

The next day they were in the Rockies following a lovely little river that fell down through pools and white rapids almost as swiftly as the shadow of the train. And still Mrs. P's mind was much on Simms. "I think he's something of a cosmologist," she said.

"No doubt of it."

"And yet I think it's not wise for an unmarried person to imagine his own cosmology. Nuns and monks in their narrow cells are wisely provided one by the church."

"Yes, I suspect you're right, but I must tell you that Simms has had two wives."

"Really!" said Mrs. P with genuine surprise. "Where?"

"Out here on the frontier somewhere. Simms tells only what he chooses."

"What happened to them?"

"They both died, one of smallpox and the other of lockjaw."

"How horrible."

"No doubt, but that's not how Simms put it, though he was at the bedside in both cases to watch the final paroxysms."

Mrs. P, who this day had her hair brushed into a long lovely falls and wore a burgundy dress, lifted one eyebrow acutely and said in a voice not merely curious, "What does he say then?"

"That they were the hosts of a vehement life not their own, that they were destroyed by too much life."

"I should never have thought of it that way," she said. And then they both were silent for a long while.

"I think you're sad to lose your cousin," said Mrs. P after a while.

The historian sighed. "Yes, but it's no surprise. I always lose him as soon as I find him."

"But you have him in mind, in memory, with almost everyone else and everything that's ever been. I've read all your books, you know." Mrs. P spoke with such directness and conviction that the historian couldn't find it in himself to take note of her monumental naivete. Yet he hardly knew what to say, and looked at the river for some while before he spoke. "It's true, Celia, that I've been a lifelong worshiper of Mnemosyne, and have always thought that history was her true liturgy. But lately I've fallen into doubt and set my pen aside."

"The world will be poorer for it." Again Mrs. P was direct and deliberate, and her green eyes were so frank that it seemed to the historian they never need blink. "But do you really think that history and society are a system with laws like those of nature?"

"Yes, I've thought that." The historian smiled. "But I've also thought many other no doubt foolish things—that history was an epic of gallantry, that it was a vast repository of moral wisdom, that it was a cosmic myth in the disguise of fact, that it was the working out of a divine covenant, and even that it was my own personal fiction that I could shape exactly as I pleased, as though I might conjure this train, this stream, and you to talk to, which is exactly what I would always conjure if I could." The green in Mrs. P's eyes brightened. "And now what do you think history is?"

"I don't really know. Perhaps it's merely man taking up one idea and then another and working each one out, as children will exhaust their games."

"In that case what's the current idea?"

"The machine, Celia. Can't you feel it? Force. The amassing of huge force, which propels us willy-nilly, which disembowels the earth, which stamps upon the earth like a giant. Don't you feel it?"

"Oh yes, I feel it. But I don't think it's what history is. Nor do you. What do you really think history is?"

"I think it's you." Mrs. P seemed offended by the historian's facetiousness. So he hastened to reassure her. "I'm quite serious. And I won't be such a bald flatterer as to suggest that you're the first woman I thought was history. But you're the latest, and you are here."

"Who were the others?"

"Many. In my youth, a fairy queen, Queen Mab, who flew about the old fields of Boston and about our parlor and in and out of my grandmother's eyes and her laughter."

"Do you find that in me?"

"Oh yes."

"Tell me who the others were."

"No. It would be tedious. I'll tell you just one other. She was a dancer, like you, with an Irish name, like yours. Her body was fashioned after the Greeks, I believe—the sunny sea-loving Aegeans. When she danced she divided light into its various colors. They floated in the air about her, like the scarves of Tiflis. I saw her again just yesterday. Do you know where?"

"Where?"

"There, on the wall."

Mrs. P craned her head to look at her own painting. Struck, she stood up, turned around, and studied it. The historian waited for her to recognize in the swirling light the dancer's limbs, the scarves of color trailing across the sunset, then he said, "You see her?"

"Yes, I do," said Mrs. P, obviously surprised.

"Good. Now I'd like to beg permission to use your study for just a little while."

Mrs. P didn't inquire whether this was the occasion for a happy return to history, but continued to study the painting. The historian took silence for consent, went into the study, sat, and began to write. Occasionally the scratch of his pen rose above the clank of the car. Outside the window the little river veered away into a canyon that already in the early mountain dusk was filled with purple shadow, so that soon painting and paper faded into darkness.

The historian left the train in Sacramento, where there was to be a considerable layover. He invited Mrs. P along, but she seemed a bit pensive and declared that she would not be fit companion that morning. She did, however, brightly sing praise of the walk out the old river road, a recommendation that the historian acted upon.

The day was warm, but there was a fresh breeze in the historian's face as he walked along the river, out to where the houses thinned and the roll of the plain grew more insistent than the peaks of roofs and chimneys. There, just at the edge of the plain, he came upon an extraordinary old house — very prickly at the top, the mansard roof spiked with a weather vane, a lightning rod, and the sharp palings of a widow's walk, and ocellated with windows thick-corniced above, like brows bent into a circumflex by surprise or intense cogitation. Below the mansard were two stories and below them the cellar, its windows squinting up from behind an iron fence. The historian had never seen a house quite like this and hardly knew where to settle his eye. At last the three windows of the broad bay of the main story fixed his attention, for they were taller and wider than the others and might, he thought, be penetrated by a concentrated gaze.

Interior darkness confounded the historian at first. Then an image appeared in the glass, but it turned out to be a reflection of something without, a boy in overalls stopped on the road and looking at him curiously. The historian was not surprised by the frank stare. To the boy, an authentic product of the prairie, his dark suit was no doubt tell-tale — decidedly eastern, even puritannical. Presently the boy's nose twitched. There was a smell of burning grass. The historian's nose twitched. Then he resumed his attempt to penetrate with his gaze the opaque panes of the bay windows.

After a while a cloud came and changed the light so that the glass was less silvered. A woman appeared inside, well forward in the bay. Virtually on the instant of her appearance the historian understood that she was imprisoned, almost as though she were a bird or a bee beating against the uncanny solidity of the glass. Actually she was only dusting, cleaning a long row of decorative green bottles on the sill with a wand of feather. Presently she paused and glanced out into the little September garden with its sparse puffs of old rose within a border of roving junipers, all surrounded by grass going brown. And then she resumed dusting, this time a thin fluted vase that contained not a rose but a sprig of syringa, from which there perhaps arose to the attuned ear a tiny screed of desperate music. The historian thought of his grandmother, the magic queen of his youth, passing through her house as lightly as a breeze off the bay—as free, he thought then, as the young republic that his great-grandfather had led into the new century and that his grandfather, her husband, had also led. He had never found her like again. Well, if only he'd gone to the frontier with Simms . . . But he hadn't. And certainly this particular woman of the West was not free.

But what was it that so obviously imprisoned her? Well, the house of course, immured within its palings, prickly counterpoint to the gentle sloping of the plain. But the woman was also personally imprisoned—flesh bound in a dark dress, hair in a snood. And no doubt she was caged by class, too, for she obviously wasn't the lady of the house. Indeed she was dark and even a bit shiny, probably from the eastern Mediterranean.

Could the woman escape? The historian thought not. There was nothing for her to escape to. The historian glanced back, surprised that the boy was still there. He must be wondering what the older man found so gripping about the image of a servant in the window—servitude to him being no doubt among the more inexplicable dooms of adulthood, but one with no grip on him yet. For he had a stout little pony who, in a mere fifteen minutes at a canter, could take him over such a roll of prairie that the house and the woman were no longer on the horizon. But the historian was without Pegasus. So he stood watching the woman work, contemplating her predicament. He wondered if his pen by some contrivance of brown or blue counterstrokes could undo the black striations of imprisonment. He feared not. He smiled wryly. The gallant writer pricking over the plain, mounted on a fiery-nostriled steed, would only, Quixote-like, entangle his lance among the cunning palings of the fence.

Perhaps Celia could free her—break her down into her constituent colors and shapes and then reconstitute her on a glowing canvas where the long lights of the plain offered liberation. But reconstitute her as what? The historian's imagination failed him. But that didn't mean that Celia's would fail her. He would talk to her about it. It set him to thinking about the arts of representation. What if he had it to do all over again? His mind ascended high above the river road and gazed back over the immense distances the train had carried him. If he had just then swooped down among the draws and rare rivulets of the great plain, he might have found Simms shambling into an Indian reservation, where the populace in their need might very well see in him a new shaman, might offer him a princess—his third and final wife. The historian smiled fondly. Being with Simms, even if only in the imagination, was always a pleasure.

But back to the question. What different representations would he make if he had to do it all over again, and if he were not wedded to his elegant old histories with their mingling of event and meditation? Where would he go to find new subjects? He thought he might go to Gotham, the very place about which a decade ago he had written so darkly— heart of the frenzy and anarchy engendered by the new Power that had outgrown its servitude and now asserted its freedom, that demanded a new type of man with ten times the energy, endurance, and will possessed by the old type. He remembered exactly his culminating sentence: "The two-thousand years failure of Christianity roared upward from Broadway, and no Constantine the Great was in sight." He savored its prophetic ring. But a moment later it disgusted him. What did he know really of that mammoth million-voiced suffering? What right did he have to speak for it? He hadn't the temperament to penetrate the secret of its woe. No, but temperament wasn't an insuperable obstacle. He was an historian, wasn't he? And somewhere in Gotham was his Clio. What if he went there and sent out his agent and found her? Oh, what a song of resistance she might sing.

The plain streamed westward under his rapid flight. But midway in his flight to Gotham his thought turned from Clio to the new man. This dread creature would not, he suspected, be easily found in the vast plush offices of Wall Street, but would more likely have his seat in one of those execrable cities of belching smokestacks somewhere between East and West—a liminal man, bestriding the threshold of a new reality that could not be described by the old history but required the marshalling of different signs: ciphers, numbers, graphs, icons capable of sustaining an enormous packing of the factual, all beyond the reach of his elegant, sententious encapsulations. So he would have to go there, too, and rub shoulders with the by-products of steel and breathe in the horrid exhausts of pure Power.

The historian sighed and came back down to earth. Of course he would go to neither place. It was too late. So he basked in a fine September elegy for some moments and then shrugged it off. Why be sad? He was an evolutionist, wasn't he? More or less like the little criminal ratman. The new history would have to mount itself on the bones of his mistakes. Not so bad, then, to have one's immortality guaranteed by a sort of archaeology of error, mummied king of a particularly appealing if unadaptive cul-de-sac.

In the meantime, the cloud had passed and the sun silvered the panes of the bay windows again. The woman vanished and in her place appeared the reflected image of the historian, alone, the boy having wisely departed for the more robust pleasures of the day. Behind, the historian heard the train whistling shrilly. No doubt he'd outstayed the layover and Celia had instructed the engineer to signal him. He glanced at the house a last time and then hurried to answer the call of pulsing steam, Power.

Eugene K. Garber's first collection of short stories, *Metaphysical Tales*, won the Associated Writing Program's Short Fiction Award in 1981 and was published by the University of Missouri Press. His stories have been anthologized in *Best American Short Stories, The Pushcart Prize, The Norton Anthology of Contemporary Fiction, The Paris Review Anthology*, and elsewhere. A professor of English at SUNY-Albany, he lives in Rensselaer, New York.

Mr. Garber's fictions have consistently explored the invasion of reality by myth. In this volume that interest takes the form of a dialogue between the empirical and the fabulous in American History of the 19th century.

The Historian was
designed by R. W. Scholes.
Typestyles are Centaur and Arrighi,
typeset by Jodee Kulp Graphic Arts.
Printed on acid-free Glatfelter
by Edwards Brothers, Inc.

More Fiction from Milkweed Editions:

Larabi's Ox: Stories of Morocco
Tony Ardizzone

Agassiz
Sandra Birdsell

What We Save for Last
Corinne Demas Bliss

Backbone
Carol Bly

The Clay That Breathes
Catherine Browder

Street Games: A Neighborhood
Rosellen Brown

Winter Roads, Summer Fields
Marjorie Dorner

Blue Taxis: Stories about Africa
Eileen Drew

The Importance of High Places
Joanna Higgins

Circe's Mountain
Marie Luise Kaschnitz

Ganado Red
Susan Lowell

Tokens of Grace
Sheila O'Connor

The Boy Without a Flag: Tales of the South Bronx
Abraham Rodriguez, Jr.

Cracking India
Bapsi Sidhwa

The Crow Eaters
Bapsi Sidhwa

The Country I Come From
Maura Stanton

Traveling Light: Monologues
Jim Stowell

Aquaboogie
Susan Straight